THE
UNICORN
GROUP

THE UNICORN GROUP

by LEE R. BOBKER

William Morrow and Company, Inc.
New York   *1979*

Library of Congress Cataloging in Publication Data

Bobker, Lee R
    The unicorn group.

    I. Title.
PZ4.B6629Un [PS3552.0256]   813'.5'4   78-23545
ISBN 0-688-03395-4

Printed in the United States of America.

First Edition

1   2   3   4   5   6   7   8   9   10

For Kate:

*". . . like the night
of cloudless climes and starry skies;
And all that's best of dark and bright . . ."*

ACKNOWLEDGMENTS . . . the example of Paddy Chayefsky, the best writer I know; the lifelong friendship of Everett Raymond Kinstler, an extraordinary person and artist; Herbert Raditschnig, who taught me much about the nature of excellence; and, most especially, Nona Gail Bleetstein, whose intelligence, dedication and love made this book possible.

On the chessboard lies and hypocrisy do not survive long. The creative combination lays bare the presumption of a life; the merciless fact, culminating in a checkmate, contradicts the hypocrite.

—EMANUEL LASKER, *Chess Grandmaster*

EXCERPT FROM A MEMORANDUM sent to the President of the United States by his aide Cyrus Wynant Harper on June 10, 1949. Document classified Top Secret and marked "For the President's Eyes Only":

. . . the new unit is now in place and operative. Code name: Unicorn. Our apologies for the delay, but it took far longer than we anticipated to identify and obtain necessary agreements from the twenty-five agents fully qualified for the work. As you know, there was no precedent for this assignment. I am now satisfied that we have in these twenty-five the very best in our entire intelligence network. In addition to exceptional intelligence and superb physical skills, these twenty-five demonstrate a willingness, as well as the ability, to do *anything* necessary to achieve an objective. They are all fiercely patriotic in the best sense of the word and show a total lack of reticence toward the more unpleasant tasks so common to our work. The phrase we are currently using is a willingness to "cancel with extreme prejudice." Their unique quality, their common denominator, if you will, is the ability and the desire to act as strongly as the situation demands—without reservation—unhindered by any humanitarian instincts. Plainly stated, this group comprises the most intelligent, able, and effectively violent unit we could possibly have hoped for. They will, of course, be used with discretion and on a highly selective basis. I am convinced that the "Unicorn" group will give us a greater flexibility and will enable us to respond to difficult situations far more effectively than in the past. It is our intention to hold the total number at twenty-five, replacements to be made as necessary. Luther will run the agents, and their identities will be known only to him and me (as your representative).

In light of continual congressional interference and the prevalence of leaks, we think this anonymity is best. One final point. I think you will agree that the Forrestal problem has been resolved in what was, regrettably, the only way possible. This was the christening of Unicorn . . . I think it is safe to say that from this point on, Unicorn will be an important factor in our present and future plans.

Excerpt from *The New York Times*, May 23, 1949:

James Forrestal, former Secretary of Defense, jumped thirteen stories to his death early this morning from the sixteenth floor of the National Naval Medical Center.

Suicide had apparently been his plan from early evening on. He declined his usual sleeping pill about 1:45 this morning. A book of poetry beside his bed was opened to a passage from the Greek tragedian, Sophocles, telling of the comfort of death.

President Truman heard the news of Mr. Forrestal's death on a 7 A.M. broadcast. He was "inexpressibly shocked and grieved." He spoke for a country shocked by the tragedy.

"This able and devoted public servant was as truly a casualty of the war as if he had died on the firing line," the President said.

The plunge that caused Mr. Forrestal's death occurred at 2 A.M. and hospital authorities announced it with a brief statement two hours later.

Pushed Open a Screen

The hospital said that Mr. Forrestal had left his room, No. 1618 in the white granite tower of the hospital, and had gone to a diet kitchen near by. There, clad in a dressing gown, he pushed open a screen fastened only by thumb latches, and plummeted to the third floor projection after hitting a narrower projection at the fourth floor.

The sound of the fall was heard by Lieut. Dorothy Turner, the nurse on duty on the seventh floor, almost immediately after a Medical Corpsman's check of Mr. Forrestal's room disclosed that he was missing. An investigation led to the discovery of the body on the roof of a passageway leading from the third floor of the main building.

There were indications that Mr. Forrestal might also have tried to hang himself. The sash of his dressing gown was still knotted and wrapped tightly around his neck when he was found, but hospital officials would not speculate as to its possible purpose.

PROLOGUE

LA RÉSIDENCE DU BOIS is a small hotel situated on the edge of the Bois de Boulogne in Paris. It is perhaps a trifle too exquisite, but on this particular spring morning as the sunlight filtered through its gauze curtains, each room fulfilled the most romantic fantasies of all those who dream of this city in April.

David Wyeth awoke, kissed his sleeping lover gently, dressed and left the room in silence. He moved quietly down the ornate staircase, noted with satisfaction the aesthetic perfection of the Persian carpet, the ebony banisters rimmed with gilt, and the small sunlit garden just off the main lobby. He nodded to the concierge and stepped out into the street.

La Résidence du Bois fronts on a small street shaped like a crescent moon that runs off the main boulevard. Early on this Sunday morning, a young woman slowly pushed a baby carriage at one end of the curved street. A little to the right of the hotel, an elderly gardener worked on his hands and knees trimming the spring flowers and shrubbery that gave this small street a special measure of loveliness.

David Wyeth paused for just a moment, reflecting on the beauty of the day, the city, and life in general. As he moved a few steps down the crescent toward the boulevard, a taxi, traveling at sixty miles an hour and apparently out of control, mounted the curb, crushed the low wire fence designed to protect the flowers, passed within a few feet of the crouching gardener, and struck Wyeth head on. Propelled backward, he was crushed between the front of the cab and a concrete wall designed to shield La Résidence du Bois from the noise and abrasion of the city. He was killed instantly.

Later, in writing his report, the gendarme noted with interest the following points: the driver of the cab, Charles Roux, had apparently suffered an epileptic fit, which may have accounted for the fact that his foot was still firmly depressing the accelerator when they finally got the car door open. The woman pushing the carriage seemed to have vanished; no one in the area remembered ever having seen anyone answering to her description. Finally, the closeness of this threat to his mortality sent the gardener, Antoine Foultz, age sixty-eight, into shock, for which he was treated at the district hospital. He neither saw nor remembered anything of value.

The death was officially labeled accidental. Wyeth's family and local employer were notified. The employer, in turn, immediately notified the parent firm by Telex and phone. The response was immediate and dramatic, for the murder of Special Agent David Wyeth, the thirty-third Unicorn, was but the most recent in a pattern of violent death that threatened to destroy that special unit so critical to the nation's intelligence capability.

PART I

OPENINGS

Your basic tactic in the opening stage of any game is to bring out pieces—"develop" them. As long as they are on their original squares they are useless. Development of the pieces gives them real scope and enables them to work efficiently for attack, defense and maneuvering—gradual improvement of one's position. There are twenty possible choices for the first move.

Which is the best to play?

—FRED REINFELD, *Two Weeks to Winning Chess*

1 SINGER

. . . the way you plan the opening will determine the kind of prospects you will have later on. If you strive for control of the center and further your development and get your King into a safe haven, you will have a promising situation for the middle game.

On the other hand, if you ignore the center, play a whole series of inconclusive pawn moves, and leave your King exposed to attack, you are just as surely headed for serious trouble.

—FRED REINFELD, *Two Weeks to Winning Chess*

SINGER LOOKED DOWN at the chessboard, studying the positions of the players, trying to fathom the design of his opponent, who was two hundred miles away. He had been playing chess by mail with Cy Harper for over thirty years, and the old man's game seemed to grow all the more deceptive and devious as the years passed.

God, thought Singer, he must be close to seventy-five, and his mind is better now than it was when he was fifty. This particular game was one of the most difficult Singer could remember: he had been analyzing the current situation for two days.

Finally—suddenly, as so often happened—he saw the pattern of play. In this single moment of illumination he perceived the past, present, and future of Harper's intricate design. He smiled appreciatively in admiration of the old man's mind.

17

He almost got away with it, Singer thought.

Once the pattern was known the response would come quickly. This was Singer's forte. Once he understood where his opponent was leading him, he could act decisively to thwart the design. He decided on an aggressive, oblique course of action, scribbled his move on a postcard, and left it on the hall table for his housekeeper to mail.

He moved through the rooms where he had lived for most of his adult life. The apartment was almost exactly as it had been when Grace was alive to care for it. A worn Oriental rug, furnishings of no particular period reflecting the eclectic taste of the 1940s and 50s—venetian blinds, heavy burgundy drapes, a grand piano open with the music of Bach's "Well-Tempered Clavier" resting on the music stand as though waiting for someone to strike the first notes. It had not been played in eight years. Only one room in the apartment gave any evidence of having been lived in.

Singer went into his study, the shelves lined with books on chess, accounting, mathematics, riddles and puzzles, classic conundrums. He lowered his heavy body into the large comfortable chair in front of his desk and returned to the work that had absorbed most of his time for the past eight weeks.

In the beginning, they had been only names. Disembodied, lacking faces and features, they were shadows whose lives had somehow produced a history of violent death and destruction. Now, as Singer sought to extract the significant elements in those lives, he painstakingly examined the minute details and minor incidents that impart to any life its texture and resonance. Portraits of seven very complex and dangerous human beings had begun to emerge.

From the moment that Cy Harper and Col. Luther Martin had convinced him to share their terrible burden, Singer knew he would enter into a world far different from any he had known. The business with the previous Vice-President would be child's play compared to what lay ahead. He knew that—yet he had accepted this assignment without pause. When Martin outlined the history of Unicorn's decimation Singer had felt himself being drawn into a whirlpool, into a darkness he abhorred and did not understand—propelled by the boredom and emptiness of his days and by the specter of the idle and purposeless years that lay ahead. He had welcomed the invitation, and the work itself had revitalized his life.

As he pored over names, dates, and events in this litany of death, he caught glimpses of the pattern. He had found a coherent structure to the Unicorn deaths within the past nine years. Singer suspected that there were even more killings than either Harper or Martin knew of, but it had been difficult to separate those deaths properly attributed to the nature of the work from those murders that seemed a part of the design—the destruction of Unicorn.

As Singer traced in time and place the sequence of death, he knew with an awful certainty that the execution of at least eighteen elite agents had been an act of war against Unicorn and perhaps against the entire Company. Once sure of this conclusion, he proceeded to the next phase of his work. An accountant who appreciated from long experience the unreliability of facts and figures, he had always sought answers not in ledgers and records but in the behavior and histories of those who kept the ledgers and the records. Morton Lionel Singer owed much of his professional success to a unique ability to discern deceit beneath the surface of apparently normal human behavior. He had, as was his way, begun his work by giving shape and form to the seven men and women who were sole survivors of the once powerful Unicorn group.

The threat to the remaining members of that group was urgent and immediate. There was no longer any ambiguity about the purpose of the Unicorn deaths. Nowhere was there any evidence that anyone or any nation had profited from the decimation of the group. Singer was, accordingly, aware of the possibility that the threat was from within, that one or more of the seven had turned cannibal. This was why he felt it essential that before any plan could be developed or counterattack launched, he scrutinize those seven lives with fresh eyes. He had decided to condense and summarize for Cy and Luther both the pertinent facts and the meaningful details. In arranging and examining these lives, in chronological order, Singer hoped that cause and effect might become clear, that hidden motivations and contradictions might then suggest answers to as yet unasked questions.

He was almost finished. The completed dossiers of Coles, Rhinehauer, Lundquist, West, Fonesca, and Jonas told an ambiguous and contradictory story devoid of any recognizable common denominator that would explain their enthusiasm for their work. But the histories that had emerged from the minutiae of these six lives were dark in every case; and even more revealing was the fact that these people were so clearly the products of the country Morton Singer had been so proud of.

The carefully prepared folders lay side by side on Singer's antique walnut desk with only the name tabs showing. He saw them as a silent rebuke for the ineffectual process that had taken too long—and had failed to prevent the most recent death. He wondered who David Wyeth had really been. As soon as Singer received word of his death in Paris, he had set aside the half-finished dossier, realizing the futility of pursuing the mysteries of Wyeth's life. The survivors demanded his full attention.

The last file to be completed belonged to Michael Trevor Gault. Having read and analyzed over a thousand pages of reports, letters, and transcribed interviews concerning this as yet unknown young man, he was now in the final process of distilling all those words down to perhaps a dozen pages.

As he wrote his summary of the life of the thirty-eighth Unicorn, Singer could feel the cold, damp winds of northern Maine. He understood the emotional deprivation of an isolated and lonely childhood that had chilled Michael Gault. Singer was, if nothing else, quite capable of assuming and identifying with another's pain.

He began to write:

File 666-30-0714 (U-38)

NAME: Michael Trevor Gault

DATE OF BIRTH: December 5, 1941

PLACE OF BIRTH: Fort Kent, Maine

PARENTS: George Arthur Gault
Marie Celeste Gault (Fleurie)

SIBLINGS: Robert Paul (34)
Lorraine Marie (33)
Suzanne Rachel (31)
Roger William (30)
Eva May (28)

MARITAL STATUS: Single

EDUCATION: Fort Kent Elementary School (1946–1954)
Aroostook Central High School (1954–1958)
University of Maine, Orono (B.A.) (1958–1962)

U.S. ARMY: 1962–1969
Vietnam (Bronze Star)
Rank: Captain

COMPANY: 1969

U: 1970

PHYSICAL DATA:
Height: 6′ 1″
Weight: 170 lbs.
Complexion: Dark
Hair: Black

IDENTIFYING
MARKS: Lateral 6″ scar lower abdomen
Broken nose (evident)

2″ scar below right eye running horizontally
toward right ear (File 49N)
2 false teeth—lower jaw (File 67321-Y)
4″ scar right thigh (File 3MR 21)

LANGUAGES: French, Spanish, German, Italian, Japanese

RATING: 209-6LM
                      internal service 43-0001

Summary and Review

To: Cy Harper and Luther Martin
From: Morton L. Singer
Re: UNICORN—Gault

EYES ONLY

I don't know how familiar you are with the area in and around Fort Kent, Maine, where Michael Trevor Gault was born and reared. It is the center of Aroostook County, one of the northernmost regions in the continental United States. The weather is generally foul, cold, damp—on the whole, bleak. Much of the local population derives from a curious blend of French Canadian and dour, parsimonious Scotch-Irish. Gault's parents worked a small potato farm near the Canadian border, scratching a meager existence out of that forbidding land.

I am deliberately overwriting this particular summary because I think a realistic image of Gault's childhood is especially important in his case. From everything your field staff was able to develop for me, Gault's mother and father were (and are) as cold and forbidding as the land they struggled with. Granted, the Maine farmer is not noted as a warm, garrulous personality, but George Gault and his wife seem extreme examples of the breed. We have on file interviews with each of them that set some sort of record for frugality of language and dearth of communication. Our field representatives were two of our very best, and the most they could coax out of these parents was a grudging admission that Gault was a "good boy." (See attached file, Gault, G. A. and M. C., Interviews 67 C-D.) A more rewarding interview took place between Hutchins, your

22

representative, and Marthe Percy, Gault's high-school counselor. She lived near the Gault farm and knew the boy for most of his youth and adolescence. In summary, she gives us a picture of a family atmosphere totally lacking love and warmth. The father worked almost eighteen hours a day and rarely, if ever, exchanged words, let alone ideas, with his family. The mother seems to have divided most of her life between fields and kitchen, also working on occasion for other, more affluent members of the community. The children were allowed to attend school so long as their studies did not interfere with the chores, which seem to me (a city boy) prodigious. Ms. Percy remembers Gault as sullen, brooding, noncommunicative, and withdrawn. Interviews with his two brothers and three sisters confirm her opinion and reveal similar personalities. Two of his three sisters are nuns who teach in Catholic schools in Bangor and Augusta. The youngest, Eva, is unmarried and, at twenty-eight, still living at home. The two brothers are married. Robert has just purchased his own farm not far from his parents. Roger is currently unemployed; it is possible that he is suffering from Hodgkins Disease, but we could not confirm this without exposing our credentials to the local hospital. It did not seem worth it. (File 5W77321-XW-Gault, Interviews 17-26-32.)

You get the picture of Gault's early years. Academically there is little to report. In elementary school he is so nondescript as to be practically invisible (three of his teachers did not remember him at all). His records show a B average in high school, with some promise in English and history. If he had any friends, we can find no evidence of it. His dating was extremely infrequent because, as soon as school was over, he was expected back at the farm (twelve miles away) to work. Ms. Percy remembers that two weeks before graduation from high school Gault announced that he wanted to attend the University of Maine and asked how he might compensate for his failure to apply earlier. Ms. Percy adds:

". . . it came out of nowhere. He had never said anything to any of us—his teachers, classmates, no one. His father came to school after I told him and blamed me for putting the notion in his son's head. What a joke that was. In two years as his counselor I couldn't coax a word out of him about himself or his plans. His father raised the roof but I called the University anyway and got him in for the fall term. He never thanked me—just went on down to Orono in September and I haven't heard or thought of him 'til you called . . ."

Singer stopped writing. As with each of the other dossiers, it was as though he had begun to live Michael Gault's life. Yet he had never understood the mentality of those who chose work centered around killing, deceit, and violence. He had written page after page describing the most destructive actions and events—reporting them to his superiors, but also seeking to comprehend why and how these things happened, where each of these people had come from, what forces had shaped their lives. As he distilled the volumes of facts into a few pages of his own perceptions, he found that it was almost impossible to work over a long period of time without turning away from the material to reflect upon himself and his own past.

The dismal sound of the rain against the windows, the damp cold that filled the room, the effect of the gray, flat light depressed him. He sensed the burden of all of his sixty-two years. His heavy body felt more than twenty-five pounds overweight; the few hours of his fitful sleep had not refreshed him. He had insisted on assembling and confronting the remaining Unicorns. The meeting he had called was only forty-eight hours away, and these reports were due on Harper's desk that evening. Before Singer would be permitted to meet Unicorn, Cy and Luther wanted to know just what his preliminary thoughts were. He now had difficulty concentrating on the material in front of him.

Looking around him at newspaper articles and photographs that filled all the available wall space in the room, he observed with some chagrin that he had never been trim, always round; he seemed to have looked the same forever, except for the hair. Upon graduating from De Witt Clinton High School in the Bronx, he had a full head of unruly black hair that had disappeared almost unnoticed over the sequence of a dozen other pictures taken over forty years. The faces of his parents looked down at him, their smiles frozen in time. Amid the nervous good cheer of his huge graduating class, the elite of De Witt Clinton blended easily enough with the somber and serious young man, framed in cap and gown, as he left CCNY with a degree in accounting.

Singer paused, permitting himself the luxury of gazing once again into the eyes of the eternally young Grace Lowenstein, fresh and hopeful in her bridal veil, looking up at Morton Lionel Singer, youngest member of the firm of Fineberg, Zeller and Cohen, certified public accountants. The adjacent picture of the wedding party—taken in front of the Concourse Plaza— showed Grace Singer, née Lowenstein, to have been lovely in a quiet, unspectacular way. That day in June, 1939, marked the first step in a thirty-year journey during which Grace and Morton were to enjoy a relationship rich in love and friendship.

The rain persisted, reminding Singer of his loneliness. Other pictures on the wall demanded attention, the progression of the photographic styles reflecting the passage of time. His induction into the United States Army at Fort Dix in October, 1941; the Whiz Kids, Singer, Seligstein, and Feldman, the best accountants the Quartermaster Corps ever had; next to this picture a montage—testimony to Grace's pride in him—of newspaper clippings, documenting the surfacing of Singer's peculiar talents. It was the story of how one persistent young lieutenant in the Quartermaster Corps had discovered and exposed Major Harold Stiles and Captain Norris Zeck, who had managed to conceal a thriving black-market operation that had diverted over a quarter of a million dollars in cigarettes, watches, cameras, spare parts, and other sundry goods intended to further the war effort. In a brilliantly obscure jungle of figures, fake bills of lading, counterfeit invoices, and nonexistent expenses, Singer saw what others had not—the pattern of malfeasance. He devised a response, baited a trap, and caught the two entrepreneurs red-handed. For his efforts he was promoted and attached to an internal investigation unit designed to prevent a repetition of such events.

25

Resisting, for the moment, the temptation to stray into the seductive warmth of memory and feeling the pressure of time, Singer forced himself to return to the rather different life that lay spread before him on his desk. How many bits and pieces there were and how goddamned hard it was to make any sense out of them!

He found Gault's childhood deeply disturbing and wondered what had propelled this isolated, lonely boy to risk himself suddenly in a new and strange environment. As with all the Unicorn lives, Singer was able to see only suggestions and hints of an answer. He resumed writing.

I now begin to find some very interesting bits and pieces concerning this young man. Again I urge you to examine all the attached material pertaining to his college life. The first thing I noticed is that the portrait of Michael Gault we have *until* he attends college is very clearly that of an introverted, silent, rather odd young man. But by the end of his freshman year, Gault has opened like a flower. His grades are excellent and continue to improve throughout his four years. In searching for the catalyst of this remarkable metamorphosis, I came across the following comment. It occurs during an interview with Myrna Larramie, whom Gault frequently dated during his first two years of college (Interview RR 4401-Larramie):

". . . he was very kind and decent and a lot of fun to be with. I think he really enjoyed everything about college. He talked all the time about his classes and his teachers, like Professor Craigie—Mike loved him, like a father. I think he made a big dent in Mike's life."

So I asked: Who was this paragon of tutorial excellence? And I turned up something I think you will agree is much to the point. The following represents a compilation of over two dozen interviews, as well as a careful study of letters written by Gault to his parents and, later, to Professor Craigie from Vietnam. The tone, conclusions, and interpolations are, of course, all mine (File corres. 4RR 17002-V):

Gault's freshman English teacher was Phillip Alexander

Craigie, La Martine Professor of English Literature. He was variously described by students and colleagues as "a philosopher," "an erudite scholar," "a humanist," "an amateur psychiatrist," and "a good guy." The man seems to have been enormously popular with both students and members of the faculty. In fact, I do not find a single dissenting voice. He conducted "at home" evenings in which students would sit with the Professor and his wife Maureen and talk of Mozart, Mahler, of Dylan Thomas and Gerard Manley Hopkins. They listened to Schubert and read aloud from Shakespeare, Joyce, and Emily Dickinson. Predictably, they argued politics and philosophy (Interviews Nolte, Wisner, Field (3C-D-E-F).

If you assemble my background material in chronological order, you will note that by the end of his freshman year Gault was virtually living with the Craigies—who had no children of their own. He took his meals with them, attended sporting events with them, and vacationed with them in Nova Scotia. Our interviews clearly indicate that the emergence of Michael Gault as a stable, attractive, integrated personality took place in direct relationship to the time spent with Phillip and Maureen Craigie. Reading a particularly significant letter (File 6749-Marks, Felice) that Gault wrote to a girl friend during a vacation in the Canadian Rockies, and correlating this letter with some of his term papers, I would say that in his four years at Orono under the tutelage and influence of Craigie, Gault learned something of the nature of love, of kindness and compassion, of warmth and generosity of the spirit. In a discussion I have had with your Dr. Milton Fineberg (staff psychiatrist 436-21-7700), the term "surrogate father" was used and explored. Dr. Fineberg said: ". . . Craigie became the parent Gault always wanted and Gault, in turn, gave the Craigies a son. *Quid pro quo.*" (See attached File 167M-Orono 1958–1962, Gault. It's all there.)

In summary, Gault's college years were a fine time for him. He made friends, dated, and enjoyed himself for the first time in his life. I can only speculate as to the effect all of this must have had on him. Suffice it to say, when asked by the yearbook editors for a quotation that would sum up his college life, Gault chose lines from Dylan Thomas's "Poem in October":

"The morning beckon
With water praying and call of seagull and rook
And the knock of sailing boats on the net webbed wall
Myoolf to oet foot
That second
In the still sleeping town and set forth."

Which, of course, was Thomas's metaphor for setting out on life's journey filled with optimism and joy. It was also Craigie's favorite poem.

Singer paused, reflecting for a moment on the poet's words. He found it interesting that someone like Thomas, whose life was so filled with self-hatred and whose early years carried in them the seeds of inevitable destruction, could have composed lines so joyous and so optimistic.

He got up and stood in front of the window, watching the rain form an endlessly changing design on the glass. He thought of how it had been in the beginning; on what a small scale he had first demonstrated his special abilities. Later had come his association with people who shaped events, who had first used Singer professionally and then become his friend—politicians and statesmen, all of whom had ample opportunities to employ his investigative abilities and whose gratitude was expressed by recommending him. His work made him financially independent and well-known among the power-brokers. It also kept him very busy.

Singer now understood how the new president of the United States had come to him. An important and high ranking government official, close to the seat of power, fell victim to the epidemic of corruption that had swept like a disease across the nation. The Boston Brahmin who served as the cleaner of the Augean stables then sought someone to scrutinize what he knew would be a dirty little tale of thievery and criminal behavior. He asked the advice of that gray ghost who had stood next to so many presidents, Cyrus Harper. Harper's immediate response had been an unequivocal recommendation of his friend and chess opponent, Morton Singer. The Attorney General was singularly unimpressed by this rotund old Jewish man but deferred nonetheless to Harper's judgment. He charged Singer, who reminded him of a Bronx candy store operator, with the critical task of building an airtight case against the transgressor.

Within three months, Singer had done the job. He discovered how the venal official had designed and executed a foolproof scheme to defraud the government in a sequence of bribery, fraud, influence-peddling, and corruption so deep as to embarrass the most hardened political cynic. Singer's work was so thorough that the culprit, upon seeing the evidence, gave up, pleaded no contest, and disappeared from public life into the friendly arms of his mistress and a few diehard industrialists who provided him with a substantial income for life in return for not being included in the man's best-selling novel.

For Singer, it was a high point in his life; above all, he hated corruption. Although he affected the facade of a dispassionate professional and seldom showed the anger and frustration he felt upon encountering those who betray a public or a private trust, his resentment revealed itself in the intensity with which he pursued his quarry. He remembered the days that preceded the sudden resignation.

The Attorney General had asked Singer to be present when this corrupt and frightened man sought to negotiate his way out of a prison term. They arrived—the fleshy, tired politician and his army of attorneys and advisers. Singer stood in the shadows listening to a legal litany of oblique conversation, the evidence he had so carefully prepared now presented to the advisers, accountants and attorneys wiping away all doubt—so complete a case that it erased any hope of expiation or ambiguity. The arrogant, vicious man who had betrayed his admirers sat down heavily, appearing to have aged ten years. His attorney suddenly addressed himself to Singer.

"I assume you are in possession of all corroborative documents that will support this summary, Mr. . . ." The pause seemed deliberate.

Singer was sure the Attorney General had given this patrician attorney his name. "Singer, Morton Singer, Mr. Bromley—I'm an accountant. Yes, we have all the checks, $100,000 each month, and we have affidavits from each 'contributor' and the deposit records from each of the banks, including the two in Costa Rica. In addition, if you'll glance at attachment B-3, you'll see that we've followed the withdrawal of $35,750.00 from Mr. Selwyn Vickery's account in the First Merchants Bank in Richmond, the conversion of that check to cash. Those bills were in large denominations and the numbers were on file—we found them again deposited to Mr. Bernard Zygof's account in Houston. We then traced the cashier's check from Houston to Panama and find it coming back into your client's account in Costa Rica."

Singer had recited this chronicle of deceit with no suggestion of judgment or any other emotion, but he had enjoyed it. He remembered how this honorable public servant had railed against "the Zionist conspiracy," he recalled how much Arab money lay waiting in the man's Swiss account—and he felt at this moment not unlike an avenging angel.

"There's much more, of course," he said. "If you want to go over it with me at your convenience, *Mr.* Bromley."

The bargaining lasted a few days, but Singer's obsession with detail left his adversaries little to bargain with. Singer found in this particular application of his talents heretofore unknown satisfaction. He also felt a sense of disappointment as he returned afterward for several years to more routine work. And so he welcomed the arrival of the President's representative, Cy Harper, and the subsequent invitation to meet with the Deputy Chief of the CIA, Luther Martin, and the President; felt elated, excited, when they told him what was required.

The past receded. This last dossier had taken much longer to complete than he had anticipated. He had found Gault's war service contradictory and as a result difficult to summarize. He began again to write.

The next item of significance is Gault's odyssey in Vietnam. In September of 1962, he was drafted; after the basic training, he was shipped with undue haste to Southeast Asia. I refer you now to an eloquent and deeply disturbing file of letters between Gault and Craigie during the 1962–1969 period. The four years Gault spent under the tutelage of Dr. Craigie, with all its pacifistic resonances, must have made the Vietnam experience extraordinarily traumatic. There are in Gault's letters constant references to the holocaust of death and destruction, the corruption of aims and purposes and people. He talks of "search and destroy operations that find nothing and destroy only innocent civilians." He describes "young Americans from decent religious homes representing every conceivable ethnic, economic, and geographic background engaging in unspeakable acts of violence." His letters to Craigie ask for answers, and Craigie's responses suggest that he too is deeply disturbed. I attach here only one of many such letters and commend you to the following excerpt. I think you can easily gauge Gault's state of mind at this point in time.

Letter dated February 28, 1964, from Michael Trevor Gault to Phillip Alexander Craigie:

". . . there are no words to describe it. Everyone seems carried away with killing, and it doesn't seem to matter who gets killed. Half of our troops are stoned on something. The officers are so damn busy getting rich in the black market that they have no time for the war. We spend days marching through mud with no plan and no purpose. Then we attack an unarmed village and it's as if everyone goes crazy at once and suddenly they're all dead—children, women, and incredibly old people all dying in a ditch. And then we're briefed on what story to tell the reporters who show up a week later. The Senators came out here last month and the brass put on a fantastic show. They took them *south* to our own area, told them it was north, let them interview some ARVN dressed up as VC, showed them maps of areas we lost three months ago and convinced them they were all ours. So the Senators went home happy and said, 'We've turned the corner.' It doesn't make any sense, Phil. There isn't any rhyme or reason or justification at all. Yesterday we wiped out a Montagnard village (they're our allies) so our Colonel could claim a victory—and *nobody gives a shit*."

Despite his feelings about the war, Gault's record is excellent. (See File 49736612RRR-Gault, Michael T., Captain, Field Force 29.) He was respected by his fellow soldiers, won a Bronze Star for heroism in a fire fight in Ban Me Thuot, and was given a field commission. In 1966, Gault seems to have attracted the attention of a Major Wilson Wald of the U.S. Army Intelligence, was transferred to his unit (USAI-49th Corps), and spent his last two years in this work. Wald reports that Gault was the best man he ever had—with a particular talent for identifying enemy agents who had infiltrated refugee groups and ARVN units (USA File 4967321-Y W, Wald Interview 392). Gault was promoted to captain and was finally discharged in February of 1969 after being badly wounded by a North Vietnamese agent. The man was hidden among a group of Montagnards who were being relocated for strategic reasons. Gault was screening them and discovered an enemy agent who, when faced with exposure and instant death, rushed Gault and stabbed him in the stomach. Only immediate medical aid saved the life of U-38.

So much for Gault's tour of duty in Southeast Asia, Singer thought, as he began to reflect on the hidden damage that war had done. How many Michael Gaults were there, men irreparably crippled by their submersion in the cesspool of Vietnam?

Singer turned his thoughts from Gault's suffering and tried to understand what had ever persuaded him at this time of his life to get involved with these vicious games, with men and women like the Unicorns. Men and women who were being systematically murdered, Singer was convinced. Dryer, Sunnyman, Ellis, Leit, Frame, Yung-Pei, Sebastiano, Whyte, Lopez-Gallardo, Matsumoto, Schmidt, Fibere, Luanda, Zynkowski, Childress, Krug, De Medici—there seemed no end. The most able and experienced agents, the best of the best, the Unicorns. Young agents with superb credentials, older agents who had survived Korea, Hungary, Nigeria, Ireland, Guatemala, Cuba, and Chile—suddenly gone, erased as though they were rank amateurs. Nine years of death by design, buried within the normal course of events in a violent world. Accidental death, line of duty, act of God, assassination, missing in action. Lost during an earthquake, drowned on vacation, felled by stroke and heart attack, by cancer and virus infection. Victims of car accidents, avalanche, and suicide—Kenneth Luanda, the best in Africa, had died by so bizarre an occurrence as being trampled to death by an elephant.

And now this last, a week ago: Wyeth in Paris. He had almost smiled as he read the report. Clearly an accident, the cab driver investigated by five experienced "seekers" and given a clean bill of health, the gardener above suspicion, and the woman not yet located. Yet beyond any doubt Wyeth's death was part of the design. What nobody knew was why.

Singer, who always began with motive, sifted endlessly through this mountain of paper without finding one. No secrets of state had changed hands; no gain had accrued to the other side, not in Moscow or Peking or Benghazi. There was no shred of evidence that either money or advantage had been the prize. European, Asian, Russian, Middle Eastern, and African intelligence systems were, in fact, deeply disturbed because they, too, had failed to discern a motive.

"We're badly hurt," Luther Martin, the CIA chief, had said at their first meeting. "We can't return Unicorn to full strength because we simply haven't that many agents who can handle this type of work. Oh, we recognized what was happening a couple of years ago, but we thought we could stop it. Now we're in real trouble. You can't train new operatives that fast. Another year of this and Unicorn is finished. Both the President and Cy Harper say you're the best. Are you, Mr. Singer?"

Before Singer could respond, Martin raised his hand silencing him. "Before you answer, I should warn you, it's no game. Whoever's doing this is mad—if you get in the way, you're just another body. That's the problem: we haven't been very effective at protecting ourselves."

Singer had already decided. "I'll take it on, Colonel Martin. Give me a few weeks to study the material and then I'll be ready to talk."

And so had begun the tedious and lengthy process that

seemed to have no ending. As he completed his analysis of Michael Trevor Gault, Singer fully realized that he had undertaken something that could, all too easily, end his own life.

He returned now to his final summing up of the thirty-eighth Unicorn. Vietnam was behind the young agent. Presumably, a new life had begun.

At this point, based on his intake testimony (G File 7Y432) and his correspondence, Gault seems to have envisioned a teaching career at the University (I would have to ascribe this to the continued influence of the good Dr. Craigie). Unfortunately, events which occurred in the months before Gault's near death and discharge interfered.

The humanist-philosopher Craigie, in addition to his many academic talents, seems also to have been an outstanding amateur cryptographer. (See attached "Letter to Editor," *Code* magazine, August, 1951—Craigie, Phillip, and articles in issues 491, 694, 720, which clearly established that Craigie had a minor reputation in this field. It seems he loved puzzles as much as I do.) In any case, six months prior to Gault's discharge, in September of 1968, Craigie takes a leave of absence from his university duties and, with his wife, moves to Washington for a special assignment in cryptography.

It took me almost a week to put this together, but it comes out like this: Your organization was struggling with a new Chinese code that proved too tough for your resident experts. Joseph Amalfitano, head of your code section, suggested calling in about a dozen civilian experts on a free-lance basis. Craigie's correspondence and telephone surveillance show considerable reluctance. He seems caught between patriotism—which, God knows, you people like to pour on—and his very negative feelings about war in general and Vietnam in particular. In the end, the Stars and Stripes win out. Playing by the rules, Craigie informs no one that he is taking this "sabbatical," so Gault never knew he was in Washington.

Now for the bottom line, to use an accountant's term: Craigie gets close to the truth as regards the Chinese code. A double agent (File 364-49-6921-Singleton, Kenneth, Top Secret) tips the Chinese residents, and they come after our pacifist professor. Using their own inimitable techniques in a basement in Virginia, they put a great deal of pressure on Craigie; as far as I can tell, their efforts go unrewarded. Discouraged but tidy, they take him to New York, rent a suite on the top floor of the Hotel Pierre, and throw Craigie out of a window at midnight on February 20, 1969.

When Maureen gets the news back in Chevy Chase, this kind, intelligent, and loving lady elects to join her husband by running her car motor in a sealed garage (Top Secret File 4446, Memo—Washington PD Report, Officer 36015, L. J. McCarthy). Of course, the Company covered up completely, took appropriate action against the Chinese residents and against Singleton, who turned up dead a few weeks later. They then issued a suicide (depression) story, which was sure to have infuriated Gault when first he heard it. Finally, they disbanded the civilian code team.

Upon being processed out of the army, Mike Gault flew directly to Bangor (Interview G7A, File 3941-X-Sarhouse, Abigail). He first heard the suicide version from Maureen Craigie's sister, Mrs. Sarhouse. She showed him the note Craigie had written shortly before his death. A verse from a Dylan Thomas poem, it held absolutely no meaning for Gault.

"Though they go mad they shall be sane,
Though they sink through the sea they shall rise again;
Though lovers be lost love shall not;
And death shall have no dominion."

I make no sense of this at all.

From the attached interviews and reports we can only approximate the nature of Gault's reactions. We do know that by the time he showed up at Langley to demand an explanation, he was deeply disturbed. Knowing the Professor and his wife so well, he just couldn't buy the suicide story. Finally, under threat of taking his doubts to the already hostile press, he was shown the entire file on the Chinese "involvement." His anger at this point approached the edge of madness.

From his intake interviews (File 49-675-Arbuss), we know the rest of the story. He recovered, with great difficulty, from the shock of discovering who Craigie had worked for. He used his intelligence skills to try and backtrack on the Chinese responsibility, but lacked the resources to discover anything. One month later, he applied for employment with the Company (that's when he had his meeting with Luther). Note the following excerpts from the fourth intake interview with Hildreth Silver (File 49-675-4, pages 39–40):

Q: Your anger, Mr. Gault, makes you a poor risk. Your judgment would be affected. We don't have time for personal vendettas.

A: That's over with now, Mr. Silver. Sure, I'm angry, but I'm neither hysterical nor crazy. Someone has to help stop all the killing, and the sooner we nullify our enemies, the sooner the massacre of innocent people will stop.

Q: Can you really forego revenge and settle down to a job that may very often involve a lot of desk work?

A: I'll do what I'm told. I just want to contribute to the end of China's and Russia's games. How I contribute is up to you.

He got the job. His psychiatric interview showed a reasonably stable, integrated personality, but if you read all the attached interviews carefully, I think you'll agree with me. I don't believe Gault ever gave up his dream of making the enemy pay for Craigie. His record certainly shows an exceptionally motivated young man (File U-38-MPS-4967-52).

To summarize that record, he spent the six months at the home base analyzing and interpreting field reports. He seems to have shown a predilection for paper work, taking the trouble to study in detail every aspect of the Company's diverse activities. We can skip much of this period because he is working very closely with Luther. I trust the material is familiar to the both of you.

Toward the end of that year, he was in an emergency in East Africa; together with another of our Unicorns (Lundquist), he was instrumental in preserving the Kenyatta regime (Kenya—X473-Field Report PL, pages 167–194 and data). He joins our inner circle in May of 1970 and really takes off. The following are representative highlights.

1970—Cambodia. Gault eliminates all opposition to Lon Nol with the single expedient of betraying their leadership to the Khmer Rouge, which then does the dirty work. Sixteen moderate Cambodian leaders were massacred in Angkor Wat.

1971—Arranged and executed sabotage that killed the three Soviet astronauts of Soyuz 11. A "stop at all costs" had been issued. Gault operated within the USSR for six months without detection.

1972—George Wallace (see attached Top Secret File GW 444673-YXPD). Obviously there were those in the incumbent administration who saw George Wallace as a threat and authorized the Company to act. Where in hell did he find Bremer?

1973—The Olympics holocaust. Gault took charge and led the action against the terrorists. He had identified the plot two days earlier, but the West German police refused to act and, in fact, held Gault incommunicado until the action began (File 92-Y, Munich).

1974—At this point Gault becomes the Company's top internal eye, cleaning out doubles and other undesirables. Again, he is working directly for Luther and peripherally for Cy, so I needn't elaborate. It's all attached, but suffice it to say that the record is exceptional.

In summary of Gault's agency work, I think we can agree it is almost flawless. As a counterintelligence agent, he is unmatched. The incidences of infiltration dropped 60 percent after Gault was given total responsibility for internal security three years ago.

Some personal addenda I find interesting. Gault lives in Georgetown in a duplex townhouse he owns with Leslie Wine (File 297-45X9-Wine, Leslie Rhonda). She is an exceptionally attractive and intelligent woman (age thirty). She owns an exclusive boutique, A Taste of Wine, in Alexandria and has lived with Gault since 1971. Although she knows who Gault works for, she has no idea as to the exact nature of his work. Her own business is moderately successful, and the subject of marriage does not surface in the five hundred pages of transcript I reviewed. The relationship seems to be agreeable if somewhat ambiguous. For some reason, their lack of passion troubles me. They met through mutual friends (File 749-Kurowski, Julian and Clara, Interview 64, pages 17–18–19) and simply seem to have drifted together. Visually, they make a very handsome pair (see attached photographs).

Conclusions (MLS):

An exceptional young man, physically and mentally outstanding, a highly effective agent. His motivation for antienemy action seems compelling. He may just be our best Unicorn.

Done. Singer closed this, the final file, and began to assemble all his material. He thought again of his brief meeting with the President and wondered once more if he had not undertaken more than he could handle.

While he had been studying and restudying the information the Langley computers had spewed out to him, a telephone call came from the White House. Without questioning Singer's availability, it was suggested that the next morning at eleven would be a good time to meet with the President.

Luther Martin met Singer at the airport with a government car, and they arrived at the White House at ten o'clock. After waiting an hour and fifteen minutes, they were invited to join the President and Mr. Harper for coffee in the Oval Office. Martin and Harper briefed the President on recent events and informed him that from this point on the entire Unicorn defense would be under the control of Morton Singer.

During the meeting, the President listened without participating. He sat at his desk, so quiet in his colorless cardigan that at times Singer forgot he was there. There was, however, in this southern farmer a presence that could not be denied. He stood and walked to the window, silhouetted in the bright winter sunlight.

"I'm impressed with what I've heard about you, Mr. Singer. Cy Harper's never wrong—at least, not that I know of. Do what you have to do, Mr. Singer, but let's not lose everything. Luther, you keep Cy informed, and he'll keep me up to date. Good luck, gentlemen."

Dismissed, they rose to leave. The President walked to the door with them, adding an afterthought. "Mr. Singer, Cy tells me you're a first-rate chess player. Maybe you'll teach me that game sometime. I think I might like to learn."

"Any time, Mr. President." Singer could neither hide his pleasure nor stop the thought that Grace would have loved to hear that.

In his apartment in New York, as the rain lessened and the morning brought no further light, Singer checked and double-checked his report and his plan of action. Then he rose, put all the papers and photographs into a large suitcase, and locked it. He left a note for Mrs. Perlmutter, his housekeeper, mentioning the deplorable condition of the apartment and requesting a light, low-calorie supper, a request she would, as usual, ignore. He put on an old raincoat and took out a large black umbrella. He ignored an attempt at conversation by Miguel Sanchez, the elevator operator, and was equally noncommunicative with Mike Riordan, the doorman. This curt behavior, so unlike him, gave the two something to talk about once Singer had left.

It was still early and the streets were empty and wet, but the rain had almost stopped. It had always been Singer's habit, when working on a difficult audit, to walk in the morning to Riverside Drive, to sit facing the Hudson River and allow his mind free rein, unencumbered by facts and figures. He saw no reason to change a modus operandi that had yet to fail him.

Still at a loss as to the motive or the identity of his opponent, Morton Singer elected, with characteristic calm and control, to open the game quietly. There is in chess a standard opening called *giuoco piano*—the quiet game. It proceeds at a leisurely pace that allows one to develop one's pieces with a minimum of difficulty. Singer only hoped that his opponent would permit him the time to proceed as he had planned.

So, thought Singer, the game begins.

2 GAULT

Forcing checkmate is always our basic goal in a game of chess. Meanwhile, our immediate aims are: winning material, checks; pawn promotion; and threats. Each of these may be a step on the way to checkmate.

—FRED REINFELD, *Two Weeks to Winning Chess*

GAULT WATCHED THE afternoon sunlight streaming through the windows, uninterrupted by draperies, shades, or blinds. The room was very quiet. Col. Luther Martin spoke first, softly, not addressing anyone in particular.

"I think we might just as well get started. We've got a lot of ground to cover. First, look around you." He paused as they all did as he asked. "You're looking at all that's left of Unicorn." Another pause.

Luther Martin, officially the number two man, sat at the head of the table. He looked drawn and tired. Close now to retirement, he seemed suddenly to have lost much of the vigorous, powerful presence that had been his trademark. Martin was both a leader and a survivor. During the long night of the agency that had begun with the Bay of Pigs, descended into Vietnam, and culminated in the backwash of Watergate, this man, unknown to the press and public, had, in effect, assumed operating control. He had held the agency together as three successive chiefs had succumbed to the corruption of power and politics.

40

"This is the first time since Unicorn's birth, almost thirty years ago, that you've been surfaced to anyone," Martin continued. "So you'll have to assume that we're under intense pressure. Each of you has operated in a vacuum, never knowing who or how many other agents were a part of this unit. All right, now you've got in front of you the service record of our Unicorn agents from inception. You've also got a very detailed and impressive piece of work describing a pattern of hostile action designed to wipe out Unicorn. It begins, so far as we can tell, in the late 1960s; the death of David Wyeth last week in Paris is the most recent killing. The seven of you are the survivors. We had no choice but to bring you together, accept the risk, and try and mount a counterattack. I don't think I have to elaborate on what the total loss of Unicorn would mean to our intelligence system, particularly with this President and this Congress."

Gault exchanged glances with Pater Lundquist, the only Unicorn with whom he had worked before joining the inner circle. He had not known at the time that Lundquist was a Unicorn. Gault considered Lundquist, an enormous, powerfully built man, the single best agent now operating.

In September of 1969, only six months after being recruited, Gault had unexpectedly been given a major assignment. A "stringer" agent in Nairobi had picked up some seemingly innocuous strands of information that were in time analyzed by an unusually astute young desk agent at Langley. When another "harmless" item relayed out of Peking via Hong Kong seemed to fit, Gault was sent to Nairobi to work with a top agent known to him only as "Viking." Working rapidly and under great pressure, Lundquist, the young giant from northern Minnesota, uncovered a Chinese-sponsored plot to assassinate Kenyatta, blame it on the Russians, and, through their local surrogates, seize control of the Kenya government.

The Chinese agents in Nairobi were superb. On two occasions, Pater Lundquist saved Gault's life. Once a crazed, drugged Kenyan ran amok in front of the New Stanley Hotel, beheaded two bystanders with a machete and turned toward Gault as his third victim. Lundquist broke the native's neck. The entire episode had been, of course, bought and paid for by the Chinese agents who had "made" Gault six hours after his arrival.

The second attempt was more oblique. Three Africans, immaculately attired as police, entered Gault's hotel room and asked him to explain some routine irregularity at the local police station. Lundquist, entering the lobby as they were escorting Gault from the hotel, recognized the charade and followed the group to the parking lot, where he dispatched the actors with a silenced magnum. Gault and Lundquist then dropped out of sight. They met secretly one night in the presidential residence with the old lion of Kenya and his lifelong friend and security chief, Joshua Mbili. The two of them listened to the old man roar outrage as they carefully presented all the details and named all the participants in the events designed to transform Kenya into a satellite of China. They listened, too, to the old man's silence as they identified Mbili, the oldest and closest of all Kenyatta's comrades, as the chief plotter. Kenyatta needed no encouragement to act decisively and with vigor. Within six hours six men were dead. Mbili was beheaded in a cellar below the President's apartments, after his eyes had been put out by the fingers of Kenyatta's bodyguard. The Chinese were sent home, and Kenyatta signed a secret agreement with the U.S. granting a chain of missile bases in East Africa and the Indian Ocean that the Secretary of State had been unable to obtain.

Gault and Lundquist, their stars in the ascendancy, continued to work effectively together. Lundquist saved Gault's life on at least three other occasions and Gault returned the favor twice. In May of 1970, Gault became the thirty-eighth Unicorn and from that point on operated alone. He had not seen or heard from Lundquist since joining Unicorn.

Luther Martin, haggard and obviously distressed, continued his presentation. "Just so there's no confusion, let me do the honors of introducing you to each other, around the table clockwise. Simon Jonas, U-36, on my left. Laura Coles, Number 40.

Mike Gault, Number 38. Emily Rhinehauer, Number 27. Dan Fonesca, Number 41. Morgan West, 39. And Pater Lundquist, 29. I'll introduce the gentleman on my right in a minute. First, take another look at the documents we've put in front of you. You'll have ample opportunity to study them, but for the moment I'll sum up very briefly. What we suspected for almost three years and have *known* for six months is all there, and it's not comforting. Just take a moment to review the pages under the heading 'Pattern.' We started in 1949 with twenty-five agents in the group, the intent being to keep Unicorn at that number. Now, notice that in each five-year period between 1949 and 1969 we lost through normal attrition three to four agents each year. I suppose we were overly optimistic in the beginning, but we couldn't quite find enough people with your special gifts to keep us up to strength. In 1969 we had twenty-two; we'd lost a total of fifteen agents in twenty years—normal for this kind of work. But from 1969 to 1974 we lost nine Unicorns—and managed to find three replacements. From 1974 up to now we've lost another nine: Wyeth was the latest, so now you are seven. We suspected what was happening in '74, but the erasing was so damned well done we couldn't find anything.

"In the last three years we've tracked every single loss. As you know, you were all alerted as early as 1973 and again in '75 and '76. Our most recent alert went out five weeks ago and it didn't help Wyeth at all. So, here we are. Someone or some agency is trying to destroy us. We haven't a clue whether it's inside or outside. Suddenly nothing is safe.

"When Wyeth went, we took special action—a little late, granted, but hopefully not too late. That will have to serve as introduction for our guest speaker. He's the author of the little novella you've got in front of you. His name is Morton Singer, and since he'll be running this particular show from here on in, I'll let him take over. Mort?"

The Colonel sat down heavily as though the effort of speaking had completely drained him. Gault now turned his attention to the overweight Jewish man fumbling with his papers.

Gault was concerned. He prided himself on his memory, and

43

he had never heard the name Singer. Nor had he ever seen a description of any agent that would remotely match this balding, aging man who now began to address them.

"Thanks, Luther."

Gault made a mental note of the first-name basis and the easy familiarity with which this man addressed the de facto head of the nation's intelligence network.

"All right, I'm Morton Singer. I'm an accountant by trade but I've had some experience at looking at facts and figures and coming up with answers. I've never done anything in your line of work, at least not until the last two months. I'm responsible for everything you've got in front of you and, as Luther said, for your being here."

Singer cleared his throat. The ride to the airport and all the rain had given him a cold and a sore throat. He felt terrible.

"When this session is over, you'll take the material I've prepared. Study it. Use it as a base for trying to figure out who's behind the killings. I won't insult your intelligence by telling you at length how important this is—we all get the message. Someone or some group is destroying this country's top intelligence unit, agent by agent. Unless we're successful in identifying and canceling the enemy, Unicorn won't survive another year.

"Someone or something knows more about you, and what you do, and how you do it, than anyone could or should. We've got no motive. The Chinese, the Russians, the Arabs are as nervous and confused as we are. There's been no profit, and no gain. And you've been helpless to defend yourselves. Wyeth was scheduled to come here. He was alerted, which didn't help him. In what order—and when or where—I haven't an idea, but it's reasonable to assume that you're next."

Silence, total and admitting no distractions. Each agent stared at Singer, without taking their eyes from his face or acknowledging each other's presence. To Gault, Singer's initial performance had been superb. It had been accomplished with a minimum of words and with devastating effectiveness.

Singer continued. "I see that we agree on a clear and present danger. The question is, What do we do about it? How do we defend ourselves against an enemy whose identity and motives are invisible? If we don't know who's moving the pieces on the other side of the board, we can't very well end the game in our favor. So far, whoever it is has managed to eliminate violently at least eighteen top agents in a nine-year period—agents whose identities no one, including yourselves, knew. We may have lost even more, but if we are correct in dating the beginning of the unnatural losses, we place the figure at eighteen. Obviously, a defensive game isn't what's called for."

He paused, coughed, put a lozenge in his mouth. His throat was sore and his voice was going.

"Old Marshal Foch came up with a pretty quotable line during World War II: 'My left is collapsing, my right has crumbled, my center is falling apart, so . . . I attack.' "

Gault watched Singer closely. The man spoke softly and not very well, but he certainly held the attention of everyone in the room. Who was he? He sounded like a math teacher Gault had studied under in high school.

"The President and your own chief have asked me in to run the game, so you're all sitting there asking yourselves—who is he? Well, as I said, I'm an accountant who specializes in catching crooks who thought they were pretty smart. If any of you wants a list of my credits, I'll see that you get them.

"For now, I'm the one who got our former Vice-President. I've spent the better part of the last month trying to figure out just what's going on, so for the moment let's assume I know what I'm doing. I've devised a game plan that depends on each of you following the rules without deviation. It may not be the way you've been operating or even the way you like to operate, but it's got to be tried.

"It goes like this. From this point on, you're responsible only to me. You've got one job—find out who's doing it and why. How you manage that is up to you.

"You're outside the agency. We don't know whether the enemy is inside or out, but we do know we've got no security at all so you go out of here and disappear. I think whoever's working you over knows all there is to know. So we don't trust anybody. You're out in the cold and you report to me and only to me. If you make contact with each other, that's your affair, but let me warn you: I'm not sure the enemy isn't in this room."

Singer paused, turning his eyes to each of their faces in turn.

"Every one of you is an agency—you make your own strategy and share only what you want to. If you need help you call me, any time. I'm the coach, the manager, the captain, and I'm the only one. That even excludes Luther and Cy Harper. I've got all the authority I need and I can make anything happen instantly, without having to go through channels. As I said, you can always reach me, but you won't know where I am. I'm going to be moving around a little. I don't feel any safer than you should. Any questions?"

Before any of the agents could talk, Cyrus Harper stood up. Now in his mid-seventies, this cadaverous man fascinated Gault. Always a shadowy figure, Harper had been born to great wealth, had remained active in international banking circles, and continued to participate in the legal affairs of one of the nation's most prestigious law firms. Often glimpsed on the periphery of critical events, he had repeatedly been mentioned for important government posts. He had been an "adviser" to presidents before the current occupant of the Oval Office called him again to service. He had never enjoyed any clearly defined authority, but Gault knew only too well that Cyrus Wynant Harper was today one of the most powerful men in the country.

"I'll just confirm what Morton has said. His authority comes straight from the President. This whole operation is his.

"Without Unicorn we lose our potential for effective action. As it is, it's going to take five years to rebuild. We're crippled. Our enemies know it and they've already begun to take advantage of it . . ."

His soft, cultured voice—the refined tones of Harvard and two hundred years of American aristocracy—echoed in the room, sonorous and measured: the sound of the apocalypse.

"While you're out chasing this phantom, the Russians, the

Cubans, the Chinese, and the Arabs have an open field. Soon we won't have a single first-rate agent left. So don't waste any time."

Luther Martin interrupted him. "I'll just add this. Singer was chosen because he's outside the family. And because his record over twenty years is phenomenal. Anybody want to say anything?"

Emily Rhinehauer peered myopically from behind her thick lenses. "The agency has all the tools, the computers, the 'research' people. Shit, how do we function without them?"

Singer looked directly at the fleshy, unattractive face. "You contact me, tell me what you want, and you'll get it. We're not going to be using the Company's resources because it's not safe, but I've already set up access to anything we might need. I'll never tap the same well twice, so no one will be able to read any patterns in what we're doing."

Now other agents began to talk. One by one, they engaged Singer. Money, guns, communication, identities . . . Martin and Harper were spectators. Together, with Singer, they seemed like three aging seers, their aura of power and calm wisdom contrasting strangely with the group now busily engaged in urgent conversation.

Gault remained in his seat, pretending to study the documents in front of him.

He felt a sense of his own power. He knew how good he was. At thirty-seven, his mind and body were at their best. Everything he had thought and done since that moment of decision eight years ago had served as preparation for this battle. Finally he joined in the debate and discussion, speaking with both Luther Martin and Cy Harper and introducing himself to Morton Singer.

After about an hour, Singer distributed the information on new codes and communication. Each agent handed Singer a list of requirements. Gault asked only for two passports with secondary identities, $25,000 in small bills, and an additional private code between himself and Singer.

Outside, the sun had begun to fade and a sullen mood engulfed the city. Laura Coles was in hushed conversation with Fonesca. The others left the room rapidly. Gault approached Luther Martin.

"How goes it, Luther?" he asked.

"Tired, Michael." Luther Martin had never called him "Mike." "Damn tired and feeling old."

"Anything wrong, I mean physically?"

"I don't know. I haven't had time to think about it."

"For Christ's sake, Luther, check it out. Without you this whole thing will fall apart."

"It has already, Michael, *with* me."

Before Gault could respond, Singer motioned Martin to join him.

"Take care, Michael. Especially now."

"I will, Luther, you too."

Gault closed his briefcase as Lundquist passed him on the way out.

"Mike, I've got to see you tomorrow morning. It's important. Breakfast at my place, or . . ."

"Sure, Pater. What's up?"

"I don't know for sure, but I may have something."

Lundquist walked away from Gault abruptly, as if he didn't want to attract the attention of any of the others. When Gault left the room, only Martin, Singer, and Harper were left. The meeting had lasted two hours. The sky was gray now with the approaching rain. The agents seemed to have suddenly vanished, as if they had been summoned from their hiding places by the sound of a magic trumpet and, now dismissed, had returned to the darkness in which they lived. Gault walked toward the center of the city as evening came to Washington.

The luminous hands of the clock showed five-thirty. Gault had not slept. Beside him in the large bed, the beautifully naked body of Leslie Wine stirred.

Gault paid no attention as he lay on his back, his eyes open, waiting for the day to begin. The tyranny of memory, uncontrolled, had forced him to wander again through the forests of that awful night that had altered forever the days of his years.

Landing in Bangor, searching the small airport for Craigie and his wife, and finding instead the messenger of death in the person of "Aunt" Abigail, Maureen Craigie's sister. Tears streaming from her eyes, running down her ugly face and mixing with the rain . . .

"They're dead, Mikie, dead—both of them. Last week, and, oh God, I still can't believe it. Phil jumps out of a hotel in New York. Maureen does it in a garage in Washington. Oh, Mikie, why, why? He was working there—in Washington. I don't know. They called me . . ."

In Washington, haunting the right corridors until he found the right button to push.

"One more day, Mr. Ferranti, I'll give you one more day and then I go to the *Post*. I've got letters from Phil"—he hadn't —"that will blow all of you sky high. Now, I want to know what really happened or you can read all about it in the news-· paper."

At Langley, again, having failed to find the killers, telling them he wanted to become a part of their world so he could in some small measure exact a price for the loss of Phillip and Maureen Craigie, making the price as high as it was within his power to demand.

The phone rang, and Gault picked it up before it had a chance to ring twice. Leslie sat up as though she had been attacked.

"Gault."

"Mike, this is Singer." The voice was even more hoarse than it had been the day before.

"What's it like out?"

"Cold, how is it where you are?"

"Snow. O.K., what is it?"

At the end of the meeting, Gault and Singer had agreed on a simple pattern of weather information to identify each other and clear the line at both ends.

"Lundquist is dead."

A minute passed before Gault could respond. "How?"

"In his apartment. Somebody broke his neck. No one heard anything."

"Christ."

"Call me at six tomorrow evening. And for God's sake, be careful."

The phone went dead. Leslie knew from long experience not to question the content of a telephone call. She lay back on the bed, reached out and touched Gault on the arm. In the darkness, she could not see his face. He finally replaced the receiver on the telephone. He lit a cigarette, then remained motionless in the shadows of the room. He cried.

Excerpted summary accompanying the individual files on each Unicorn agent prepared by MLS for review by Cyrus W. Harper, Col. Luther Bishop Martin, and, if requested, the President of the United States:

> Classification—Top Secret
> Basis: NTK

Under no circumstances copy. These individual files will be the subject of our next meeting.

Acknowledge receipt as per standard procedure established for this investigation.

MLS

File 022-71-3005 (U-27)

NAME:	Emily June Rhinehauer (m. Sindell)
DATE OF BIRTH:	October 25, 1929
PLACE OF BIRTH:	Minneapolis, Minnesota
PARENTS:	Herbert Wallis Rhinehauer Martha Sophie Rhinehauer (Norton)
SIBLINGS:	None

MARITAL STATUS:	Husband deceased
EDUCATION:	West Park Elementary School (1934–1941) North High School (1941–1944)
EMPLOYMENT:	Minnesota Mining First National Bank of Minneapolis (1953) U.S. Department of Agriculture, Washington, D.C. (1954)
COMPANY:	1954
U:	1956

PHYSICAL DATA:

Height:	5' 5"
Weight:	145 lbs.
Complexion:	Sallow
Hair:	Brown

IDENTIFYING MARKS:	Birthmark across lower back Small mole on neck
LANGUAGES:	None
RATING:	206-44 (c)

Summary and Review (MLS)
Project UNICORN

Ms. Rhinehauer came to us some forty-eight years ago on October 25, 1929, charitably described in history as Black Friday. She was an only child, a belated arrival to parents (both over forty) who were at the time employees of the United States Postal Service.

I find nothing in the somewhat skimpy record to indicate that her parents were not kind, pleasant, loving. From all that your excellent research staff has been able to gather, we must assume that our beloved "Cook" was from birth a singularly unattractive child almost totally devoid of charm. In all our background interviews, we find words like "cute" and "adorable" totally absent (File 477-X-Cutler, Emma). There is, in addition, evidence that Emily June, thanks to the wide disparity

51

in age between her and her parents, spent a great deal of time alone.

Her elementary- and high-school history shows us the portrait of a shy and quiet child, liked by her teachers, never causing anyone any trouble, her homework always prepared. Academically, the operative word is "ordinary." Our researcher had trouble finding any friends or classmates who remembered her. (Note attached excerpt from "The North Star," the high-school yearbook, in which she is labeled "a good friend" by the editors, who have then proceeded to misspell her name.) One might say that in these formative years of childhood and adolescence she made little or no impression on anyone.

She seems to have been as undistinguished socially as she was academically. A lengthy interview with a classmate (File 542-317-6-Hooper, Ursel) reconstructs the following event in this agent's life—an event, by the way, for which she was probably totally unprepared. Our informant was an eyewitness whose memory seems excellent. Some three weeks before the Senior Prom, a tall, awkward boy approached Emily as she was closing her locker and mumbled an invitation to that gala event. When she finally realized what he had said and recovered sufficiently to respond, she managed a nearly inaudible acquiescence. It turned out to be the best night of her young life. Reconstructing the chronologies, on their second date Emily June Rhinehauer succumbed to Steve Sindell's charms (up to now unnoticed by his female classmates) and was initiated into the mystic rites of sexual love (Intake interview VVY 73216 EJR).

Steve and Emily spent the next three years in a quiet, uneventful, yet intense courtship. He completed two years at the local community college while Emily went to work as a file clerk at Minnesota Mining. Upon graduation, Sindell got a decent job with a management future at the largest department store in Minneapolis; the happy couple celebrated at Murray's, the "Home of the steak you can cut with a spoon." This was, without exception, a good time for both of them, based on Emily's testimony to friends and relatives. I see no reason to doubt this. Their relationship in and out of bed was romantic and in all ways excellent. (All this information is culled from our agents' own recollections as given to our resident Freud.)

In 1950, Ms. Rhinehauer's beloved was drafted. He served with a combat infantry platoon in Korea (Service Record). He managed to survive MacArthur's energetic charge north from Seoul to the Yalu River and his equally swift retreat in the opposite direction. He saw his friends die of bullet wounds, of frostbite, of hunger, and of neglect. He was, as are most soldiers, frightened almost constantly and he wrote Emily and his parents of his fears and of his love for her. (See attached letter salvaged from his mother's "memory book.")

On the day the truce was signed at Panmunjom, a North Korean sniper blew the top of Steve Sindell's head into a thousand pieces of bone and brain. Ironically, Emily's husband was the last officially recorded casualty of the Korean police action.

While Pfc. Sindell was defending our honor in Korea, Emily seems to have found an outlet for her loneliness by cooking superb gourmet dinners for her friends and family. She was, in fact, in the kitchen when the news came from Korea. Testimony from all those present is in agreement: she did not cry then, nor does anyone remember her crying when the flag-draped coffin was lowered into the frozen earth.

For the next six months Emily June supported herself by working as a teller at the First National Bank of Minneapolis while taking a variety of Cordon Bleu cooking classes at night. To all outward appearances, she seemed to have resumed a normal life. With two exceptions. There is no evidence that she ever again at any time mentioned her husband to anyone. She assumed her maiden name. She moved out of the apartment they had shared into a furnished room. She destroyed every picture of him as well as every shred of evidence of their shared life. To new friends, there was no sign that he had ever existed. (See interview with Sindell's parents.) In addition, during this period, her speech patterns seemed to undergo a bizarre change. For all of her life Emily had been a soft-spoken, extremely shy person who stayed in the background at social gatherings. Now she began to speak aggressively, to tell off-color jokes often centered about a sexual or ethnic anecdote. She also liberally sprinkled her everyday dialogues with excessively strong language. She put on weight, her already poor eyesight deteriorated further, necessitating the thick glasses she wears today. She seldom saw her parents, and never saw her dead husband's mother and father (Interview XX43-1-16-24-39).

In 1954, with no warning or explanation, she suddenly left Minneapolis for Washington. She surfaces in our files as a clerk-typist working for the Department of Agriculture, but, as far as was known, we find few if any social relationships. She took intensive courses at night in karate and judo; she joined a rifle club and enrolled in a course given by an electronics expert who had been fired from a sensitive government job for using his expertise to blackmail his employers (File 900-19-Y-Cross, Xerxes).

Finally, in November of 1954, this lady applied for work, citing her fury at those who robbed her of her husband. In a series of extensive interviews, she seems to have convinced several members of your membership committee that she would make a compatible and useful addition to the club. (See attached intake interviews 439-440-441YY.)

She was accepted and the rest, in the words of the bard, is legend. Our "Cook" has probably the best record of achievement over a longer period of time than any other of our Unicorns.

With the help of her new employer she established what was to be her permanent cover. She wrote food articles and restaurant reviews for *The Washington Post* and, in 1957, established what was to become her immensely successful cooking school, "Emily's Gourmet"—twenty students once a month, one thousand dollars per student. She began to attract attention in the food field. She traveled all over the world, collecting recipes and meeting the great chefs. She wrote several successful books, including *Soups of France and Germany* and *Fifty Gourmet Dinners.*

Despite her success and its concurrent residue of tremendous demands on her time, Emily June Rhinehauer did become one of the most consistently effective of our general agents. In 1956 she was invited to join Unicorn. The file of this agent, who is given only very special, complex, and dangerous assignments, is unmarred by a single failure. The agency psychiatrist who did the intake study on this short, fat, unattractive woman has noted that much of her success was probably due to the fact that her emotional self was as totally anesthetized as anyone he had ever seen. He emphasized what appeared to be a total absence of any recognizable human emotion, including anger (Intake D Report 97463127 AS-Canowitz, Sheldon, Dr.).

An example of this lady's operating style was the identification and nullification of Hoerst Luckmann, a rising young political figure in West Germany who seemed well on his way to becoming that nation's next chancellor. Actually he was a top KGB agent, and his death in a tragic fall down a flight of stairs was greeted with satisfaction in many corridors of power once his true allegiances were exposed. One hour and thirty minutes after Luckmann's back was broken and before his body had been removed, Emily Rhinehauer gave a brilliant demonstration of regional American cooking to Munich's leading chefs, gathered at the Walterspiel Restaurant. Her Shrimp Jambalaya was particularly well received.

Ms. Rhinehauer has never engaged in any serious social contact with a man since the news of her husband's death, but she has managed to establish a circle of devoted friends who are amused by her loud, pungent conversation—which, by the way, I find disgusting—and who consider her to be a good and loyal friend.

Conclusions (MLS):

A very obsessed and dangerous lady. An absolute professional with a deep undercurrent of violence and rage. A "nun," if you will, dedicated to the death and destruction of everyone on the other side. Very close to psychotic. I'm glad she is on our team. I'd hate to have her angry at me.

3 RHINEHAUER

Premature attacks—usually with the Queen in the fore-
front—are likely to recoil on the attacker, resulting in
considerable loss of time and sometimes of material as
well. Every player has had the experience of succeeding
with an unsound attack against weak opposition; but
this is clearly something that cannot be recommended.

—FRED REINFELD, *Two Weeks to Winning Chess*

EMILY RHINEHAUER WAS A very angry woman. For twenty years
she had lived the most dangerous life possible, surrounded by
death, and she had survived. She believed she had survived
because she had jealously protected her anonymity. No hint
of her real vocation had ever surfaced; nor did she have
contact with anyone else inside the Company except Martin.
Now, because they were scared, she was blown. She glared
out from behind her thick glasses in hatred for those who had
placed her in jeopardy. She had listened to Martin and Harper
and that weird old accountant and had been overwhelmed with
a sense of apprehension. Nothing had felt right. How the hell
could this agency with all its brains and computers and controls
take three fucking years to figure out that the loss of eighteen elite
agents was no act of God? And then bring in an outsider with
no hard experience, tell him everything, put him in total charge
—*show* him the agents who never surfaced. It didn't make any
sense, and what Emily Rhinehauer didn't understand, she didn't
like.

She had left the meeting as quickly as possible and gone directly to her five-room apartment in Georgetown. The only sound in the room was from the fire and from the occasional distant traffic that moved slowly through the tree-lined streets. She placed Singer's manuscript, together with all his supporting documents, on a small Eaton desk near the fireplace and began to study it. Her silent and thoughtful meditation by the fire was, for Emily, a satisfactory response to many difficult problems.

At nine-thirty, four hours after she had begun, she completed her consideration of the Unicorn crisis, then placed Singer's opus in the fire and watched it burn.

Emily, who believed in aggressive action as the best and safest course, was determined not to provide a passive target. She made three telephone calls. The first was to her secretary/assistant. She arranged to cancel her cooking classes for two months, pleading illness and exhaustion. She then booked a one-way economy seat on the TWA night flight from Dulles to Paris and asked the airline to reserve a room for her at the Régina, Place des Pyramides, Rue de Rivoli. Finally, she dialed Singer at the number he had provided. The phone rang seven times before Singer answered.

"Singer."

"This is Emily Rhinehauer. I'll assume you know enough to arrange a clean wire. I want all the stuff I asked for at the meeting delivered here by midnight. My apartment."

"That might be difficult, Miss Rhinehauer."

"Don't give me any crap, Singer—you made a big thing about being able to get anything done."

"All right. What else?"

"I'm going to Paris right away. I'm going to start with the last killing. Wyeth—that whole thing stinks—if you're half as smart as you say you are, you must have seen it. I'll attend a cooking seminar and I'll give a couple of lectures. I'm staying at the Régina but if I drop out and you need to reach me, leave a message at the Amex office on the Rue de la Paix for Doris Finestein to contact her aunt. It'll get to me. If I don't answer that, I'm out for good. One more thing, I want the name of one absolutely reliable line into the Sûreté. Someone who speaks English and whom we can trust—totally. Don't slip on this one, Singer, because the goddamn frogs are as crooked as corkscrews. They'll double and triple so many times you can't tell who's playing for which side. Just figure out how that bastard Arab terrorist got out. The last co-op I was given was guaranteed to be their number one Ivory Soap agent and I find out he's getting a weekly paycheck from the Saudis, from Sadat, from Israel, and from Iran. If you can't give me a name, say so, but if you give me one you better be sure you're sure."

"You'll get a name, and I'll be sure," said Singer. "Anything else, Miss Rhinehauer?"

"Some ideas—for whatever they're worth. The stink of this whole thing is like the morgue. Wyeth was too damn good to get caught like that *after* he'd been warned. Somebody's mad at us, or mad, or both. I don't think this has got anything to do with the games we play—I think we've got a crazy on our tail, but I can't find the common denominator—so I'm going to try and take the Wyeth thing apart. And Singer . . ."

"Yes?"

"I'd watch my ass if I were you. Because if I were crazy and I thought you were as good as you think you are, I'd make damn sure I got you first."

"Thank you for the advice. Now let me give you some news. Lundquist's dead."

Emily absorbed this without comment.

"How?" she asked finally.

"A broken neck, not accidental, in his apartment sometime earlier this evening."

Her reply: "Shit."

At three in the morning, the extra passports and money Emily had requested arrived with a short note from Singer.

Your line into the Sûreté is Charles du Plessis. Guaranteed. The driver of the taxi that killed Wyeth is now living at 39 Rue Monsieur Le Prince, Apartment 6, with his daughter.

She sent a Telex to Maggie Vaudable at Maxim's to say she would, indeed, be pleased to attend the seminar on Thursday. She then cabled an old friend, Georges Bisquet, the only Frenchman she had ever trusted.

Georges. Arriving Charles de Gaulle tomorrow 11 PM TWA 331. Urgent. Meet me.

Emily

She went to sleep a little before 4:00 A.M. She dreamed she was lost in an unknown city, a city of interlocking tunnels that had no entrances or exits. A city of subways. She asked directions, but no one could understand her. When she woke at six, she felt anything but refreshed. Emily Rhinehauer was, for the first time since she had joined the Company, very frightened.

She hated flying, hated being confined in a small space with her life in the hands of someone whose competence she was in no position to judge. She hated the plastic food served on plastic trays by plastic bitches who were never available when you needed them and hovered about when you wanted to read, work, or sleep.

This particular seven-hour flight was made even more unpleasant than usual by the presence in the adjoining seat of a senile Armenian-born attorney who recounted the saga of his life in an interminable and endless stream of boring conversation. His legal specialty was immigration law, and he had spent the greater part of his professional life rescuing fellow Armenians from the clutches of the Turkish government. (Liberally sprinkled throughout his conversation was evidence that the weight of his good deeds lay heavily on his frail shoulders.) Despite her rudest efforts, Emily was unable to stem the flow of stories, anecdotes, and uninvited opinions on a variety of uninteresting subjects. Finally, she had terminated his monologue by moving to an empty seat as far removed from this garlic-breathed old bore as possible.

The plane's arrival at Charles de Gaulle came as a welcome release. As always, Customs and Immigration procedures here were perfunctory; Emily charged through the last official barrier into the usual crowd of Parisians waiting to welcome friends and relatives. She searched their faces but did not see Georges Bisquet. Then she noticed a powerfully built man in a chauffeur's uniform moving toward her. He carried a bouquet of anemones which, for many years, had been Georges' gesture of welcome.

"Madame Rhinehauer."

"*Oui.*"

"I am Alain Paul. Monsieur Bisquet is outside in the car. He asked me to meet you and bring you to him."

His English was heavily accented and a little clumsy. He spoke very softly for so large a man.

"Fine. That's my luggage."

She motioned to the porter who had picked up her bags in the Customs area. The chauffeur gave a sharp command and led the two of them to the front of the terminal, where a large black Mercedes-Benz limousine was standing in the "Absolutely No Parking" zone. Emily knew of no policeman in France who would disturb, let alone ticket, that car with its GBXYOO license plate. She entered the car and settled herself beside her old friend as they glided away from the curb and moved toward Paris.

The bond that joined these two disparate people had its roots in a chance crossing of their professional lives. Following the war, as Georges' influence in the French underworld grew, it was inevitable that he would make powerful enemies. Finally, he became a serious threat to Lorenz Marti, then in control of the criminal life of Paris and the rest of France. Marti was a Corsican whose brutality and wealth were equally legendary. After several attempts at reconciliation had failed and a final peace conference ended with Marti's top lieutenants kidnapped and killed, Marti felt impelled to eliminate his younger rival. Using all of his power and influence, he spun a web of evidence around Bisquet that clearly linked him with a nearly successful attempt on the life of de Gaulle.

As the government was readying its case against Bisquet, Emily Rhinehauer, while investigating a NATO double agent, stumbled over evidence of the entire plot. Because she possessed an unfailing instinct for mutually beneficial associations, she took her information to its intended victim and offered to assist Bisquet in nullifying Marti. In return Emily, being a devout believer in *quid pro quo*, asked for Georges' assistance in framing the double agent.

Their first collaboration proved eminently successful. The NATO official committed suicide, and a dismembered Lorenz Marti was found in a Paris sewer, along with the rats of Paris and the heads of his two Corsican bodyguards. With this successful beginning as the base, their association continued. They came, finally, to respect and trust—perhaps even to like—each other.

As the car approached Paris, Georges questioned Emily about her cooking, her books, and her *succès d'estime*; she inquired as to the health and happiness of his wife Stephanie and his five children, all well established in the professional and social life of Paris. Despite the innocuous conversation, Georges Bisquet sensed the tension and fear that was unlike the Emily Rhinehauer he had known for so many years.

"I do not know you like this, Emily," he said. "What has made you so afraid?"

Accepting what she knew to be an offer of assistance, Emily told her friend of the events leading to her telegram—of the deaths, of the meeting in Washington, of her own perceptions as to what was happening.

"Georges, I can't give you all the details, but you've known me long enough to trust me. I'm not dealing with an ordinary killer or group of killers, or even some foreign superagent. This is different. You know how good Wyeth was. Well, he was *warned*—and it didn't help him. I got out of Washington as

61

fast as I could and covered myself every step of the way. But I'll tell you, I've been followed every fucking minute since I left my place this morning."

Bisquet's patrician features were hidden in the darkness of the car. There was no response. Emily went on.

"I doubled back twice in Washington, went to the wrong airline first; I was the last one on the plane and the first one through Customs here. I'm still sure I've got a red-hot poker up my ass."

"What can I give you, my friend?"

"Protection while I'm in Paris. I want the best bodyguard you have, and I want him with me all the time. I've got a lot to do without much time to do it. I don't want to waste a goddamn minute looking over my shoulder."

Bisquet motioned toward the silent driver.

"Alain Paul is the very best I have. He is the best with a gun and a knife. He has the physical strength of ten men and is very intelligent. Alain has been with me for twenty years, since he was fifteen—since Marseilles. I've trusted him with my life and will now trust him with yours.

"Also, my eyes will watch you. And the eyes of those who serve as my *cercle intérieur*. I will know where you are—always. I will know if you are followed, and I will know if you are in danger. I can, as you know, act instantly. No, my dear Emily, you will be safe in my city. What else do you need?"

"Two things, Georges. Run a very careful check on a top Sûreté agent named Charles du Plessis. I've been guaranteed he's totally clean, but I won't go near him until you confirm."

Georges took a gold pen from his pocket and noted the name.

"Now the final, the toughest thing. When Wyeth was squashed against that wall, there was a woman outside La Résidence du Bois pushing a baby carriage. I think she fingered him. No one's been able to locate so much as a piece of her, and I don't believe in coincidence. She's got a key to the lock, Georges, and I want you to find her for me."

"It's done, *ma chère* Emily. You will have the name in forty-eight hours. What else can I do for you?"

"That's enough for the moment, Georges. If I need more, I'll ask—and again, thank you."

She sat in silence for the remainder of the journey, lost in her own thoughts and fears. The car moved into Paris, glided noiselessly through the darkened boulevards and past the closed shops on the outskirts of the city. It had begun to rain, the light rain that softly watered the city throughout April and May.

The limousine stopped in front of the Régina Hotel; Alain Paul and Georges helped Emily out of the car and inside the hotel. While she registered, Georges gave Alain the details of his new assignment. The big man listened without comment. At the desk, Emily was given a message: "There is a ticket for you for the Paris Opéra Saturday night. Suggest you try the Canard aux poivres verts at Lasserre. Caveat Emptor. S." She completed her registration and turned to Bisquet.

"How do we communicate, Georges?"

He handed her a piece of paper with a number written on it. "Alain can reach me any time. This is my most private number. There is always someone to answer. If I want you, you will either get a message here or you will be told to call home." He drew her into a more private section of the slightly shabby lobby. "I agree with you, Emily. I do not like this thing. Be always at attention, my friend."

Bisquet left quickly, and Emily and Alain followed the night porter to her room in this hotel that catered neither to Americans nor to tourists. It had an outdated ambience: a cage elevator, worn carpets, and musty furniture, as well as a wonderfully rude and disinterested staff. Emily had been given her usual room on the mezzanine floor, overlooking the noisy Rue de Rivoli and a corner of the Tuileries. Alain had arranged to stay with her until a connecting room became available. Alain made himself comfortable on the floor.

It was nearly three when Emily fell into a fitful sleep. This time she dreamed of wandering through endless corridors, seek-

ing doors and windows without success. She appealed to faceless people for help, only to find that they were deaf-mutes; she
found it increasingly difficult to walk, as if the thick air had become a solid mass.

When the telephone woke her at seven with her morning call,
she had the distinct feeling that she had been crying.

Bisquet delivered her favorite weapons, an ugly .38 caliber
pistol hidden in an oversized Louis Vuitton tote, and a small
knife. But for two days Emily remained, as she had so many
times before, totally immersed in her cover. She lunched with
her old friend Maggie Vaudable, co-owner and public relations
director of Maxim's. Over Coquille à la neige, spring asparagus,
and Laurent Perrier champagne, they discussed such pressing
matters as the rise of a new young chef in the Auvergne, the
decline of New York's French restaurants, and the future of
frozen vegetables in haute cuisine. Roger, the maître d', hovered
invisibly to assure perfection. Maggie was well into her sixties,
but still projected the Parisian charm, intelligence, and vitality
that made her a legend. Emily spent Wednesday afternoon in-
specting kitchen equipment and examined yet another new,
cheaper version of the Cuisinart which she found to be inade-
quate. On Wednesday evening she dined with Raymond Oliver,
author of one of France's best-selling cookbooks and proprietor
of Le Grand Véfour. She toured the kitchen and met Oliver's
newest chef-protégé. On Thursday morning she wandered
through Le Jeu de Paume, enjoying the French Impressionists.

Wherever she went, Alain Paul was close by—at times invisible, at other times very much in evidence. When she ate,
he sat at the bar or at a nearby table. For her seminar at
Maxim's, the bodyguard was introduced as a former student.
Emily participated vigorously in a rousing exchange of opinions
at this semiannual "Dialogue des Maîtres de Cuisine." The discussion was heated and passionate, centering about Emily's attack on the latest repercussions of Guérard's *cuisine minceur*.

The evening lasted until after two. When Emily returned
to the hotel, she found a message from Georges: "Call home,

mother very ill." She went immediately to her room and dialed the number she had been given. A strange voice answered.

"Identify."

"Cook."

"From Monsieur B. I am reading. Du Plessis OK. Telephone 74-3215. The woman you look for is Micheline Solière. She disappeared the morning of the killing from her apartment at 36 Rue St. Denis, Neuilly. Disappearance total. Mother only relative and lives in a nursing home two blocks from her at number 58 Rue St. Denis. She has not heard from her daughter. Expect more information Sunday. You have not been followed, but we have disturbing information. Must see you tomorrow noon. Lunch at Chez François, Rue François 1er, near Plaza-Athénée. Be careful. Tell Alain condition is *noir*."

Emily held the dead line for a few moments before passing the information to Alain, who neither reacted nor commented. During the forty-eight hours they had been together they had not exchanged a dozen words. For a big man he had an uncanny ability to blend into his surroundings; there had been times when she forgot he was there.

That night, for the first time since the meeting in Washington, she slept well. Tomorrow she would be able to take some aggressive action. The waiting was over.

On Friday morning at eight-thirty she called Charles du Plessis, an inspector attached to the "Special Branch" of the Sûreté's internal security section. He answered after the first ring.

"Du Plessis."

"Rhinehauer. When?"

"Ten sharp, Le Pont d'Alexandre. I am crippled, and not pretty."

He hung up, the brief conversation having increased Emily's confidence in the man.

A little before ten, Emily and Alain Paul strolled across Le Pont d'Alexandre, stretching over the Seine like some relic of a forgotten age, evoking all the elegant men and women who had crossed this romantic span talking of nothing, carrying parasols, riding in carriages, and staring into the waters of the river that has always flowed through Paris. As she reached the center of the bridge, carrying her lethal Vuitton tote, she noticed a short, dark, incredibly ugly man walking toward her. One of his legs was several inches shorter than the other and he wore a black orthopedic boot with a thick sole. He was short and stocky, and his limp distorted the movements of his entire body; he reminded Emily of a malignant spider inching across a concrete pavement. When he reached her, he offered his hand. His thumb and forefinger were missing.

"Madame Rhinehauer? I am Inspector du Plessis."

"Could I see some identification, Monsieur?" she asked.

He almost smiled. "But of course." He showed her his Sûreté identification and a coded note from Singer that could only be translated by a Unicorn agent.

So Singer's using the Company after all, she thought. It took her a few minutes to decode the note: "Emily, if the bearer is du Plessis he will answer your question about the traffic with a reference to the weather. Otherwise he's not."

Emily sighed. "Is the traffic always this bad in Paris?"

"Only because we have had so much rain this month. The wet streets make accidents."

They stood now leaning on the rail, looking at the river. For all its romantic associations, Emily still saw it as a dirty river crowded with barges, houseboats with laundry on their decks, and phony little *bateaux mouches* moving forever up and down. Alain Paul stood at a discreet distance, watching.

"You know why I'm here, Inspector."

"Monsieur Singer has said only that you look for information in the matter of David Wyeth and I am to help you in all ways." He had a harsh guttural voice, bad breath, and a disconcerting habit of clearing his throat as he talked. He also projected an aura of directness and honesty that Emily found reassuring.

"What do the authorities know that we don't?"

"Very little, I think," said du Plessis. "The file is very—

meager. The woman is totally disappeared and we have no description. The cab driver, Charles Roux, has moved last week from Ansières to La Rue Monsieur Le Prince on the Left Bank, as you know. He is not fully recovered from the accident and has come to live with his daughter who is divorced. He does not leave the apartment. One thing I have found out since Monsieur Singer called. Wyeth was a homosexual—or at least bisexual. The night before he was killed there was a man with him at La Résidence. He too has disappeared, and the night receptionist who may have seen him is dead." Rhinehauer let this flood of information, so casually dispensed by du Plessis, wash over her.

So Wyeth was a fag, and they had another dead body. She stared at the crippled policeman.

"You certainly have a bag of goodies. Where in hell did you find this stuff?"

"I have made my own inquiries, Madame."

Why the fuck did all Frenchmen call her Madame? It was just one of the things she didn't like about them.

"O.K., I've got a luncheon appointment and then I'm going to try and smoke out that cab driver. Can you get me something on a woman named Micheline Solière, 36 Rue St. Denis?"

"I will try. One more thing I have discovered. There was no faulty mechanism in the taxi. Roux must somehow have jammed his accelerator, have known how to fake the accident without putting himself in serious danger."

"Fine. Roux and I will have a nice little chat. As they say in show biz, don't call me, du Plessis, I'll call you. You've been very helpful. Thank you, Inspector."

"*Je vous en prie, Madame.*" He turned abruptly as though dismissed and limped with surprising speed across the bridge in the direction of the gray, faceless buildings bordering the Seine at Quai d'Orsay.

At noon she joined Georges Bisquet at a sidewalk table at Chez François. The spring flowers formed a lovely barrier, fencing in the restaurant. A bottle of La Doucette was chilling on the table. Georges rose to greet her. He looked worried.

"Ah, Emily—*comment ça va?*"

"Fine so far, Georges. I liked du Plessis—he seems to know what he's doing—and I'm moving something this afternoon."

Bisquet leaned forward. "What?"

"I'm going to put the screws to that cab driver. By tonight I'll know something. Now. What's bothering you?"

"My organization has sprung a leak, as you would say, and it is connected with you."

"What the hell are you talking about?"

"Emily, you know how perfect my operation is. I have a thousand safety devices. Now I find that my cleanest phone, the number you use, was tapped." He was more agitated than she had ever seen him. "And one of my best men is gone. I also have had three monitors accepting reports from those I have placed to follow you on where you are at all times. They work in double shifts and call my central control every thirty minutes. My telephone makes a record and at the end of each day, the paper is put in my own safe. This way, should anything happen to you, we will know everywhere you have been. Because only myself and my closest partners are to know that, our copy machines leave a mark on any document that is duplicated. This morning, when I received yesterday's sheets, I see they have been copied. This is the first time in a dozen years that my club has had an uninvited guest, and I don't like it. Whoever arranged this is technically exceptional and has also reached one of my best men. I now fear for you, Emily."

The waiter arrived for their order. "A salade Niçoise for two," said Bisquet. Then, "I have nothing yet on Solière, but I will tell you this—she is alive and still in Paris."

"How do you know that, Georges?"

"She has in this city two sisters and a brother whom she would call every day. They have neither sounded the alarm nor asked any questions. They know somehow that she is all right. Her mother in the nursing home received a pneumatique from Solière yesterday. It was destroyed before we could trace it, but pneumatiques can only be sent within Paris."

Emily thought about this as she watched the waiter prepare and serve the salad and pour the wine.

"O.K., that helps. I've got du Plessis on her too, and maybe he'll turn up something. I'm supposed to meet Singer at the opera tomorrow night. Keep a close watch, Georges—everyone tells me I've got no tail, but I can feel it. Somebody's breathing down my neck."

They finished their brief meal with little additional conversation. Emily was preparing her approach to the taxi driver, and Bisquet was obviously troubled at the breach in his impregnable fortress. He left in his Maserati, driving himself but accompanied by a bodyguard; as the car disappeared into the traffic, Emily thought of how far Georges Bisquet had come from his beginnings on the Marseilles waterfront.

Almost without exception, no important criminal activity took place anywhere in the country without either his active involvement or tacit approval. He was sixty years old and had been born in Marseilles, the only child of Fernande and Hugo Bisquet, owners of a small, unprofitable waterfront bistro called, cheerfully, Le Perroquet. At the age of fourteen, a local pimp, whose confidence and ego were inflated by an excess of Pernod, had attempted to extort from Hugo Bisquet some special privileges for his women. It was impossible for the elder Bisquet to make such an accommodation without offending other, more powerful friends. The pimp's response to Bisquet's refusal was in the vocabulary of the waterfront. He dragged Hugo from behind his bar and, in full view of customers, friends, and Georges, proceeded to beat him to a pulp.

While his mother, Fernande, ministered to her husband, Georges left the bar and visited the parents of one of his less respectable friends. Here he obtained a fully loaded .45mm revolver. Georges then lured his father's tormentor to an alley where he identified himself and proceeded to empty the contents of the revolver into the man's groin. From that moment forward, Georges' upward movement was rapid and without interruption. Within ten years, Georges Bisquet had become the single most powerful man in Marseilles, controlling all of the drug traffic and most of the prostitution and exercising strong control over elected and appointed government officials. During the war and subsequent Nazi Occupation, Bisquet worked effectively for both sides. He served the Allied and Resistance causes by providing the Allies with a superb intelligence network covering all of southern France; he cheerfully collaborated with the Germans by supplying their carnal needs, such as women and drugs. After the war he was given France's highest civilian honor and as the Marshall Plan began to influence France's recovery, Georges Bisquet resumed his drive to become the most powerful criminal in that nation.

As soon as Bisquet's car was completely engulfed by traffic Emily and Alain took a cab to the corner where a narrow street called Monsieur Le Prince joins the Boulevard Saint Michel.

"I'm going into the apartment alone," said Emily. "If our information's accurate, his daughter is at work and he will be alone as well. If he's not home, we'll come back. You watch my rear. If I need you, you'll know it. And, Alain, I don't care how good you think you are, keep in mind that we're up against a real pro."

For the first time since she had met him at the airport, he smiled. *"Vous aussi, Madame."*

Together they approached Number 39, a four-story building that showed the results of a half-century of neglect. Emily waited across the street while Alain went inside the building, came out and walked around it, then returned.

"The front is the only way in or out. No concierge. Number 6 is in the back on the third floor."

She nodded, and they went in. The smell of cabbage filled the hall. Somewhere in the building a child sang of an owl and a mouse. They paused at the third-floor landing. Alain positioned himself at the top of the stairs; Emily walked down the hall to Number 6 and knocked. She waited. The child stopped singing in the apartment above. She knocked again. The door opened slightly, and Emily could glimpse a man's face.

"Oui?" he said.

"Monsieur Roux, could I speak with you just a moment? It's important."

Having counted on his curiosity to open the door, Emily immediately stepped inside. The apartment was dirty but seemed strangely empty. A half-empty bottle of wine stood on a bare table, and a shabby chair with a pillow on it faced an old television set. Roux wore loose baggy trousers, an undershirt, suspenders, and old slippers.

Emily struck Roux suddenly with the palms of both hands on his narrow chest, propelling him into the chair, then moved close to him, holding him in place with her strong hands. She did not raise her voice.

"I want to know about La Résidence du Bois and David Wyeth. And the accident. I want to know, Monsieur Roux, who hired you, and I want to know right now. If I don't get it all, you're a dead man."

To emphasize the point she took the revolver from her shoulder bag, jamming the barrel into the man's mouth.

"Who hired you, what did you do, how did you do it—and why? Right now, Monsieur taxi driver."

Roux's eyes bulged with fear. He believed her. She took the gun out of his mouth.

"I'm listening, you son of a bitch, you cocksucker." For Roux now, as for Luckmann just before she pushed him down those stairs, as for Marti just as she shot him in the mouth, as for all the others Emily June Rhinehauer had eliminated, the sight of her eyes magnified behind those thick glasses was terrifying.

The taxi driver tried to speak.

"Nothing—*rien de tout*—*rien*. I assure—an accident. I could do nothing, my pedal sticks, I swear to you, Madame, by the grave of my wife . . ."

There it was again—that goddamn *Madame*. She reached to her leg and took out the knife. Without hesitation she cut his cheek horizontally from the base of his ear to the corner of his mouth. For Emily, speed was now essential. The man was in her control for the next few minutes. The sheer audacity of her violent onslaught would either pay off immediately or he would collapse or begin to fight back. He screamed as the blood ran down his neck, soaking his dirty undershirt.

"No, *mon Dieu*. Please, I know nothing. I am innocent. Please . . ." He began to cry. With one hand she held him in place, pressing him against the back of the chair. With the other she placed the point of the knife under his eye.

"Last chance, Roux. Who? Why? And how?"

The man stared wildly into those distorted eyes, and he knew.

"Money—500,000 francs. I have been a cinema stunt driver, many years ago, *un autre nom* . . ." Now it all flowed out— words tumbling on words as if the torrent of them might somehow save him. "I know how to make the accidents."

Emily pushed him closer to the edge. "Who, damn you? Who hired you?"

As he opened his mouth to say the name, Emily saw in his eyes something beyond terror. She threw herself past him onto the floor just as Roux's entire head exploded, scattering blood, bone, and brain all over the room. A second shot broke the plaster on the wall just behind her. It sounded as if a cannon had gone off in her ear. A crazy thought flashed in her mind: Christ, this was how Steve went. She flung herself to the side, whirled toward the door just as it closed. She got up, moved toward it cautiously, opened it—and looked out at the empty hall. She heard the footsteps echoing down the stairs. Where the hell was Alain? Confident in his excellence, she had not locked the door behind her. She reached the stairwell and saw her bodyguard sprawled head first on the steps.

Alain Paul would never again serve Georges Bisquet. An almost invisible wire was buried in the flesh around his neck.

Emily listened for any sign of alarm. A dog was barking and the child continued to sing. She retreated to the apartment and examined it carefully, paying no attention to her blood-splattered clothing. She understood it now.

72

She knew she had to get out very fast. She picked up the phone and dialed Bisquet. A strange voice answered. "Identify."

"This is Cook—where the fuck is he?"

"A moment, Madame." Her nerves were shot. She heard clicks that sounded like gunshots.

"Emily. What is it?"

"Trouble, Georges. Alain's dead and so is Roux—at Roux's place. I'm swimming in blood and Alain's lying on the stairs. It was a setup and I fell for it—Roux was put here for me to find. Get me out, Georges."

He whistled softly. "You must get Alain into the apartment before he is found. Someone will come from me in ten minutes. Do not open the door unless you are called Fernande."

His mother's name. Christ, she thought, he's nuts too. She managed to move Alain Paul from the stairwell to the apartment, then locked the door and turned to view the carnage. Roux was sprawled over the TV chair with half his head gone; Alain was as silent as he had been while alive. Emily Rhinehauer stood frozen against the wall in the far corner of the room, waiting for the knock on the door, and almost didn't hear the whispered voice when it came.

"Fernande."

She opened the door to three men and a woman who came in quietly. The woman gave her a pair of slacks and a blouse and helped her change; the men opened up sleeping bags, zipping the dead men inside and carrying them out.

"Monsieur Bisquet says you must return immediately to your hotel. You were right—this was arranged. Roux's daughter is in Provence on vacation. She thought he was still in Ansières."

Emily did not respond to this disturbing confirmation of what she already knew.

When she reached her hotel, the young bodyguard she had seen with Georges earlier was already in her room.

"I'm very sorry, Madame."

"So am I, but sorry doesn't mean shit. Your friend's dead and I almost joined him." She now felt she had made a serious mistake in relying so heavily on others. It was not the way she usually worked. The phone rang.

"Du Plessis. I have heard."

"News does travel fast in Paris."

"Are you all right?"

"Fine, considering. Which isn't saying much. What have you got?"

"I think I have Solière."

Silence. Emily had been set up once. Now she would be more cautious.

"Where?"

"I will know Sunday morning perhaps. I will breakfast with you at your hotel. In the meantime, do you wish protection?"

"Not from your boys. They're worthless." As soon as she said it she was sorry. "O.K. for breakfast," she said in a conciliatory tone.

"*Bien—à toute à l'heure*, Madame Rhinehauer."

She went into the bathroom and spent the next half hour in the comforting confines of a hot bath. Little by little, she put herself together and began to make some sense of the situation as she now knew it.

Saturday she spent in her room. Her new bodyguard, Marcel Girard, reported hourly to Bisquet. Emily sat alone at the window all day, watching the spring sunshine falling on Les Jardins des Tuileries until the gentle shadows came, making the park look as if it had been recreated by Cézanne or Pissarro.

At seven, Emily dressed for the evening, took a taxi to La Place de l'Opéra, picked up her ticket, and went to her seat. Just as the lights were dimmed, Morton Singer arrived dressed in a slightly worn, out-of-date tuxedo. He settled himself next to her as the opening strains of the overture to *La Nozze di Figaro* began.

He leaned toward her and whispered, "I understand we almost lost you. What happened?"

"You did and it doesn't matter now. I was set up and I fell

for it. It won't happen again." Her tone did not invite further discussion.

The music rose to a crescendo, ending the conversation. At the end of the first act, with Cherubino on the way to the Army and Figaro firmly in command of the action, Singer escorted Emily into the Grand Hall. He leaned toward her as if they were discussing the failure of the baritone to approximate Mozart's vocal instructions.

"Any ideas on who, Emily?" For the first time he used her first name.

"A few. For starters, I think it's one of us. The only people who knew everything about Wyeth's death were at that goddamn meeting you called. The French authorities lost interest in Roux a long time ago, and whoever hired him had no damn reason to kill him unless he knew we were moving. So, only one of us would have set him up like that."

"Reasonable, but hardly conclusive. You know, in chess even the best players are deceived by thinking their opponent is more devious than he actually is."

"Goddamn you, Singer, fuck chess and listen to me. Whoever infiltrated George Bisquet's closed company had to have the equipment and very good connections. Georges' phone was tapped and his intelligence intercepted—all to keep tabs on me. The only people who know me at all were at that meeting. Excepting du Plessis, who *you* guarantee. Georges is the only person I trust, so where are we?"

Singer moved to the bar. "Champagne?"

"No thanks."

"I love it—can't get enough." He ordered a glass and looked at her. "Suppose you're right. That poses a very serious situation, but it does narrow the field."

"I'm waiting for some new information, which I should have tomorrow morning. If I don't get it, I'm getting out. You'll never see me again. Somebody around that table's better than I am. Somebody who set up Wyeth, broke the neck of that bull Lundquist, and almost got me. If I get what I need, I'm going after the last key in the Wyeth killing. I'll let you have what I've got tomorrow night and if it's worth anything I'll hang in. Otherwise I'm out. Permanently."

"Your decision, Miss Rhinehauer, but try and keep me informed. I think I agree with your conclusions. You're the first piece to attack and too often that's the first piece to go. I prefer a game where the attack is better supported by the other pieces."

She was in bed and asleep before two. She dreamed of being sucked into the vortex of a black hole. The darkness was so oppressive that she awoke at four and could not sleep again. Hours later, when she descended in the elevator cage, she saw du Plessis waiting for her by the reception desk. They sat down to a continental breakfast—the black French coffee Emily hated and the croissants she loved.

"Do you have anything, du Plessis?"

"Quite a bit, Madame. I have found Solière."

Emily showed no emotion. "Where?"

"La Clinique St. Estèphe. It is a private sanitorium for those who are incurably and criminally insane. It is well known and has an excellent reputation. It is presided over by a very excellent psychiatrist of a first-class name, Professeur Maurice Gangelle."

"How did she get there?"

"Hard to say. Apparently she went home immediately after Wyeth's death and made two telephone calls. One to a number in the United States—Washington—that has been disconnected. It was only, how do you say, borrowed, not rented . . ." He leaned forward and lowered his voice as if the old waiter who had just poured Emily a second cup of the loathsome coffee had some interest in what they were saying. ". . . the second call was to the clinic. This is how I found her. Because the number is in the book still in her apartment, and I check their record of incoming calls, and her name is there two hours after Wyeth is

76

smashed. Then I think where I would hide somebody, and this hospital seems a perfect place." He was obviously pleased with himself. "I know in every mental hospital there are those who work there because they cannot find work anywhere else. I find one like this at St. Estèphe and I offer him a *good* job in Nice if he finds Solière in his hospital and *voilà*. There she is under the name Javotte Mirelle—her mother's name before she married. And she speaks English perfectly."

Emily watched the ugly crippled man finish his third cup of coffee and wondered just how far she could trust him. She quickly made up her mind.

"Get me inside—today."

"Impossible. They let no one inside who is not a relative whom they know or a doctor they have seen before and checked."

"Du Plessis, I've got a feeling if I don't see that lady today I never will. Get me in."

Carefully, thoughtfully, he buttered yet another croissant.

"*Eh bien*, you will be from the States. The Sharpe Foundation. You will be on a surprise inspection, to give money—grants, you say—and you will want to speak alone to patients. I will show you a picture of Solière."

He extracted from his wallet a small snapshot of a pretty young woman in her mid-twenties.

"Why the hell didn't you show me this before?"

"I only found it yesterday in her apartment. All other pictures were gone. I would not show it to you unless you needed to see it because I, too, do not trust everyone."

"Fair enough." Her estimate of the man continued to grow. "How long to set up this inspection?"

"Three hours. I must get someone with whom they can check your credentials, and three or four people to go with you as part of the team."

"Nobody else—just me. Tell them Sharpe is doing it with individuals so we get better responses from the patients. If they

77

don't like it, tell them a five-million-dollar grant is in the works and show them proof. There's no loony bin in the world that can't use that kind of money."

"D'accord, Madame. Wait here. I will return."

Emily sat at the breakfast table, watching du Plessis make phone calls for over an hour. Finally he returned.

"Done. You are Christine Moore. You are there by permission of Gaston du Brey, the chief of the Bureau de Sanitaire Publique. He may be called at home. Your identification and papers are on the way here. Your bodyguard can go with you as driver, but I do not believe they will let him into the women's section. You will be interviewed by Dr. Gangelle. Can you convince him?"

"I'll have to. If you don't hear from me by eight tonight, notify Singer and Georges Bisquet. They'll know what to do."

"Be very careful, Madame. I do not think it will be easy."

"Nothing's easy in this business, my friend. Ask Dave Wyeth."

Du Plessis looked at her for a moment and then returned to his cold coffee.

They waited in silence in the lobby until the papers arrived. She told Marcel their plan and called Bisquet.

"I don't like it, Emily," he said when she had told him.

"Neither do I, but there's not much of a choice. How good is Marcel?"

"Very close to Alain. Very, very good."

"But Alain wasn't good enough, was he?" There was a pause on the other end.

"Be careful, Emily. I will wait to hear from you."

She considered calling Singer, but decided against it. She had no way of knowing how much he was passing on to the others, how much he really believed her theory. At two, Marcel drove her to La Clinique, about a half hour from the center of Paris in St. Cloud.

They entered the clinic; after a thirty-minute wait, they were ushered into the office of Dr. Gangelle. He was a tall, humorless man, with penetrating eyes. She could imagine the strength and comfort his patients derived from that deep, melodious voice and those slender hands. Emily disliked him instantly.

"We were not informed of your visit, Miss Moore," he said.

"I know, and I do apologize. But your Monsieur du Brey thought I was leaving Tuesday, and I leave tomorrow. We're making some special research grants to private clinics abroad and he did feel I ought to consider your operation."

Emily had adopted the flat, Midwestern accent of the bureaucrat who has migrated from Ohio to Washington and speaks only in official jargon. Gangelle was attentive.

"You understand we deal here only with the most disturbed patients—incurable, criminal, and violent. Their privacy must be protected."

"Of course, Doctor. But Monsieur du Brey was so insistent and . . ."

"May I see your credentials, Miss Moore, while I try to reach my colleague?"

She gave him the passport, the Foundation letter, and other official documents along with a curriculum vitae. As he glanced at them, he dialed Du Brey and spoke rapidly in French. When he was finished, he reluctantly addressed himself to Emily.

"Unfortunately," he said, "even private hospitals are at the mercy of the government. You may tour our facility at will. An attendant and a nurse will accompany you. I am told you must be permitted to talk with whomever you wish. I will comply, but I would like to see you before you leave. Your driver must wait in the hall. Please sign this release freeing us of any responsibility for your physical safety."

She hurriedly signed the paper in the name of Christine Moore. She acknowledged the curt dismissal. She waited another half hour in the sterile reception room before being approached by a massive nurse, whose tag read Mlle. Suzanne Forestière, and an equally large male attendant named Hans Pourse.

She moved down silent and noisy corridors for over an hour, past locked doors with tiny barred windows, past rows of silent men and women sitting on benches staring into space, past those who shrieked and moaned and cried, past those who struggled and those who only slept. She noticed that each corridor had two massive steel doors, one at either end. At a desk in front of each door sat a white-suited attendant, a ring of keys on his belt, keeping the corridor under observation at all times.

For Emily, it was a nightmare beyond description. She played her role, investigating case histories and methods of treatment, seeking in the files the name "Mirelle." The smell of urine and feces filled her nostrils. Hands clutched at her; once she stumbled over a child. Her two watchdogs said nothing. At one point a patient sprang toward Emily; the nurse, three hundred pounds of white starched uniform, enveloped the patient and carried her off to some adjoining chamber.

Finally, when Emily felt she could bear no more, she found in the records of Ward 62Y the file of Javotte Mirelle. She asked that four patients be pointed out, among them Mirelle. She talked with the others first, using the nurse as interpreter, asking sympathetically about friends and relatives, exercise and books. The first patient remained mute; the second sang, in Latin, liturgical music of the sixteenth century. The third, in answer to Emily's questions, was rational and charming. Finally, Emily became impatient and inquired of Mirelle. The giant nurse explained that this patient was separated from the others —so violent that she had to be confined in a private room. Emily insisted on seeing her. The nurse shrugged and beckoned her to follow.

Again, an unbearably long walk past horror and misery and pain.

They entered a corridor lined with rows of small windows in steel doors; the attendant opened one of the doors, and Emily stepped inside. The room was empty. Before she could touch her purse, the nurse and her companion had seized her. Within seconds her clothes were stripped off and Emily was strapped to the bed, naked and helpless. She had no chance to use her karate skills, no chance to extract that deadly knife. She lay staring at the ceiling, terrified. Without warning, the steel doors opened and the reputable and charming Dr. Gangelle stood before her, tall and slender, gazing intently at her.

"So, my dear Cook, you must wonder what has happened and why. And what we can look forward to, eh?"

Her eyeglasses had been broken in the brief struggle. She saw him dimly.

"They know I'm here, Gangelle."

"Who. Du Plessis? He put you here. We are both controlled by the same source. Our debts go beyond our reputations and our impeccable lives, Madame. Bisquet is dead, of a heart attack. Unfortunate, but certainly not uncommon in so tense and violent a man of sixty. Marcel Girard, too, will stay with us. You see, we have known from the beginning. We knew one of you would call seeking the killer of Wyeth. That boring old man who followed you on the plane is one of us. The concierge at the Régina read all your messages. And we still have two members in that close club of which Monsieur Bisquet was so proud.

"You see, Miss Rhinehauer, there is someone who has come to hate your group and its games beyond all reason. That person hates violence, you may be surprised to hear. You, all of you, are no match for my client, whose anger is now turned against all of you—against killing and killers, against all the little charades you play with human life." The doctor spoke quite dispassionately, as if he were presenting an interesting diagnosis during grand rounds. "As a psychiatrist, I assure you that this person's anger is the most terrible I have ever seen. And that you will all be forced to end your games of violence and death."

"You're going to kill me?"

"Hardly, *ma chère cuisinière*. My employer has something else in mind for you. You will stay here, as my guest. Your name: Javotte Mirelle. Monsieur du Plessis has supplied the suitable papers. No one will ever ask for you here. This is, as you know, not uncommon in institutions for the mentally ill.

"A French court, alas, has ruled Javotte Mirelle incurable. You will retire to the halls and corridors through which you have just walked. You will not find escape through suicide. No one ever has.

"In the halls and corridors, in the bathrooms, in your room —you are watched by those whose job it is to care for you and also by those who monitor patients through the television that sees everything. You will be given drugs to make you more tranquil, more peaceful, but be assured that they will in no way prevent you from knowing where you are. The only exit for you is, in fact, through that one portal open to all our patients— the one we call madness. But I suspect you have glanced into that corridor before.

"I will look in on you from time to time. *Au revoir*, Unicorn."

He left. The nurse entered, unfastened Emily's straps, and left. Emily stood up and walked to the door. She looked through the small glass window and saw only the corridor, crowded now with women who paced endlessly back and forth. She began to cry, quietly at first, and then more violently. Finally exhausted, Emily Rhinehauer slid to the floor and stared into space.

4 SINGER

The single strategic theme usually will not dominate a game, but will have to share top billing with another, or with several others. And what commonly happens is that one strategy sharply pursued convinces the defender that he must take the game out of the course that is evidently going to succeed for his opponent.

However, in sidetracking the original strategy, the defender expects not to solve all of his problems, but to test the flexibility of his opponent, his adaptability to a new situation, which calls for a new strategy.

—ROBERT BYRNE, "Chess"
The New York Times, February 20, 1977

HAVING ENDURED THE long, dull flight from Paris to Washington, Singer had come directly to the law offices of Cyrus Harper from Dulles International Airport. It was almost six when he arrived, and Harper's secretary informed Singer that her employer was dining with Luther Martin at a small Italian restaurant nearby if he wished to join them. Singer, who was not hungry, decided to wait. The secretary, an elderly and attractive woman who had served Harper for almost forty years, invited Singer to make himself comfortable in Harper's private office.

Within half an hour, the other attorneys and the rest of the office staff had left Singer to share Harper's opulent chambers with two black cleaning women. He was tired and depressed. He placed the contents of his briefcase on the large mahogany conference table that occupied one corner of the room, sat down,

and began to read again that lengthy document he had so enthu-
siastically prepared and presented with such pride only two
weeks ago. It was as if he hoped that the words would suddenly
provide some new and startling revelation, an illumination that
would bring the matter to a quick and decisive conclusion. He
found nothing in the dates and facts that he had gathered so
meticulously.

Restless, he rose from the table and began to pace around
the large office of oak and leather, gazing at the evidence of a
legendary life spent in the corridors of government. Unlike his
own study, where photographs and letters had been framed with
the love and pride of his wife, these trophies and testaments
seemed to exist only as the credentials of a life passed in the
vortex of power. More persuasive than any biography that would
ever be written, they confronted Singer with the central theme of
the life of Cyrus Wynant Harper—service to the nation.

At that moment Harper and Luther Martin came through
the door, startling Singer.

Harper extended both his hands warmly. "Morton. Were you
waiting long? We thought you'd join us."

"I wasn't hungry, Cy. How are you, Luther?"

"I've been worse, Mort, and I've been better."

Harper went to the bar and poured three glasss of a superb
old Armagnac. The three men settled down around the table and
tasted the brandy. Harper was the first to break the appreciative
silence.

"I gather it's not going well, Morton."

"An understatement. Cy, we're less than two weeks in, and
I'd say we're under siege. No matter what we do, we're anticipated. Whoever it is stays a good light year in front of us."

Martin sat, staring at the report Singer had placed in front of
him. It contained a step-by-step review of everything Singer had
done and seen in Paris.

"What happened to Emily?" Martin asked.

"I don't know, and that's the worst part of it. Maybe nothing.
She said if things didn't work out, if she couldn't locate that
woman, she'd take herself out of it, disappear. But I don't be-

lieve it. I think she was scratched somehow. First of all, Bisquet's death was just too convenient. I couldn't act fast enough to get an autopsy, but I'm not a great believer in coincidence. She trusted him, totally, and we know her instincts were generally damned good. Du Plessis can't find a trace of her. Her hotel room was untouched. Bisquet's man Girard is also gone. And that, gentlemen, tells me I've lost two very strong pieces—Rhinehauer and Lundquist—before we've even gotten started."

Luther Martin got up and began to pace. He hated conferences; he hated sitting around tables talking. A soldier, he was at his best when initiating action. Now he looked old and sick; it was as if all the years of danger, of watching men and women die, of planning and seeing plans become events had suddenly exacted some terrible price. At sixty-four, he looked eighty. He interrupted Singer.

"It doesn't make any sense. Absolutely no one other than the three of us even knew where or how Unicorn was going to respond or what we were trying to do."

"The Unicorns knew," Singer said.

Harper looked up sharply. "Is that what you believe, Morton?"

"Emily believed it and she played it very close to the vest. Very safe. I see no other possibility, Cy. One of our Unicorns has gone mad—it's the only explanation that makes sense. Who else could get that close to Lundquist in his own place, who else could pick off Emily, given the way she was covered? She knew she was tailed from the time she left Washington, but she couldn't locate it. She was one of our best, so who was good enough to get her? Only one of them.

"Gentlemen, we've got a fox in the hen house, and I suggest we face that very unpleasant fact."

Suddenly, despite the comfort and elegance of Harper's office, the room was cold and forbidding. The last remaining daylight had faded, imperceptibly, and the office was now quite dark. Harper got up and turned on a few lights.

"Which one is it?" he asked of no one in particular.

"That, my old friend, is the riddle. Which one indeed, and

how do we come by the answer before we're all dead?"

Luther Martin moved to the silver carafe of ice water that was on Harper's desk across the room. He took a pill out of a small ivory case, swallowed it, and drank two glasses of water.

"Twenty-nine years ago, when Cy suggested Unicorn, I was opposed. Too much power, not enough restraints. But, hell, they've done an incredible job. The original twenty-five are all gone, but we've been able to find others just as good. And now you're telling me one of them's turned cannibal. It doesn't make sense—what the hell's the motive? No, Mort, it won't wash. I can't buy it."

"There's only one other possibility, Luther, and that's that it's either you or Cy. Will you buy that?"

The silence reverberated in the shadowed office.

Singer continued. "We're old men, the three of us. When I started this, I approached it as a puzzle, a chess pattern. Find the game, you find where the attack is coming from—which piece has the ultimate power. Then it's relatively easy. You blunt the attack, box the piece in, turn it around, remove it. Checkmate. But I'll tell you this: we're in a war and we've lost both the initiative *and* the advantage because I didn't really believe it could be one of them. That mistake could prove fatal, and I won't make it again. It's either one of them or one of you." He looked at Martin and his old friend.

Harper finally spoke. "Any ideas, Morton?"

"Cy, I've been playing chess by mail with you for a long time. Let me try an analogy. White begins every game. That first move gives White an advantage. If it is maintained throughout the game, White will probably win. So Black is, in the beginning, on the defensive. Black's response to White's initial attack is critical. It is designed to turn back that attack, force a retreat, regain the move advantage, and initiate an attack of its own. That is precisely our position at this moment. We can retreat and move onto the defensive, or try and mount another attack.

"My initial plan, the product of a conceited old accountant who didn't take the game seriously enough, failed. I sent our seven Unicorns on a search and destroy mission without proper support. A beginner knows better. Now, before we attack again, I suggest we accept our defeat, move into a strong defensive posture, and see if we can encourage our opposition to show a little. We need to see more."

"How the hell do we do that, Morton?" Luther was still visibly upset by Singer's insistence on his thesis, the guilt of one of his best agents.

"Try this. We've got five strong pieces left—Coles, West, Jonas, Gault, and Fonesca. There's nobody else. I've got to proceed on the assumption that it isn't either of you. If it is, I think the game is over. O.K., now I want to bait a trap. I want to expose one piece and see who comes running."

Martin began to pace again, revitalized now, some of the weariness gone, almost a picture of another time and a younger warrior. "Go on, Morton."

"I'll set up a Judas goat—staked to a tree. I'll get word to each of the other remaining players that one of your Unicorns has something. If my hunch is right, one of them will try to eliminate the bait. Ever see a Bishop or a Knight naked in the wrong square? Stands out like a neon sign. I'll place each of them where they should be and see who ends up somewhere else."

Harper went to the bar and poured another Armagnac. He swirled the amber liquid slowly, until it clung to the sides of the snifter, running down in uneven patterns. His eyes never left the glass as he spoke, so softly that it was difficult to hear him across the room. "Suppose your Judas goat is in reality the lion?"

Singer smiled for the first time in a month. "Then no one will come, and we'll know."

"Which one, Morton? Who do we set out in the sun?"

"When I began this, Cy, I did a very thorough job on all our pieces. Unicorn—past, present, and future. I studied each of them from a dozen different vantage points. I'm not in your business—as an accountant, I'm used to looking at figures, which, contrary to popular belief, always lie. The way to get at the truth is to look at people. Who they are, who they were. Hell, figures don't tell you anything, they can be manipulated, distorted, changed until they'll say anything you want. So I refer you again to my work—it's in front of you. We can scratch Rhinehauer, Wyeth, and Lundquist, but you've still got five to look at."

The two men looked at each of the folders.

Singer continued. "The choice we make is critical, so let's take our time in deciding which Unicorn gets staked to that tree. It'll be a long night, gentlemen."

They began at the beginning with what they had read and studied just a few weeks before: Singer's biographical details merged with physical and psychiatric profiles; his short summaries of their lives, interspersed with his own opinions and comments; his queries of those items that either disturbed or interested him.

The night passed slowly. Few words were exchanged save for an occasional question or answer. Harper continued to sample his Armagnac, Luther Martin coughed and paced, sat down and rose again, unable to find rest. Singer made copious notes and left the room occasionally to relieve his bladder. He smoked cigars, and their noxious fumes blended with the more pungent aroma of Harper's meerschaum. Martin, a chain smoker, had gone through two packages of cigarettes before morning.

Then the three men talked quietly about things they thought they had known. They went over the material exhaustively, examining ambiguities and inconsistencies. Finally, as the night blended unnoticed into first light, they were agreed. Harper framed the words.

"Gault, then, I would agree. Next to Lundquist, I think he is, or was, probably the best of the group, so he's best able to take care of himself . . ."

"Also," said Martin, "his specialty has been keeping an eye inside. I think the others will believe it, that he's the one most likely to get close. Christ, Mort—I hope you don't lose him."

"You run that risk whenever you expose a piece deep in enemy territory, Luther. This time we're going to lay it out very carefully. Gault won't know what he's being used for, but we'll try and take very good care of him."

Singer's colleagues were not reassured. Harper turned out the lights and opened the curtains. It was daylight, a little past six-thirty.

Luther Martin turned to Singer. "Is there anything I can do? I'm not used to sitting on the sidelines cheering."

"Not now, Luther. Just keep all our channels open on a twenty-four-hour basis, and this time I'll feed you everything you need to know. We agreed on locations. Fonesca operates out of his home base in Tokyo. Jonas probably won't move from Big Sur—he seldom does. West will go to ground in Nairobi on the assumption that a black piece is best hidden on a black square. And Coles should work her Chilean connection either on the spot or from here. If any one of them begins to roam, we'll have something to watch."

Harper closed the meeting. "You'll keep us informed, Mort."

"When it's profitable. Right now my instinct is to play this game out alone. It seems to me that we've been on a party line without knowing it. I feel very unsafe."

Martin buttoned his uniform and ran a comb through his disheveled hair. "O.K., Mort, but don't play it so close that we can't help if you need us."

"I'm no hero, Luther. You'll know what you need to know when you need to know it. To keep us all alive and well."

The three men placed all their documents in their briefcases. Harper returned his to his safe. They talked easily now, of old friendships and other times. They left the offices and the building, signing out with the security guard. Harper's limousine glided silently to the curb as he said his good-bye.

Luther Martin watched the car move away toward the Potomac and Virginia. "A lift, Mort?"

"No thanks, Luther. I think I'll walk a little. Between the plane and our little meeting, I'm stiff from all the sitting. Grace always wanted me to exercise more."

Another car, this one an official Army vehicle driven by a uniformed soldier, moved into the space vacated by Harper's limousine. The soldier opened the door for Luther Martin.

"Be very careful, Mort. This is no damned chess game."

"I will, Luther. And you too."

The car pulled away. Singer stood for a moment or two, his figure bathed in the light of the Washington dawn. The sun was rising now, and a few people appeared in the deserted streets. He walked rapidly to a phone booth on the corner and dialed a number.

The voice answered in a whisper. "463-5702."

He hung up and dialed the number he had been given.

"Yes."

"This is Singer. It's all set."

"They bought it?"

"They probably think it was their idea."

"Any problems?"

"None."

"You're good, Singer. You're very good."

"We'll see. We haven't got any real answers yet."

"Go slowly, old man, and don't make any mistakes. For both of us."

"Same to you, my friend."

Singer hung up and began to walk slowly in the direction of Dupont Circle. He would check in to the Washington Hilton, breakfast, shower, and try to sleep for an hour or so. It annoyed him that his hands had been shaking when he dialed those numbers. He was tired.

There were moments in chess when you were forced to take great risks. You began an unsupported attack masked by feints, by misdirection and diversion. You knew that the game might end very suddenly if your opponent discovered the true purpose of your move. Thus it was important that the move appear to be somewhat less complex than it was. If, as you reached for a piece, your hand trembled even slightly, or your eyes dropped and your mouth tightened, the opponent was alerted and your plan jeopardized.

Singer knew he must control the wave of terror that now swept over him like an avalanche.

90

PART II

MIDDLE GAME

Once the mobilization of the forces for both sides has been more or less completed, and the basic features of the position have taken shape, the time has come to formulate a plan of campaign for the Middle Game. It is imperative to have a plan; to shift the pieces about in the vague hope that something will turn up is worse than useless. It is even better to have formed a bad plan than no plan at all: from the failure of a bad plan there is something to be learned, and you can benefit from the experience thus painfully acquired to help form a better plan the next time.

—A. I. HOROWITZ, *Learn Chess Quickly*

FILE 473-24-5617 (U-40)

NAME:	Laura Susan Coles
DATE OF BIRTH:	November 8, 1946
PLACE OF BIRTH:	College Station, Texas
PARENTS:	Franklin Victor Coles Janet Linda Coles (Briggs)
SIBLINGS:	Foster Bruce Coles (32) Jody Lynn Coles (27) Martha Mary Coles (22)
MARITAL STATUS:	Single
EDUCATION:	Fernwood Elementary School (1951–1957) Sam Houston Junior High School (1957–1960) Lakeland High School (1960–1963) Bennington College, Vermont (1963–1967)
EMPLOYMENT:	Foster's Burger Palace, College Station (1962–1963) Library Services (Bennington College) Dr. Wilfred George (Chairman, Dept. of Fine Arts, B.C., 1967) National Gallery of Art, Washington, D.C. (1967)
COMPANY:	1971
U:	1973

PHYSICAL DATA:
Height:	5′ 7″
Weight:	125 lbs.
Complexion:	Fair
Hair:	Blond

IDENTIFYING MARKS:	Lateral scar under left shoulder from service-connected injury (1973). See pages 14–15 and Addenda 46 for details.

Summary and Review (MLS)
Project: UNICORN

This agent's background seems to embody the best of rural America. Her father, Franklin Coles, was born and raised near Imperial, Nebraska. He graduated from the Agricultural Extension course at the State University, married Janet Briggs, and moved almost immediately to Lubbock, Texas. Coles tried raising cotton and soybeans on a thousand-acre farm for ten years and finally gave up under financial pressure. He accepted a job as the County Agricultural Agent at College Station and is now in his twenty-second year in this job.

The Coles had five children, four of whom are still living. (One was killed in 1961 in an automobile accident.) We have on file (attached) interviews with fifty residents of both Imperial, Nebraska, and Lubbock and College Station, Texas, who have known this family well at some stage during a period of sixty years—longer, in fact, than the parents have lived. They are well-liked, active in their community. (All photographs are attached in your folders marked P6A-B-C.) As you can see, the agent is exceptionally attractive and has been since she was born. The entire family could accurately be described as "handsome."

The agency files on Laura Coles were unusually complete, so I was able to project a very clear biographical portrait. She enjoys and has enjoyed a very healthy family life. She remains quite close to her brother and two sisters as well as to her parents. They admire her success in her chosen field (art) and consider her loving, thoughtful, and attentive.

She did quite well academically and was among the most popular students during her elementary- and secondary-school life (see attached copies of yearbook and letters). Socially active during high school, she still managed to graduate in the top one percent in her class. During her junior and senior years, she enjoyed a busy social life without any single attachment. From her intake interview (File 6-X9), her first sexual experience occurred in June of 1962 (Junior Prom) with one Paul Peter Linke (MIA-Vietnam, 1964). From this point forward, her sexual relationships seem quite normal. (See attached interviews 47, 48, 49, File 5-V4.) She was, I have concluded, neither overly reticent nor promiscuous.

Our first inconsistency in this otherwise uneventful recitation is her decision to attend Bennington College in Vermont. This surprised her parents and friends, who assumed she would attend either Texas A & M at College Station or, at least, the State University at Austin. Upon graduating from high school, she does not appear to have any career interest (see attached interview with Claude Wendt, her adviser).

Coles' college career was what one would expect from her high-school life, with one notable exception. In her freshman year (1964), she seems suddenly to have developed an interest in fine arts; from this point on, she studied this field with unusual intensity. Despite the lack of support data, I suspect an affair with one Dr. Wilfred Lanseer George, then twenty years her senior, a professor of Fine Arts and later head of the Department at Bennington. (Current status: deceased. Coronary on April 10, 1975.)

Coles graduated with honors, and Dr. George recommended her to our friend CB at the National Gallery in Washington. From the hyperbole of the attached recommendation, I suspect that the good Professor wanted to get rid of Laura. And one would think, given an oblique reference in the college newspaper, that there was a Mrs. George who was making noises (no verification).

According to CB, Laura Coles was so impressive as to be hired immediately. She moved to Washington, where she comes into the Company's orbit for the first time. She has six months of considerable social success in our nation's capital (by this time I think it fair to describe her physical attributes as spectacular) and meets one of ours, Scott William Lambell (File 731-22-4949 attached). The attraction was instantaneous on both sides (letter L. Coles to Mrs. J. Coles, February 4, 1968). They become roommates; based on all supporting evidence, I would judge the relationship as stable.

On June 18, 1970, Lambell was terminated by a hostile in Bangkok while on assignment. Three months later Coles applied for employment with the Company. The following items I think are significant and worthy of discussion.

* 1) Excerpt from initial application form:
    21. Why do you wish to work for this agency (answer completely)?

I am anxious to find some work that is interesting and challenging in both an *intellectual* and *physical* sense. Also, I believe I have some *special qualifications* for the kind of work your agency does.

Interesting?

* 2) Also refer to her Psychiatric Profile (PP 1437YY-Paine, Gregory, Dr., Ex. P.).

   ". . . in summary she is extraordinarily controlled, but I suggest that she is successfuly hiding some damage."

Dr. Paine did, however, recommend her employment.

* 3) Excerpt from her final interview. Control agent Harvey Trask (921-34-769, called "Linden")

Q. One thing still troubles me, Laura. Why do you really want to get into this kind of work?

A: I'm angry, Mr. Linden. I've lost something, and I want them to pay me back. I'm very intelligent and I'm not squeamish and I don't want a desk job. Look, I know what you people do and I've got a damn good idea of how you do it. Try me—what the hell have you got to lose! I'm patient and I learn fast and I'll do what I'm told. Take a flier on me, Mr. Linden, and maybe you'll get more than your money's worth.

Q: Do you think you can kill someone? (There is no pause in the tape.)

A: For Christ's sake, I read the newspapers. I don't believe in Christmas or the Tooth Fairy. I know the kind of world we live in. Give me some credit for intelligence. The answer, Mr. Linden, is yes. I've got a pretty damn good idea of what I'm getting into.

Q: Could you kill someone?

A: I already have, my friend.

I have no record of any follow-up to that comment on the part of the Company. It seems to me a significant omission.

Coles was hired on November 10, 1970. Her training record —outstanding—is attached. She continued to use CB and the National Gallery of Art as cover. I won't review her operative record, which as you know is extraordinary. She became the fortieth Unicorn in 1973 (October). I would, however, like to draw attention to her Chilean activities because I find some highly suggestive and even disturbing facts here. I've outlined them as follows:

(1) There is no question that the whole operation was an organizational masterpiece. She executed her role in the affair superbly and can be said without exaggeration to have made a major contribution to the downfall of the Allende government.
A. She recommended our withdrawal through IMF, WB, and OAS of all economic support at exactly the right moment, after leading SA to believe we could not act.
B. She nullified Frei's attempts to pour oil on troubled waters by seducing Tobar, Frei's political adviser. The man fell insanely (not too strong a word) in love with her and gave Frei some very bad advice.
C. She arranged and supervised the assassination of General Schneider—thus removing a stabilizing and moderate alternative—and created the illusion that A had ordered the event.

All the above can be categorized as good work. She seems, however, to have been somewhat overzealous:
1. She suborned and seduced Col. José Luis Cruz, A's top security officer, and supplied General Augusto Pinochet Ugarte with the names of all A's security agents. None of them survived the ensuing holocaust.
2. She insisted on being present at the Villa Grimaldi during the torture and death of her lover Cruz. The circumstances were particularly unpleasant and included the use of the "Planton."
3. It seems that it was Laura Coles who made sure that Allende's pathetic exit from his headquarters, in an attempt to surrender, was greeted by a fusillade of automatic fire that literally erased the old socialist.

One eyewitness account (attached, Waldemar Shurz—security adviser to General Pinochet) suggests that our lovely Laura is excited by certain kinds of torture and death. As a theory it is worth examining in light of our current problems.

To bring you up to date:
Coles is currently Assistant Director of Public Relations at the National Gallery and is, according to her superiors, doing a superb job. She lives with Walter Du Quoin Parsons, a rising

young legal light (Patterson, Fielder, Wistreth and North). There is no evidence to suggest that marriage is being contemplated. Her last psychiatric examination—two years ago—shows nothing of interest. Her main strength seems to lie in organization and implementation. She has never refused an assignment and gets along with any agent with whom she works.

Conclusions (MLS):
A strong, dedicated, talented woman—well able to take care of herself. On the surface highly stable, but I suspect a deeper disturbance than we have any evidence to support.

5 COLES

Each of the chessmen has a different way of moving.
This variety adds a great deal to the charm of chess,
and allows the chessman to cooperate to produce
stunning effects . . .

The Queen, like the King, can move in any direction.
But there is a very important difference—the Queen
can keep right on moving until she is blocked by some
obstacle to her further progress. The Queen captures
by displacing the hostile chessman she is eliminating.

—FRED REINFELD, *Two Weeks to Winning Chess*

LAURA COLES HAD, in the three weeks following that first meeting in Washington, drawn a complete blank for the first time in
her professional life. The morning after Lundquist's death, she
had gone to his apartment and done her own scan. With Singer's
permission, she remained in the apartment for almost twenty-
four hours, searching for some sign of what Pater Lundquist had
found or thought he had found. Having overheard his whispered
comment to Gault, she was convinced that someone else had
also heard that conversation, someone who then decided to
eliminate the giant Swede from the game. She had hoped, at the
very least, to discover some clue as to the identity of the intruder
who was able to nullify U-29 so easily.

Nothing. Not a whisper, not a memory. Whoever had been

here was now totally invisible. She had asked Singer to keep everyone out of the apartment for at least a day and a night. In the end, the silence of the place had become increasingly oppressive; when the rooms and the possessions and the furniture had failed to reveal anything at all, Laura became oddly depressed.

Her next response was to call in all outstanding accounts. She made a person-to-person call on a safe wire to Chile's Chief of State, General Augusto Pinochet, who owed much of his power to her covert activities on his behalf. She knew that there existed among a group of "undesirable" nations a secret but highly effective network of interacting intelligence services; she knew this alliance conducted joint operations without communicating with their counterparts in more powerful countries. Included were the Korean CIA, Iran's Savak, Qaddafi's Special Force, Brazil's Unit 5, and similar covert agencies from Argentina, Thailand, and Indonesia. She asked Pinochet to get her an accurate assessment of what these groups were reporting with regard to the Unicorn deaths.

Pinochet immediately dispatched Carlos Steiner, his intelligence chief, on a three-week global tour; Steiner met with his counterparts in thirteen small anti-human-rights nations in Latin America, the Middle East, Africa, and Asia. At the end of his trip, he arranged to meet Laura at the Chilean Embassy in Washington.

The meeting took place in a corner of one of the large ornate reception rooms used for affairs of state. The room was rich in dark woods, medieval tapestries, and native art from the Andes. Carlos Steiner and Laura Coles were old friends who had worked together for many months to help destroy the old professor's Socialist regime. Laura dressed for the meeting in a beige suit that suggested the exceptional outlines of her body without offering Steiner anything more specific. She knew that in Chile he had wanted very much more than a working relationship; at the time, however, Laura had employed her considerable sexual talents in a direction more closely related to her mission. Together, she and Steiner suborned and helped destroy the protective intelligence ring that had surrounded Allende, but not once in all those months did this young intelligence agent cross the line that Laura had drawn so clearly. Later, when it became imperative that Ambassador Orlando Letelier be silenced, Steiner and Laura again worked together in Washington with excellent professional results—and no change in their personal relationship.

Now, as they sat talking quietly, Laura felt his eyes following her smallest moves. A young Chilean woman served pisco sours and some unidentifiable hot pastries.

"You are an exquisite woman, Laura," Steiner said when the woman finally left them alone. "I'd almost forgotten."

"Thank you, Carlos. It's very, very good to see you. How are things in Santiago?"

"Good, Laura, quite good. Except for the public relations problem, we proceed very well. Most of our enemies, at least the powerful and influential ones, are either dead or in deep confinement. Those few that remain free are far too frightened to cause us any real trouble. It will, of course, take us much time to repair the economic damage, but we will succeed if your new President sticks to words and does not actually interfere."

He paused and walked to the window as if to place some distance between them. "Laura, exactly what was behind my fact-finding mission?"

"I really can't tell you much, Carlos. We've got someone or something trying to hurt us and I'm simply trying to get a line on it. Did you turn anything up?"

He returned to the sofa they shared and reached under the coffee table for his briefcase. He opened it and handed Laura a thick folder.

"This is the result of all my meetings. I'm afraid you will find very little. The Iranians didn't even know what was happening to Unicorn. Savak is too busy chasing their own people. Koo's group in Seoul had heard a little, but couldn't help at all. The Libyans were the most helpful. Starting on page 161, you will find a transcript of their report. You must already know most of it, but they did say that one of your people, from the description probably Lundquist, had contacted one of theirs in Washington. He asked some unusual questions concerning the death of an agent named Singleton in 1969. They think there was some Chinese involvement, which seemed particularly interesting to the Swede. Other than that, the trip was a total waste. I am sorry."

Laura watched Steiner closely as he spoke, thinking how difficult it would be for most people to identify this blond, handsome young man—who was rumored to hold the future of the Junta in his hands—as Chilean. His files were filled with the outpourings of those who had enjoyed his hospitality at the Villa Grimaldi, and yet here, in the civilized environment of the embassy, Carlos Steiner was the epitome of European charm and civilization. Laura lit a cigarette.

"Maybe not," she said. "I'd like to follow the Chinese kite a little. I've never heard of it before. Who can I see?"

"I'm not certain. I can arrange a line to Peking through one of our stringers who works as a houseman at the Peninsula Hotel in Hong Kong. His name is Fung Ka-Wai. Ask for a front room in the old section on the fifth floor. We're not too well staffed in that part of the world but the Taiwan boys are excellent, and they are in debt to me. When do you wish to go?"

"A couple of days. God knows, we've got no time to spare. Set it up for me and I'll take the Pan Am flight out of Kennedy Saturday morning."

"It is done, Laura."

"Thank you, Carlos. Very much."

She leaned over and kissed him, touching his cheek lightly with her hand.

They left the room together and separated in front of the embassy. Massachusetts Avenue was deserted, though flanked on either side by the lights of the embassies. The silence was oppressive.

Laura had her own car; Steiner's ambassador had provided him with an official limousine. She sat in her parked car for a moment or two, watched Carlos drive into the darkness, then drove home to the apartment in Chevy Chase that she shared with Walter Parsons, her current lover. She entered the apartment silently, undressed without turning on the lights, and slipped naked into the bed. The young lawyer stirred and mumbled.

"Everything O.K., Laura?"

"Fine, darling."

"Call the number on the telephone table. He said it was important."

She kissed him and went into the study, where Walter had taped the message to the phone. She dialed and was answered by a male voice.

"Yes."

"This is Laura Coles. Who is this?"

"Mike Gault, Laura. I didn't expect you to call so late. I'm sorry if I've interrupted anything."

He spoke softly, and she liked the voice. She retrieved the image of a dark, introspective face.

"You haven't. What's up?"

"I'd like to see you as soon as possible. I think it's important."

She hesitated for just a moment—this type of direct contact on an open wire was highly unusual. She quickly decided to follow his lead, if only to see where it would take her.

"Tomorrow, around noon. Lunch, if you want."

"All right. Let's try the garden at the Hyatt. It's noisy and crowded and very public, and the food and service are terrible."

"With that kind of buildup, how can I refuse? See you then, Mike."

She hung up and returned to bed. Walter was asleep again, but it was quite some time before she could follow him. She was aroused, and she didn't know why. She placed her hands between her legs and stroked herself gently.

Laura spent Friday morning preparing for her trip to Hong Kong. From the time she joined the Company, she had used her job with the National Gallery as her primary cover. Now, working through the Special Events section at the gallery, she arranged an exploratory trip to the Far East relating to two major exhibits of Oriental art. The Company would provide the necessary flow of reports, photographs, and other supporting documents that would satisfy the head of her department and her co-workers—and would also provide a stand-in to travel and interview key authorities in Japan, Korea, China, and Thailand. This would leave Laura free to follow the Chinese kite wherever it flew. The entire operation was arranged within two hours.

At ten-thirty she called Carlos Steiner.

"Good morning, Carlos."

"Hello, Laura. Everything is arranged. I've alerted the Taiwan group to expect you in Hong Kong on Saturday. You will stay at the Peninsula, and they will contact you there. The code subject for purposes of identification will be philosophical in nature. I urge you to exercise extreme care—it is impossible to be safe in Hong Kong where so many others are operating and where you are so close to Peking. Also, Laura, remember that you have never operated in the Far East. It is altogether different from our part of the world."

"You know I'm always careful, Carlos. I'm all set on the Saturday Pan Am flight. I'll talk to you whenever all this is over. And Carli, my dear, I can't thank you enough."

His voice softened to a whisper.

"*Por nada,* Laurita. *Vaya con Dios.*"

Laura showered quickly, put on a tailored gray suit, left a note for Walter, and took a cab to the Hyatt Regency in downtown Washington, arriving deliberately early to make a call that had to originate from a public phone.

"Singer, this is Laura Coles."

"Yes, Laura."

"Anything on Julia Child?"

"Absolutely nothing."

"O.K., here's what I've got. There seems to be some kind of Chinese involvement that goes back about nine years. Lundquist was nosing into this. I've got a very light lead, but I'm going to chase it into the Crown Colony, then take a few from column A and B and whatever. I leave Saturday. Don't announce me to anybody out there, but set up a drop so at least you'll know what I'm doing. I'll try and keep you current. I'd like to see you tonight, around nine at Kennedy; we can talk outside on the terrace. I've got something for you, and I'll want something in return. A .38 police special, just like mine, delivered to me at the Peninsula."

"No problem. Where are you now?"

"At the railroad station they call the Hyatt. See you later."

She stood on line for a table in the coffee shop. A few minutes after she was shown to a table, Michael Gault sat down next to her.

It had been an interesting experience for her to put faces to Unicorns she had known only as numbers prior to Singer's meeting. While reading the dossiers, she had tried habitually to imagine the physical appearance of her peers. She had been wrong in almost every case, but never more so than with Michael Trevor Gault. His biography as prepared by Singer had not in any way prepared her for the strength she sensed he possessed. There was something hidden in his dark, handsome face, something in the veiled eyes that she found hypnotic and very sensual. Several times during the meeting she had covertly glanced at him and at least once had been embarrassed to have been caught by the object of her interest. His return glance had had the hint of a smile in it. Now, in his presence, she felt the memory of that initial attraction. As if he had access to her thoughts, he said, "I must admit, I never imagined what our U-40 looked like."

"How *does* she look, Mike?"

"Very special and very inviting."

"Thank you, sir." She shifted, beautifully, in her chair. "Now, why are we here?"

Give it to them, Laura, then take it away. You learned a long time ago, and it always works. Just when you're getting the familiar response, remind them who the hell you are. Remember how Cruz looked at you when he first met you and when you first let him see you naked and touch you, and remember how he looked at you when Steiner hung him upside down in that stinking room at Grimaldi.

Gault's tone of voice now matched hers.

"You know Emily's been scratched."

"Yes. I got Singer's message."

"O.K. I think I've got something real, but I can't follow it alone for a lot of reasons. I had to choose among the Unicorns that are left. You're my first choice."

"What did I win?"

"Be patient, will you, and I'll lay it out."

The waitress arrived with that sense of timing peculiar to her job, the ability to materialize at the worst possible moment during a conversation. Laura ordered a chef's salad and Gault asked for a rare minute steak. The noise and frenetic atmosphere of the coffee shop seemed to reach a crescendo. Had they been talking through a megaphone, no one could have overheard.

"You know what I've been doing for the Company since 1974?"

"No."

"I've been our inside man. Right after the Olympic mess in Munich, Luther Martin brought me home to clean up our own house. Checkers was clearly out of it, mad as a hatter, and that tightass Haig had his hands full playing President and trying to keep the whole thing from going down the tubes. Kissinger was spying on everybody. Thanks to Hoover and Gray, the FBI was dead. Martin saw the agency going the same way. He gave me a free hand and asked me to look around and report only to him. I won't bore you with all the details, but we did quite a sanitation job. It was more like cancer surgery. Corruption and disease every goddamn place."

He paused to sip his iced tea. Laura was fascinated, not so much by the words as by the man. As he talked, his anger and passion began to force their way through the reserve of his professional training.

"I was the first one to see a pattern to the Unicorn deaths. At first nobody listened. Even Martin was singularly unimpressed. Admitting that it was very well done and allowing for the fact that no one but he and Harper knew who the Unicorns were, it still seemed clear to me. I couldn't understand why the damned numbers didn't cause more excitement. Christ, from 1969 to 1974, we dropped nine. Up to then, we'd never lost more than four in any comparable period. When U-11 and U-17 were scratched in a two-month period in 1975, I raised hell with Martin and he finally agreed it was worth looking into."

The noise of the room seemed to fade as Laura listened to Gault.

"He promised to put a special team on it, but asked me to keep after the termites that were eating at us from inside. It went pretty high and kept me busy for the rest of the year. In '76 and early '77, I did all I could to complete the sterilization of what was left of this agency. The Sorensen nomination scared the hell out of all the old hands, including Luther and Harper, so I got involved with killing that off and had no time to defend Unicorn. The next thing I know is Singer's on the scene and we're all blown to each other at a goddamn PTA meeting. Luther never gave me a hint as to what he was going to do. O.K.—so far, what's your conclusion?"

Unprepared for the question, she did not respond immediately.

"I don't know," she said finally. "I was out of the country most of the time. I had no access to any of this. I didn't know who any of the Unicorns were until they showed up at the meeting. Those two old men put this whole thing together almost thirty years ago and just didn't see any reason to mess with it.

"So what's the point, Mike?"

"Analyze it, Laura. No one but the agents and Harper, Martin, and the President knew of Unicorn's existence until the meeting. No one but Harper and Martin knew the identities of the individual Unicorns. That raises a very interesting question: Who the hell could be wiping us out if nobody knows who we are?"

Laura shifted uncomfortably in her chair. "If I'm following you correctly, Mike, you're pointing at Luther Martin."

"Laura, that man is as close a friend as I've ever had. He hired me and in a way I love him. I also admire his integrity— what it's meant to the agency and to the country. But damn it, right now I can't see anything else that makes sense. Now let me give you something else. Lundquist approached me just as Singer's meeting was breaking up. He wanted to see me. We'd worked together before I was in Unicorn and we traded lives at least three times. We trusted each other totally. I never saw him after the meeting because somebody got there first. Afterward I backtracked on what he'd been doing just before the meeting. Pater had been glued to Luther Martin like a Siamese twin."

"How the hell did you find that?"

"I picked up a coded report in his place an hour after I was told he'd been killed."

"And six hours before I got there."

"When Singer called, I went right over. The report was in a double false pocket inside his briefcase. He had it made when we worked together in Africa—it's like a double kangaroo pouch, a false pocket inside a false pocket."

"Even if I had found the second pocket, it would have been empty. You were there first."

He smiled for the first time since he'd begun his recitation. She felt that smile inside her. She thought, Christ, Gault, don't start that. I closed that out a long time ago.

"We're not competing, Laura. I'm telling you this because I need you."

"Why me?"

"There's no safe way I can follow this track by myself. Whoever's doing this to us is capitalizing on our goddamned insistence on operating alone. Wyeth, Pater Lundquist, and Emily found that out. O.K., I've got to work with somebody. Jonas won't move off his ass to go anywhere, West hasn't shared anything with anybody since the Preacher was killed, and I think Fonesca's mad as a hatter. So it's you by elimination."

"Thanks for the compliment. I win because the others all lose. Why don't you take this to Singer?"

"As far as we know, he was hired by Martin and Harper. I know absolutely nothing about him. If he turns out to be clean and we build a perfect case against Luther, we can show it to him. For now, I won't take any unnecessary chances. I think he's O.K., but I also think Luther is using him.

"Singer thinks he's a genius. You learn early in this game that there's no such thing—you're never good enough, and there's always somebody better. How about it, Laura, do we go the rest of the way together?"

The ubiquitous waitress reappeared, cleared the dishes with a maximum of noise and a minimum of efficiency. She refilled Laura's coffee cup and spilled Gault's iced tea before vanishing into the crowd.

The interruption gave Laura a chance to think. She had stayed alive in Chile when agents with far more experience had died badly because she trusted no one while they trusted a few. The fact that he appealed to her as a man only made her decision more difficult. Laura's romantic liaisons had, almost without exception, ended badly. She had given too much of herself away to someone she had respected and admired when she was at college. The affair ended at the edge of scandal when her lover's wife threatened him with exposure. He had turned his back on Laura without pause or regret or even a word of explanation. Then, when the professor had faded into memory, there was Scott Lambell, whom she had learned to love and to whom she had looked for a rebirth of emotional health; he had, just before he was drowned in a klong in Bangkok, told her not only of his work with the agency but of his passion for a fifteen-year-old Thai boy. (The same boy, in fact, who lured Lambell to his death.) There were others, though none who mattered so much.

And so Laura, tempted by Gault's offer and troubled by the attraction she felt for him, distrusted her feelings. Somehow she felt manipulated. God, she thought, I've talked to this man for less than an hour and I'm wet. Finally, she answered Gault.

"I don't know, Mike. I've always preferred working alone."

"So have I—like all the Unicorns. That's one of the reasons we were chosen. But we can't afford it any more, Laura."

"What if we're wrong about Martin?"

"Then we'll find that out. Alone, we're very naked. Together, we can cover each other. I read the Chilean story in Singer's report. You're very good, Laura, and so am I."

"And so is whoever's after us."

He put his hand on hers and spoke very softly. "Laura; we live our lives isolated from normal people. We've each got our own reasons for doing what we do, but that doesn't change the fact that it's an isolated existence. Because we're Unicorn, we don't even have the support or friendship of our own kind. I think we've got to change the way we operate. Very honestly, Laura, I want some help."

She felt his hand on hers, and it burned. It was almost as if a lover had proposed marriage. In this declaration of weakness, Michael Gault communicated instead an incredible aura of male strength. She felt feminine and vulnerable; she felt him, here in this crowded, noisy restaurant, between her legs. Not sure what was happening, she removed her hand.

"O.K., Mike, let's give it a try. I'm not a hundred percent sold, but at this stage anything's better than being alone. For openers, listen to what I can give you."

She took a kind of refuge in sharing her information, telling him of her entire conversation with Steiner and of her plans to pursue the Chinese connection. As she talked, he became increasingly quiet and thoughtful.

"Interesting," he said when she finished. "What could Pater

have found in the wok? 1969–70, that's a long time ago. I can look at our Top 'S' files if you want. I've got open access."

"I don't think they'll tell us much, Mike. After all, Singer's been through them, and I'm sure Harper and Martin have had a pretty careful look. I want to chase this down myself."

"Where?"

"Hong Kong maybe. My Chilean friends can set up a line to Peking, but I've got to be there."

"O.K., Laura, let's try it together. We'll travel separately but work as a team. No secrets. I know the city and have a few friends there."

Suddenly Laura was thinking not of her reason for going to the Crown Colony but of Jennifer Jones and William Holden making love in a romanticized Hong Kong. She forced herself to listen to Michael Gault's outline and approach.

"You go Pan Am Flight 1 tomorrow and book the Peninsula. I'll go JAL, get in a few hours later, and stay across the harbor at the Mandarin. I'm Michaels. Message me that you're in safe and I'll make contact."

They got up to leave. Mike, as if he were a friend of many years' standing, put his arm around her shoulder.

"Let's make it good, Laura. Good *and* safe."

For that, she had no reply.

Gault paid the check, and they left the hotel separately. Laura returned to her apartment, packed, arranged for a seat at the evening performance at the Kennedy Center and tried to call Steiner. He was not in. From a small safe in her study, she removed a .38 caliber custommade pistol, tooled to accommodate a short silencer. She put it in a special pocket of her Givenchy raincoat. She also carried two fountain pens; one was equipped with Mace, the other with the Company's newest version of cyanide vapor. The latter was instantly lethal. Last among her unique accoutrements was a set of false fingernails tipped with RS46, an inert biological poison that was, when scratched against human skin, lethal within five seconds. Laura had used these to dispatch Letelier's bodyguard when he discovered her placing the bomb inside the Chilean exile's car. She packed the nails in with her cosmetics for the trip to Hong Kong.

At nine o'clock, while a performance of Samuel Beckett's *Waiting for Godot,* starring John Gielgud and Ralph Richardson, was boring the fashionable Kennedy Center audience, an overweight gentleman in a rumpled black suit stood on the terrace overlooking the Potomac River, talking with an exceptionally beautiful young woman.

Laura told Singer the details of her conversation with Steiner, then gave him the specifications for a duplicate of her own gun and asked again that he have it delivered to her hotel in Hong Kong. Singer didn't comment until she had finished.

"This whole thing seems to get more complicated all the time, Laura. We are now faced with a Chinese involvement going back almost ten years. All right, follow it—but keep me closely informed. Your drop is the Crown of Hong Kong, an Oriental art gallery in the Peninsula. The woman who runs it is Yang Lin-Shi. Identify yourself with a reference to Chinese erotic art; she will respond by showing you a pertinent example. Code all your messages and let me know in advance if you're going to be away from the hotel for any substantial length of time. I can't afford to lose any more pieces."

"One question, Singer. How much do you really know about Gault?"

He looked at her strangely. "Why?"

"Just curious. Can you tell me anything?"

"He's been our top inside eye since 1974. Martin says he's our best now that the Swede is dead."

"I know all that. I want some real background. Not a rehash."

"I gave you everything I had in that report. You all got the same thing."

"It's not enough. And I don't believe it."

"It's all I have, and it will have to do."

Now there was clearly some antagonism between them.

Singer was tired of playing Court Jester. He didn't like them, any of these arrogant agents, and it was obvious that they didn't like him. If he were to succeed in this impossible job, he had better establish just who was in charge.

"Anything else on your mind, Laura?"

"Yes. Why did Gault join in the first place? There's something in your stuff that doesn't quite make sense."

"Why did you join, Laura?"

"I needed a job."

He smiled. "Nonsense. You joined to get back at us. The old professor threw you out in favor of his ugly wife, and your boy friend dumped you in favor of a Siamese queen. Not what you expected when you were throwing batons in the air and giving all the boys wet dreams. You just couldn't make it, Laura, and now you want to get yours, from all the men in the world."

For a moment she just stared at Singer. He was still smiling. Then she spoke quietly, in a soft, cold voice. "Don't push it, old man. I advise you very strongly not to push it."

She turned and walked away, leaving Singer to contemplate the words of John Fitzgerald Kennedy etched in the marble facade of the Center, illuminated now by a full Washington moon.

He smiled to himself as he watched her disappear into the building. Press enough buttons and you find the right one, he thought. Nothing like letting them know they have no secrets left. If she's part of it, maybe now she'll make a mistake.

He stood staring at the river long after Laura had gone.

Laura moved rapidly down the stairs to the garage. She was furious at having allowed the old bastard to bait her. No one had gotten at her like this, certainly not the dummy who had conducted her psychiatric intake interviews. How could the old accountant have known which rock to lift?

Had she not been so angry, Laura might have noticed that the rear window of her locked car was open about one-eighth of an inch. This was to provide a little fresh air for the figure that lay huddled on the floor in the rear of the car.

She got in, put the key in the ignition and started the engine. Covered by the sudden sound, the figure uncoiled with tremendous speed and looped a wire around Laura's head. Only a second had elapsed before the wire was drawn tightly about her throat.

She would have been dead in a minute but for her training and instincts. At the precise moment she felt the presence behind her, she began a counteraction in anticipation of the garroting wire. She pressed her elbows against her sides and, with all the speed and strength she could command, jammed her extended thumbs toward that area where she saw the Oriental face in the rearview mirror. Just as the wire loop was touching her throat, a terrible scream filled the Audi. The loop slackened and Laura lunged for the door, pushed it open, and hurled herself out of the car onto the concrete floor of the garage. She drew her gun from the pocket of her raincoat and crouched beside the car, waiting to see if there was a backup. The screaming continued. She opened the door and fired three shots into the figure lying across the seat. The screaming stopped and the deserted garage was silent once more. Quickly she took off her raincoat and threw it over the sprawling, twisted figure. Then she drove to the exit, paid her parking fee, and left Washington along the MacArthur Parkway. About ten miles out, she stopped at the first service station and dialed the number Mike Gault had given her at lunch.

"Gault."

"Mike, Laura. Let's start our partnership a little early. Somebody just tried to erase me. I've got what's left of him in the back seat. Any suggestions?"

For a moment there was no response, then:

"Drive into the night garage at Foggy Bottom. Go in on C Street. Show your standard ident card and park in space 31. I'll be there."

It took her twenty minutes to reach the State Department Building, where she pulled into space 31. In the adjoining space was a Volkswagen minibus with State Department insignia. Gault got out of the back.

Laura did not leave her car. "He's in the back seat."

Gault opened the rear door. The man's eyes were open, weeping blood mixed with a colorless fluid that ran down his face. Laura's bullets had formed a tight triangle in the area of his chest.

"You want to see my necklace?"

She removed the wire loop that still hung loosely around her neck and gave it to Gault, who then motioned to two men standing in the shadow of the VW. They quickly moved the body into the van and drove away.

Gault looked at Laura, reached into the car and put his hand on her shoulder. "Anything else, Laura? Do you want me to go home with you?"

"No, I'm fine now."

"He was Chinese, Laura."

"Christ."

"I've got my seat on the JAL flight. I'll contact you after you arrive."

"See you in Hong Kong."

She turned on the ignition and drove off without waiting for a reply. He stood in the dark concrete space, looking after her for a long time.

She put the car in her own garage, checked the rest of the vehicle, and, out of habit, opened the trunk. It took her a full minute to comprehend what she saw.

Carlos Steiner lay in the fetal position, his legs and arms tied together. He had been dead for many hours, garroted by the wire that was still imbedded in his neck. His eyes bulged and his swollen, purple tongue protruded from his mouth.

Laura immediately closed and locked the trunk. She went to her apartment, where Walter was working in the study.

Without looking up, he called to her as she came through the door. "Laura, there's a message on the pad by the phone. Doesn't make much sense, but I had it repeated."

"I'll get it, Walter," she said, trying to control her voice. She found it: *Steiner was for Bon Voyage. The rest we save for Hong Kong.*

She dialed Gault, but got no answer. She went to the bathroom, straightened her hair, and washed her face. Back in the study, she kissed the young lawyer and asked if he had had supper. He said he had and returned to his work. When preparing a tax case he often worked most of the night. Walter Du Quoin Parsons was considered promising by his senior partners.

After a shower, Laura called the Chilean Embassy on a private line that was open twenty-four hours; she was connected immediately with the resident intelligence agent, Armando Pais. She reported Steiner's death and told him she would leave the keys to her car with the doorman. Pais thanked her and ended the conversation without comment. She then called Singer, who sounded sleepy.

"Singer, this is Laura Coles."

"Yes, Laura."

"Someone tried to cancel my trip, and my Chilean travel agent has gone out of business."

"Permanently?"

"Quite."

"I'll look into it. Who closed up the office?"

"A friend. Quite clean."

Singer sighed. "Fine, Laura. We've got some interesting information coming in from our branch offices in California, Africa, and Tokyo. I'll keep you informed. Are you traveling alone?"

"Yes."

"Well, keep the home office posted."

* * *

116

Singer had asked Luther Martin and Cy Harper to meet him by the Reflecting Pool. Waiting for them, he tried to pinpoint the source of his uneasiness. The pace of events seemed to be quickening; consequently, the danger of a single misstep also accelerated. Singer was becoming increasingly less confident of his support systems. He no longer felt he could talk freely in Martin's office at Langley, and he felt neither comfortable nor safe in Cy Harper's offices at the law firm and at the White House. More and more seemed to depend on Singer's ability to maintain total secrecy. Control of the entire operation, once shared among the three men, had shifted into his hands. No one was above suspicion, and recent events confirmed that his opponent remained a move ahead of all Singer's plans and efforts.

A premature heat wave had engulfed the capital, and Singer was very much aware of his years and his excess weight as he walked alongside the water. In his seersucker suit that had barely survived five years of summer service, Singer was perspiring profusely.

He had been in the park for about ten minutes when Cyrus Harper arrived. He saw Harper's Daimler pull up to the curb and watched intently as the tall, almost cadaverous figure emerged and crossed the grass in his direction.

Harper, walking briskly despite his age, waved a greeting as he joined Singer by the side of the pool.

"I'm getting a little long in the tooth for these kinds of games, Morton, and so are you. I trust there's a reason for this charade."

Singer smiled. "Just remember who got me into this, Cy. That should put an end to the complaints."

"But why in God's name all this trenchcoat drama? My office is the safest place in Washington."

"I would hope so, Cy, but I'm past taking chances. I've got some . . ."

He stopped. Luther Martin had entered the park from the

Monument side and approached without being noticed. His large, black Cadillac stood by the curb. He was talking as he walked toward them.

"Morton, I think you've gone off your rocker. You know what you two looked like from back there? Two dirty old men trying to look up little girls' skirts."

For the first time, Singer noticed the group of uniformed school girls chasing each other near the fountain. He imagined what the three of them must look like: Harper, wearing a custom-tailored dark pinstripe suit; Martin, in a tweed sport jacket over flannel pants; and Singer himself, round, rumpled, and sloppy—his bald head shiny under the glare of the hot sun. A trio to strike fear in the hearts of our enemies, he thought.

"Hello, Luther," said Harper. "How are you feeling?"

"Can't brag and can't complain, Cy. What's all this about?"

Singer took control of the meeting. "I won't keep either of you long. The fly has landed on the flypaper. I think our bait is taken."

Harper winced at Singer's mixed metaphor; Martin was suddenly quite attentive. "You've heard from Mike?"

"This morning. He's in Hong Kong with Laura Coles. They've joined forces. Her last night in Washington was quite eventful. She left a bloody trail behind her, including one dead Chinese contractor. Gault cleaned up that mess with a minimum of fuss. It also seems that her Chilean connection has disappeared—their embassy's playing dumb. I don't make much of it. Anyway, Coles seems to have responded to the bulletin we put out on Gault, and I anticipate a lot of activity in the next few days."

"Any word from the others?" said Martin.

"Fonesca has gone underground with his network in Kyoto. He claims he's following the Chinese connection from his side. His lead is identical to the one Coles says she turned up. He also says he's got an interesting idea, but isn't ready to share it with me. West is stalking something in the African bush, but refuses to give me a clue as to what it could be. He said he should have

118

something interesting in a week or so. Jonas is sitting on a cliff in Big Sur trying to think. My last conversation with that cerebral gentleman took place an hour ago and consisted of my talking and his listening. After a singularly unrewarding thirty minutes, he finally consented to give some evidence that the line had not been disconnected. He said 'thank you' and hung up. I don't know where you found your mythical beasts, Luther, but they are a very strange group."

Before Luther could respond, Harper suddenly took over the session. "I think the fun and games are over, gentlemen. I've seen some alarming reports from State and Defense—by now all our enemies know just how badly crippled we are and they're all moving to make profit. The President is more than concerned. He's angry, and if you've never seen this cracker lose his temper you've got a treat coming. Nobody's talked to me that way in my life. We're considering postponing the next SALT session and our garrulous UN ambassador's going to be asked to stay home and stay quiet for a while if we don't get Unicorn on the road to recovery soon."

For Singer, this was a new Cy Harper. This was the regal authority, speaking angrily from his position to the right of the throne the way Richelieu or Wolsey or Rasputin must have addressed their subordinates.

". . . I want affirmative action, gentlemen, and I want an end to the Unicorn deaths. I want to know who it is and why and, above all, I want it stopped. If you two can't do it, I'll get someone who can."

Martin was stunned by this frontal assault from the man he had known and worked closely with. "For Christ's sake, Cy, I'm doing the best I can. If you've got any brilliant ideas, let's have them. What's the point in attacking us?"

Harper's voice softened to a more familiar tone. "I'm sorry to have to put it so strongly, but there just isn't any time left. Luther, Morton, let's finish it."

There was nothing more to say. Harper turned abruptly and walked straight to his car.

Martin put his hand on Singer's shoulder. "He's right, you know, we're losing the whole damn thing. Maybe we just can't cut it any more, Morton."

In the short time they'd known each other, the two men had grown very close.

Singer turned to face the intelligence officer. "Not so, Luther. We're quite good enough to do what has to be done and we're getting there. Take my word for it and trust me. We've had some setbacks and it's been slower than I had anticipated, but I think we'll have some positive progress very soon. I'll handle Cy."

They parted, walking in opposite directions. A Washington Gaslight van that had been double-parked across the street moved slowly away from the park. Inside the van, a complex battery of electronic equipment recorded what the sensitive ears of a Sennheiser 450 shot-gun microphone had picked up over a five-hundred-yard distance. The quality of the recording was excellent.

As the van was moved through the city, the tapes were duplicated, individually boxed, wrapped, and addressed. Within the hour, they were on their way to two separate overseas locations.

6 COLES & GAULT

Chess mirrors more than warfare. It symbolizes the romance of Kings and Queens and chivalrous Knights . . .

. . . Caissa, the Goddess of Chess, is the daughter not only of Mars but of Aphrodite.

—ANTHONY SAIDY, *The Battle of Chess Ideas*

LAURA COLES HAD LOST track of time. She arrived at Kai-Tak airport in the late afternoon on Pan Am's global Flight 1 from New York and was met by a uniformed chauffeur whose cap bore the insignia of the Peninsula Hotel. She cleared customs within thirty minutes, and her luggage was removed to a Rolls-Royce Silver Ghost. In light of the hysteria at the airport and the fact that Hong Kong was the gathering place for smugglers from all over the world, Laura considered the speed and ease with which she reached the hotel something of a minor miracle.

Upon arriving, she was greeted personally by Max Keller, the manager who was largely responsible for the Peninsula's continuing reputation as one of the four or five great hotels in the world. Keller escorted Laura to a large room and introduced her to the five Chinese staff members who would be responsible for her welfare during her stay in Hong Kong. They ranged in age from the nine-year-old boy who would carry messages, flowers, and gifts to an aged, stooped woman who would wash and iron Laura's clothes. All five were under the command of

Fung Ka-Wai, a short, stocky man of indeterminate age. As a group, they had prepared her room and put away her clothes; in the tradition of the hotel, the houseman served jasmine tea to welcome her to Hong Kong.

Once the servants had gone, Laura went to the window and, for the first time, looked out over the harbor that separates Hong Kong from Kowloon and China. As she watched, she became fascinated with the ferries and the sampans and the junks that worked the waters between the island and the mainland. She did not notice the fading of the light as the sun set behind the mountains; she was hypnotized by the emerging city lights. As darkness fell, they became more clearly defined, their colors more readily recognized. The color and motion then combined with an almost inaudible sound rising from the city to create a mystique that enveloped her.

Laura let herself drift and finally gave herself up to this strange city. By the time the darkness was complete, she stood immobilized, staring out of the window, wondering exactly what she was doing here.

It was only now, as she watched the boats move back and forth in the harbor, that she confronted the violence of her last night in Washington. A knock on the door startled her, almost as if she had been asleep and was suddenly awakened from a bad dream. She glanced at the table clock. It was eight. She had been at the window for almost two hours. The knock was repeated; she roused herself and opened the door, expecting Fung Ka-Wai. It was, instead, the bellboy, carrying an arrangement of exquisite red and yellow tea roses. A note was attached.

> Welcome to Hong Kong. We hope you will visit our shop in the lobby while you are a guest of the hotel. We are open all hours until midnight, except noon to one.
>
>   Yang Lin-Shi
>   Crown of Hong Kong
>   6 Lobby Plaza—The Peninsula

This was an invitation to visit the shop between twelve and one the next day. She tipped the boy; as he was leaving, Fung

Ka-Wai came to the door and asked if he could turn down her bed. Yes, she said, and waited: this was Steiner's man in Hong Kong.

As he moved silently and efficiently about the room, he said, "The Chinese philosopher Lao-tse has remarked that the longer the journey, the more welcome the visitor."

"Thank you, Mr. Fung. I bring greetings from Carlos Steiner."

She was annoyed to find herself addressing him in that formal, stilted tone that Americans use when confronted with Orientals.

"And I return my greetings to my good friend Carlos. He has told me only that I am to help you in all things. What can I do, Miss Coles?"

His tone and manner suggested nothing beyond professional service. Apparently, news of Steiner's death had not yet become general knowledge. She had decided to keep the information to herself lest it compromise her entry into the shadow world of the Chinese intelligence community.

"I want direct contact with a double-A Peking agent who can give me some information that's about ten years old and related to something that happened in Washington. I'll go in if I have to."

"Not easy to do, but I will try. You will be here for a while?"

"As long as it takes. But, Mr. Fung—time is important."

"I quite understand. Meanwhile, I suggest you enjoy our city."

"I intend to. And thank you."

He left, and Laura immediately undressed and went to bed. She was tired after the long trip, more so than she realized; within a few moments, she was in a deep, untroubled sleep. The drug that had been placed in her tea insured that the figure entering her room in the early morning would encounter no interruption. The purpose of the visit was accomplished in less than two minutes; as daylight filtered through the draped windows, there was no evidence that anyone had violated the security of Laura's room.

The insistent ringing of the telephone slowly brought Laura to consciousness. It took several minutes for her eyes to focus, for her to realize where she was—and that she had been drugged.

She reached across the huge bed with considerable effort and placed the receiver to her ear. Her voice was unnaturally thick. The hotel operator identified herself and apologized for the call. It was after eleven, and there were several messages marked urgent as well as a small carton labeled for hand delivery. Laura said she would pick up the package and the messages within the half hour. She wanted to recover from the effects of the drug before leaving the room or seeing anyone. She did, however, want to alert Gault, so she asked the operator to place a call to the Mandarin Hotel.

"Mike."

"Yes, Laura."

"Short and simple: the sandman paid me a visit last night and left me something to remember him by. I'm just now coming out of it."

"Do you want me to come over?"

There was nothing in his voice to suggest concern or anxiety. She might just as well have been reporting the details of a successful shopping expedition.

"I think not, Mike. I need at least an hour or so. I'll call you when I get myself together."

"Whatever you say. I'll be right here."

She struggled out of bed and subjected herself to an ice cold shower—and to reflections on her stupidity. Christ, she thought, the first lesson you learn in kindergarten is not to trust any environment until you've had a chance to check it out.

She was still furious with herself when she finished dressing. She called the reception desk and asked them to send up her messages and the package. The first message was simply a confirmation from Mike of his arrival and location; the second, in code, was from Singer. It was fourteen hours late to be of any use.

Your Chilean friends see a Chinese connection in Steiner's accident and suggest that your Eastern residence may not be as secure as was represented. Advise continuous contact via the art gallery. Also, a certain amount of urgency has been presented by our employers. All Unicorns are being copied.

Like a kid in a candy shop, she thought. God protect us from the amateur spy.

She destroyed both messages and opened the package. It was the weapon she had requested, beautifully concealed inside the false bottom of an antique jewelry case. The enclosed note was simple.

Hopefully you will find more use for the container than for its contents.

The signature was a simple calligraph underneath which was printed "The Crown of Hong Kong, Fine Oriental Art." The weapon was identical in all respects to her own, down to the deceptively complex but unusually small and effective silencer. Since airport security had forced her to leave her own weapon behind, this duplicate increased her sense of security. Her priority of the moment was to determine if Fung Ka-Wai had been responsible for the drugged tea. Until she knew, he was useless to her.

She dialed the Mandarin. "Everything's O.K. now," she said.

"Good. Any ideas who?"

His voice stirred the now familiar feeling of excitement and tension inside her. "Some possibilities. My Chilean friends may have been indiscreet. But I can't see the profit—I can't figure why."

"Check everything very carefully." He paused. "What's next on our tour of the mysterious East?"

"I have some shopping I'd like to do. I'm not sure you'd

be interested. Let's have dinner together somewhere. By then I may know whether the purchase will take place."

"Whatever you prefer. Let's meet on my side of the ferry landing at about seven. Keep in touch."

"I'll try and call in a couple of times. And Mike—thanks. I'm beginning to like traveling together."

Before going out, Laura loaded the gun with the soft-headed bullets Singer had provided and clipped both her pens into the pocket of her jacket. She left the lethal nails in her cosmetic case. She did not feel she was in any immediate danger, since the tea could just as well have been poisoned as drugged.

She then began an intensive search of her room. The drug had been subtle, gradually taking hold as she stood mesmerized by the view from her window. It had sufficiently impaired her professional reflexes so that she had not engaged the chain on her door. But whoever was responsible for the drug could not have counted on that. She checked the chain; it had been carefully altered so that it could be disengaged from the outside. Which meant at least one of the servants had an outside employer who wanted inside. The whole incident didn't seem to make any sense. Despite her skill at this type of sweep, she found no evidence of anything having in any way been disturbed or rearranged. Nothing was missing, nothing added.

It was close to noon when she abandoned her search and installed her own safety alarms. She went downstairs for her appointment at the art gallery.

Singer's local control Yang Lin-Shi was perhaps the most beautiful woman Laura had ever seen. She was a slightly taller version of the classic Eurasian female: a perfectly clear complexion, luminous dark eyes, hair that seemed a mixture of black and dark blue and fell in a perfectly straight line below her shoulders, and long legs revealed in glimpses through the slit in her turquoise and gold cheung-sam.

The two women faced each other across a small desk in the center of the gallery.

"Miss Yang, I am Laura Coles, from the National Gallery

126

in Washington. I believe you wrote to us concerning a new painting."

"Ah, yes, we have been expecting you. I hope your journey was pleasant and that now you have rested well in our city, Miss Coles."

The young woman spoke the impeccable English which is heard in the more affluent sections of the Crown Colony: the best of Oxford flavored with a subtle trace of an older, alien heritage. The voice itself was delicately modulated, yet seemed to fill every corner of the room. She smiled gently as she spoke and Laura wondered how many men had been impaled upon that smile.

"Please call me Laura," she said. "I understand that you've obtained an authenticated example of Chinese erotic art from the period of K'ang-hsi."

"That is what I said in my letter to the curator of your Oriental art section. Would you like to see the work? I believe you will agree as to both its authenticity and its perfection. I find it wholly extraordinary."

As Laura was led to a small room off the main gallery, where Yang Lin-Shi closed and locked the door behind her, she was disturbed by the tension she sensed in the woman. Yang Lin-Shi carefully selected a Chinese painting on silk from a suspended rack and showed it to Laura.

"It is called 'In a Garden on a Rocky Seat' and is an almost perfect example of the period."

As the Eurasian woman described the particular virtues of the painting, she gently touched her own lips. She then spoke of the evolution of Chinese erotic art and of the conventions that reached a cul-de-sac of rigidity during the period in which this particular example had been created. As she talked, she handed Laura a map of the city and a message.

I have arranged for you to meet with a Mr. C. T. Loo at a private table at one-thirty in the dem sem parlor at 63 Wing Kut Street. He owes us a very great favor; we have elected to let him repay us now. He will be sitting alone at a window table on the second floor. He is a very large man, so you should have no difficulty in finding him. At that hour, the teahouse will be quite crowded and noisy—you can speak freely there. The Company owns the restaurant, and you will be positioned so as to have no concern regarding the eyes and ears.

Their discussion of the painting remained natural and fluent. The note continued in the same stilted style.

Act as most Americans do. Sit down timidly at Mr. Loo's table and ask the waiter to bring you exactly what your unknown table-sharer is eating, as you neither read nor speak Chinese. Then, if all is quite safe, Mr. Loo will introduce himself in perfect English. If he says nothing, leave at once. The danger will be most extreme. Mr. Loo is an employee of our Company, but he has excellent and high-ranking credentials with the other side. He is considered to be their best local director. A superb double agent and most useful. A word of caution: I arranged to meet you here because this room and this gallery was ours and a hundred percent safe. Until last night. Someone donated to my gallery a few small pieces of modern art.

As Laura read this, Yang Lin-Shi pointed to a tiny microphone imbedded in the intricately patterned bamboo frame of the painting rack. Laura glanced again at the paper.

I found five of these microphones when I arrived this morning. I felt it best not to alert whoever was responsible by changing the place of our meeting. I must urge you, however, not to come here again, not to contact me under any circumstances. The Company will arrange for a new local control. The identifying word will be "chase." Be alert—we have never before been penetrated. The intrusion is most expert.

Without pause, they continued their comments regarding the painting, to which Laura found herself strangely attracted. It depicted a garden off a room that was suggested in the upper left-hand corner of the work. A gnarled tree crossed the scene diagonally, from the upper right to the lower left. A Chinese nobleman and a Chinese girl, young and quite lovely, reclined against the tree trunk, he with his back to the tree and she about to mount him. His penis, fully extended, was the focal point of the painting. The colors were muted, ranging from a pale brown to a delicate aquamarine. Occasional pink blossoms enlivened the total effect, subtly transmitting a grace and romance to the strenuous sexuality. The penis, harshly painted in a strong red, was an angry intrusion on this pastoral mood.

Laura handed the note back to Lin-Shi, keeping the map on which the tea parlor was indicated. She closed the discussion by saying that she would want to think about the possibilities of purchase, since the price and terms quoted were beyond her authority to authorize. Yang Lin-Shi informed her that the National Gallery's option was valid for forty-eight hours, after which period other interested buyers would have to be notified. The message was clear enough: Laura was to conclude her business in Hong Kong within two days. Not only could her safety not be guaranteed beyond this period, but the threat she posed to the stability of the Company's own local operations would have to be terminated as soon as possible.

Laura left the Peninsula Hotel and took the Star Ferry across the harbor to the island of Hong Kong; the trip took about fifteen minutes, giving her a brief respite in which to plan ahead. If Singer had risked arranging her meeting with the five-star double, somebody sure as hell had valuable information. It was highly dangerous to let anyone see, much less talk, with a covert agent so placed inside the People's Republic.

The harbor at noontime was a tapestry of color and motion. In the distance, a group of gray freighters under Liberian and Panamanian flags rested alongside two sleek British cruisers, motionless, as if silently guarding the entrance to Hong Kong. They seemed fixed to the deep blue waters of the South China Sea.

The graceful junks and sampans moving between those distant shapes and the ferry provided a collage of bright colors as they proceeded in all directions, overloaded with passengers and cargo. Their oddly shaped sails were lit from behind by the sun, and Laura tried to imagine what this harbor must have been like before the West imposed its culture and its civilization on the mystery of China.

The ferry was crowded with cars and people, with tourists endlessly taking snapshots, grinning like idiot children into the lenses of cameras that would ultimately reveal little of this place or its beauty. Pictures proudly displayed in the living rooms— out of focus, the backgrounds obscure, and the faces hidden by shadows. Thus, thought Laura, Eastman Kodak's contribution to our life and times.

The twang of Indiana and the drawl of Georgia echoed throughout the ferry and mingled with the quieter, yet intense conversations of the Chinese who used the ferry daily. Boys and girls darted by, begging coins and cigarettes from the tourists, who either turned their backs to stare blankly at the sea or traded the desired commodities in return for having their snapshots taken with Chinese children. An old man sold hot chestnuts and cold meat, patiently touring the deck in search of customers. Laura sat calmly as the soft breeze blew through her hair. For these few moments, her acute sense of danger and death relaxed; a long forgotten part of a young and vulnerable girl from Texas returned—and with her, some capacity for trust and wonder.

As soon as he finished his second conversation with Laura, Michael Gault sent wires to Tokyo and Washington. He informed Fonesca that he was leaving Hong Kong on Singer's orders and would be arriving in Tokyo to provide back-up. He would register under the name of Trevor at the New Otani. In his second wire he provided Singer with a brief, incomplete report on the drugged tea and explained that he would leave for Tokyo to provide the support the Unicorn there had requested. He added that Fonesca had also asked that Singer suspend all communication for three days, unless informed to break silence. Once the messages were dispatched, Gault listened to the tapes which had arrived by pouch from Washington. He then called the Peninsula and gave his instructions without identifying himself.

"She should be leaving her room in the next few minutes. Stay with her. I believe she'll spend some time in the art gallery. I'm on my way over. If she leaves the hotel before I get there, I'll pick you up at the teahouse. I don't want anything to go wrong, so stay on your toes."

"I understand, Michael."

"Did you change the nails?"

"Exactly as you requested."

"I hope so. That lady knows how to use them. No slips, Ka-Wai, please."

The Chinese voice replied, "I will not disappoint you." He hung up.

Gault, unlike so many in his profession, had always based his working relationships on such positive values as reward and friendship. It was a simple matter to turn Fung Ka-Wai—who had served Steiner's Chilean net out of fear and profit, but who owed Gault his life and was more than willing to serve him without question.

Gault took a cab at the front of the Mandarin and arrived at the Peninsula while Laura was still inside the art gallery.

"Is she still inside?"

"In the small room."

"All right, I'll cover her now. What is the name?"

"Loo."

"How did you find that out?"

"We let Miss Yang find the microphones to reassure her that the room is safe, but there is still one other ear she cannot find. We picked up her call to the Chinese net and we know the code. It is Loo."

Mike was impressed. "Really, that's very interesting."

"Do you know him?"

"Quite well. He is very dangerous, but knowing makes things

easier. You disappear now, Ka-Wai——I'll reach you if I have to. For now, good work—and thanks."

The Chinese houseman disappeared quickly into the stream of tourists who were windowshopping in the hotel arcade. Gault went inside an antique store directly across the corridor from which he could keep the door of the gallery in view and wait.

It was almost one-thirty when Laura entered the teahouse on Wing Kut Street. Hong Kong is filled with thousands of such establishments, the dem sem lunch being a ritual in the life of most Chinese businessmen. They leave their offices or shops a little before noon and arrive at their favorite restaurants, where they occupy the same tables they have occupied for many years. No one ever takes another's place, and women—other than the wife or visiting friend of a Western businessman living in Hong Kong—are seldom in evidence.

Laura, of course, transmitted all the necessary signals that marked her as an adventuresome yet insecure tourist, a woman traveling alone in search of the real Hong Kong. She carried her map, a guidebook, a copy of *Gourmet* magazine recommending restaurants of the city. At first she looked in at the ground floor, seemingly in search of a seat. They were all shared by groups of businessmen who had talked and argued over lunch for ten years, or by strangers who might occupy the same table for two decades without exchanging a single word.

Laura attempted to inquire of a passing waiter if there were other tables. With no warmth of welcome or interest in assisting her, he pointed upstairs and Laura mounted the narrow steps. The second floor was identical to the first—a tile floor, small wooden tables and wooden chairs. The odors of ginger, coriander, onion, and garlic mingled with the occasional billows of steam, rising from the bamboo trays that floated throughout the room.

There were on this floor a few empty chairs, but no completely free tables. Laura attempted to take a chair at a table occupied by three Chinese men in the center of the room, only to be instantly descended upon by three waiters all talking at once in strident Chinese and waving their hands against her incredible rudeness. Throughout the commotion the three Chinese studied their papers and ate their food, never once looking up.

Laura, appropriately intimidated, noticed a single empty place at a table for two opposite a huge Chinese man totally immersed in his newspaper. The table was near the only window in the room. She pointed to the chair, using her hands and eyes to question the attacking waiters. One of them went over to the gross figure, spoke deferentially to him in Chinese, and interpreted his total disinterest as license to beckon Laura to the table.

She sat down—clearly nervous—and was handed a ten-page menu. She tried to engage the attention of several passing waiters; they rushed back and forth, carrying empty dishes and returning from the kitchen with trays of food, pausing, occasionally, to converse with old customers. The room seated some forty people, including a handful of Westerners who obviously lived and worked in Hong Kong and who exhibited a comfortable familiarity with the ritual and traditions of the dem sem lunch.

Laura hesitatingly leaned forward and spoke at the Chinese newspaper behind which her table companion was hidden. "Excuse me, sir. Could you help me?"

Her request, delivered slowly and distinctly, elicited neither recognition nor response. At that moment, the man's food arrived: fried dumplings bathed in a hot chili soy sauce, small steamed meatballs liberally peppered with bits of scallion and cloaked in rice. Laura recognized a favorite dish—large steamed buns stuffed with chunks of braised pork. She quickly played out the charade of identification, touching the waiter on the arm and pointing to the food on the table.

"I'll take those, just like that, please."

And she kept nodding and pointing like a retarded child.

The waiter stared uncomprehendingly until her table companion dropped his newspaper and spoke to her in perfect Oxford-flavored English.

"May I be of some service, Madame? My name is Loo, Mr. C. T. Loo."

He handed Laura a card with his name and that of his company, The East-West Trade Corporation, engraved on a silk parchment base. The letters were in fine black script. The reverse side was printed in Chinese.

Mr. C. T. Loo must have weighed well over four hundred pounds—he was, without question, the grossest man Laura had ever seen. His face was a perfect circle from which peered two tiny black eyes; his small nose was almost invisible; his red mouth was moist and thick. The immense bulk of the man prevented him from sitting close enough to the table to handle his food comfortably, so that he was forced to cover himself with two napkins and transport his meal across his expansive girth. This he did with dexterity and skill. As Laura read his card, he delicately placed a small dem sem in his mouth, savored and swallowed it.

Laura offered a sigh of relief. "Oh, thank you. I was just about ready to give it up and go back to the hotel for a hamburger. I'm Laura Coles. Could you tell the waiter I'd be happy with exactly what you're eating?"

Loo instructed the waiter with unmistakable authority. The stooped Chinese, who was every bit as relieved as Laura, seemed to have escaped into the relative safety of the noisy, crowded kitchen. Loo also beckoned one of the passing bamboo trays and selected an assortment of tiny dumplings which, together with a bowl of thin brown sauce, was placed in front of Laura. She began to eat immediately.

Loo and Laura continued their performance for about ten minutes. He described the food knowledgeably and expressed interest in her work; she questioned him about the city and its life. He remained cordial if reserved as he helped her select more food and explained in detail the ingredients of everything they ate.

Suddenly he changed both the tone and the content of the conversation. "I trust, Madame, that you are fully aware of the risks involved in this meeting." Before Laura could respond, the man leaned forward and continued. "This is the first time since I became an employee of the Company that I have been visible to anyone, which means, in your own vernacular, that it had better be worth the cost. The secrets which I have carefully guarded for twenty years are now placed in great jeopardy. I am very angry."

Yes, thought Laura, both angry *and* frightened.

"I wish for you and those for whom you work to know that I agreed to this preposterous meeting only because I have been told that you are all in grave danger. I hope that danger has not been exaggerated—because if it has, I shall feel ill-used. I do not meet with others in my work. I trust no one and, thus, have outlived many."

The man resumed his meal; despite the clumsy image he presented, he wielded the chopsticks with dexterity, even grace. Laura spoke directly to the purpose of this meeting, ignoring his complaint.

"No game, Mr. Loo. This is real and very serious. Over the past nine years, the Company has lost eighteen, maybe twenty, of its top executives. It's no accident. You must have heard something."

He nodded.

"If we don't find out quickly who's putting it to us, the Company will be, at best, crippled beyond repair. If that happens, you too are in trouble."

Loo continued eating, but his eyes were on Laura.

"On April 10 of this year, an agent named Pater Lundquist was killed in Washington. We have some fairly reliable information that, at the time of his death, he was exploring some old territory—a Chinese action going back to the first months of

135

1969 in Washington. The only name that shows is a Company agent named Singleton; that's a real name, not a code or a cover. I would like to know what Lundquist was interested in and what the hell he was up to. And, Mr. Loo, I need to know this very fast."

He looked up for a moment from his shrimp toast and smiled. The flesh in his face fell into creases and folds, and the beady eyes disappeared completely. His smile was as incongruous as it was inappropriate, giving off neither humor nor warmth.

"I will obtain the necessary information tomorrow. It will not be my privilege to meet with you again. The information will be delivered to you by an unlikely but totally reliable courier; she will identify herself by speaking to you of an age-old recipe for Beggar's Chicken, much beloved of discriminating Western gourmets. How you proceed with the information I give you is a matter of no concern to me. However, let me give you one additional piece of information about myself. I have been made a very rich man as a result of my success in serving two masters simultaneously. In 1966 the current leaders of the Chinese People's Republic, a name, by the way, that has little to do with people or republics, in a fit of pique had my brother and his entire family tortured and erased. This was in response to a false accusation made by that most delightful of women, Chiang Ching. The death of my beloved brother and his family became my goad and compelled me to offer my not inconsiderable services to your delightful organization. I was, at that time, second in command of all internal security forces in Canton Province. Since then I have risen to a position of some modest power within the Chinese intelligence community. In my current position I am able to repay those who robbed me of a beloved brother. If anything you do here threatens this, you may, my dear young lady, add the name of C. T. Loo to your undoubtedly long list of enemies. Now let us continue our warm and altogether fascinating conversation that will help to bridge the gap between East and West."

They did just that. He was a dealer in antique jade, and he showed Laura a magnificent example of the stone, rare and much desired for its light and subtle coloring. Laura had never seen so beautiful a piece. Laura, in turn, talked of her work with the National Gallery and described the painting for which she was negotiating. Finally, after almost three hours at the teahouse, Mr. Loo glanced at his watch, apologized for putting an end to this most pleasant lunch, and paid the bill over Laura's protests. They left the restaurant together.

The enormous Chinese maneuvered himself with great care down the narrow staircase, bidding farewell to at least a dozen waiters and the owner. Once outside, he hailed a taxi for Laura; as she was about to enter the cab, Loo stopped her.

"The very nature of our enterprise, Miss Coles, demands undue haste in all things. It is ironic that in a discipline where patience and time play so important a part, we are always asked for speed and haste. I should think that a very large portion of our current problems and disasters can be attributed to this senseless dichotomy. Our business is dangerous in the extreme, let me assure you. You are young and very confident of your abilities; yet I have seen far better than you lying in alleyways or stretched in agony on wooden racks and others whose mistakes have driven them quite mad. You lack sufficient caution and humility. These two things alone can bring about your death."

"What are you really trying to say, Loo?"

"You were followed here, you foolish woman, and in so doing you have compromised me. You are not one who can expect a pleasantly advanced age."

He almost pushed her into the cab, waving it away with his right hand. Laura's last view of Loo was out the rear window as the cab crawled through the crowds in Wing Kut Street; he was standing on the sidewalk as a giant Bentley pulled around a corner and picked him up. Laura's cab turned the corner on to Queens Road and headed in the direction of the ferry.

It was almost five when she returned to the Peninsula. She

called the Mandarin and left Mike a message that she'd had a fine day and would meet him as planned at seven o'clock. This time she checked her room carefully, finding all the warning devices were undisturbed. She cabled Singer that the Crown of Hong Kong had been penetrated and that she had opened a highly promising line of inquiry. She then pressed the button that would summon Fung Ka-Wai. The room porter responded immediately, entering the room with a large bouquet of yellow roses.

"They arrived just after you left, Miss."

The accompanying note was simple:

So you do not feel alone in the mysterious East.

Morton Singer

She smiled, thinking that Singer must be feeling guilty for that last night in D.C., and turned her attention to Fung. She could not trust him until she knew exactly who had drugged her tea, but she had to maintain the illusion of partnership.

"Have you got me a line into the other side?"

"Not as yet, Miss. It is quite difficult. I believe there is some closing of doors since you have arrived."

"Well, we don't have time to wait, Fung. Do something soon or it will be useless. I've got to talk with an inside agent. Carlos Steiner thinks very highly of you, and I trust him."

"I will do the best I can. Is there anything else?"

"No. If I want anything further, I'll let you know."

The houseman left the room, and Laura took advantage of the time to relax. She lay immersed in the long and deep marble bathtub, its water scented with the jasmine bath salts provided by the hotel.

Almost without willing it, she began to think about Mike Gault. He had touched her, and she did not know why. Perhaps Mike had reached her somewhere back before the days of death and rage to call forth something that she had never really stopped hoping for. Whatever he had done, Gault had not only offered male strength, support, and protection—he had promised something more, something as yet withheld, waiting beyond the next few hours. It frightened her, but it also gave her a feeling of expectancy that she had not known in a long time.

Lying in the tub, Laura drifted between past and present: her feelings during the Chilean action, the electric excitement of those days and nights, the way she had felt as she watched the agony of José Cruz—and how depleted, how empty she had felt after it was over.

She thought of Walter Parsons, that thoughtful but passionless man with whom she lived in a singularly pragmatic arrangement. She couldn't even remember his face. She kept returning to Mike Gault, and as she did, she gently stroked herself until, under the expert manipulation of her own hand, she achieved a welcome release.

They sat on the deck of the *Tai Pak* in the small harbor at Aberdeen. Laura had again crossed the harbor from Kowloon to Hong Kong; Mike had been waiting at the ferry slip. They had taken a cab through the crowded streets that ran parallel to the harbor, down Desvouex and Queens Roads, finally turning inland for a short distance on Pok Fu Lam Road. It was still light, but the sun was beginning to infuse the landscape with a burnished golden color that softly illuminated everything it touched. Chinese workers were hurrying home on foot and on bicycles. Laura had sat silent in the cab, overwhelmed by the variety of costumes and faces, surrounded by cabs, small trucks, overcrowded buses and cars, and an occasional Rolls-Royce or Mercedes limousine.

The cab had raced past Telegraph and Waterfall Bays in the southeast corner of the island; as the driver turned into Shek Pai Wan Road, his passengers once more looked out over the South China Sea. This road, winding far above the water along the cliff, reminded Laura of the Amalfi Drive in southern Italy, and their driver took the curves like an Italian, never dropping below sixty miles an hour. As the ancient taxi shook, rattled, and swayed from one side of the road to the other, Mike touched Laura's hand.

Laura's first view of the tiny harbor was a collage of extraordinarily beautiful shapes and colors, an Eastern fantasy. The sun was setting, joining water and land in a violent blending of red and purple.

Hundreds of small boats crowded the landing, waiting to carry diners to the floating restaurants that stood anchored some five hundred yards off the dock. Outlined in colored lights, they seemed to promise a festival along with an exotic cuisine. The women who ferried diners back and forth called out, vying for business.

Mike selected one of the tiny sampans at random; he and Laura sat side by side in the front, while in the rear a young woman, clad in the traditional coolie hat and black pajamas, propelled the boat by stroking a long oar back and forth in the dark waters. In the center of the boat, under a canopy of bamboo and wood, a young girl held a baby in her arms and sang lullabies. Laura felt Mike's arm tighten around her.

"Mike, I've never experienced anything like this. It's beyond beauty."

"I haven't been here in over three years, but you never forget it. I like it better than Paris, or any of the Western cities, though I'm never quite sure why." He turned to look at her. "You look sensational, Laura."

She had seen to it; her coral silk blouse emphasized her full breasts, and the white slacks clung to her hips, buttocks, and thighs. Her dark brown hair, which seemed to reflect the lights of the harbor, fell in soft waves almost touching her shoulders. The only jewelry she wore was a pair of small gold hoop earrings and a very thin gold chain around her neck.

They reached the *Tai Pak* within five minutes and were effusively welcomed aboard by the Chinese owner. The ritual of greeting began with his explanation of the origins and lurid history of the large junk. Giving the impression that he had no other customers, he led Mike and Laura to the side of the vessel and proudly asked his staff to display the variety of fresh fish that swam in cages fastened to the hull. One of the Chinese deckmen reached into each cage with a long-handled wire net and scooped up samples of the fish that were on this evening's menu: groupers and blowfish, giant crabs, crayfish and large prawns, pink and blue and gray fish of every size and shape, all exotic varieties taken earlier in the day from the sea.

Mike, politely rejecting the standard recommendations of the owner, requested a more authentic and exotic sampling of the seafood cuisine of China. The owner, obviously pleased at the opportunity to demonstrate his art, called out the menu to the waiter. They would begin with a crab soup with a trace of curry, then giant prawns, grilled in their shells on a bed of coriander, to be dipped in a thin sauce of vinegar, ginger, and hot sesame oil. This would be followed by crayfish and crab, braised in a sauce smelling faintly of star anise, fermented black beans, garlic, pepper, and perhaps the suggestion of an aromatic wine. The climax of the meal was proudly displayed for Mike and Laura: a large red snapper, to be baked with shredded ginger and scallions, surrounded in a deep platter by a thin, pungent sauce which gave to every part of the fish its own curious taste.

Laura and Mike lingered over their food for what seemed like hours. In this ancient, magical port city, the danger in their lives receded, and they welcomed the time and the moment.

Toward the end of the meal, Gault, as if anticipating her mood, spoke first. "It's been a long time, hasn't it, Laura?"

She looked at him, framed by the colored lights of the boat, and placed her hand over his. "I'd forgotten just how long it has been, Mike. It happens so gradually, you don't notice. And coming back is very . . . painful, because you begin to get some idea of what you've missed."

141

"Regrets, Laura?"

"Some. That maybe I've lost something I can never get back."

"I'm not sure I'm following you."

"Doesn't it ever get to you, Mike—the killing and the goddamn pain? Don't you ever wake up at night so scared that you think we'd be better off dead?"

"Sometimes." He said the word so softly that she hardly heard it. "But then I remember why. I don't think we really have a choice."

She heard something behind his words and looked directly into his eyes. In them she saw nothing, at least nothing she could read. Empty and cold—like a grave.

"What does *that* mean, Mike? Everybody's got a choice. That's what makes us human."

A smile crossed his face, so briefly that she was not sure she had seen it.

"We're all driven, Laura," he said. "By loss or anger, maybe by need. The truth is, we're getting what we need from what we're doing. That's why Unicorn has always been special. And why there aren't many of us around."

She stared at him, deeply moved by the depth of his feeling, yet powerless to understand him or touch him.

"What, Mike? What got you started? If we're all driven, what's behind you?"

He told her in a rush of words, everything from his beginnings in the chill of his childhood to his experiences with the Craigies and in Vietnam. He told her of happy feelings and memories—most of which had turned bitter along with his life. He had never revealed himself in this way; it was as if the flood of memory, once begun, was as involuntary as it was momentous. Laura Coles listened—and fell in love.

"Oh, Laura, I stood staring at this skinny old woman, Phil's sister, Abigail Sarhouse, tears running down her ugly, old face. The rain and the cold were drowning her, and I can still hear every word she said. She screamed over the sound of the frozen wind—'They're dead, Mike, both of them. Don't you understand, we'll never see them again. They killed themselves.' And then she cried, and I cried, and we stood there on that little airport landing field getting soaked, holding each other and crying."

His eyes were dry, as if negating the passion and the pity in his voice. He spoke then of how diligently, obsessively, he had pursued the simple facts of their deaths and found instead, at the base of it all, his first visions of an unredeemably complex apocalypse.

When he had finished, they sat together without speaking, looking out at the harbor for several minutes. The boat swayed slightly, stroked by a warm breeze; in the distance hovered the *Tai Pak*'s sister ship, the *Sea Palace*, outlined in the same garish lights that ringed their own boat.

It was Laura who broke the silence. "Sometimes, Mike, at night or when I've been alone too long, I think about the things we do and I'm not sure. When I started, I loved the work—it seemed to have an important purpose. I felt powerful—and useful. I hated them, the enemies, and I loved being smarter and tougher and always a couple of steps ahead. I did a perfect job in Chile. I played them all. I let them use my body until they cried out in the night, and then I took the joy I gave them and killed them with it. There was one, a clever young policeman who was supposed to keep Allende and his government secure. God, Mike, how I played with him. While he was spying and manipulating and arresting, I was using him to set the old man up. When Allende walked out of his palace with his hands over his head, shaking and pissing and crying, I had fifty of his own palace guards on my personal payroll waiting for him. And you know who had to fire the first shot—Laura Susan Coles, the all-American pompon girl from Texas. It felt great, Mike."

"And now, Laura?"

"Now I'm beginning to have second thoughts. The thrill is definitely gone, or at least going. I'm getting edgy, and I'm not sure that what we do does anybody any good. We arrange Beirut—and now everybody's dead and everything's the same as before.

"I was beginning to feel this way before Singer laid out the Unicorn deaths. When you stop to think of all the things we're personally responsible for, aren't you surprised? And this only makes it worse. You just cried over the death of a decent man. Don't you ever take a body count?"

He reached across the table and took both her hands in his. A shiver ran through her body. "No, Laura, I don't do any counting and I don't think about it too much. As for our enemies—I see each of them as the one who threw Phil out of that window, who put Maureen in the car and turned on the motor and left her there. The more of them to die, the happier I am."

"Do you care for anyone who is alive . . . now?" she asked suddenly.

"Not really. I live with a lovely, intelligent woman who provides what I need. And you, Laura?"

He was hedging, she knew, talking to prevent her from getting too close.

She replied in kind. "I've got a roommate who's someone to talk to and relieve the tension. It's better than masturbating, but not much. Ever see someone with scar tissue from being burned in a fire? Well, there's no feeling left . . . and it hurts when it heals. Right now, Mike, a part of me is trying to heal, and I'm not sure I can handle it."

She began to cry, quietly at first. The waiters, alarmed and curious, kept a discreet distance, assuming a lovers' quarrel. Her face twisted and distorted itself, trying to stop the tears. It was no use. Gault moved closer to Laura, holding both her hands in his. They sat together, awkwardly, until the crying finally stopped. Gault paid the bill and led her to the rail of the now nearly deserted restaurant.

Away from the inquiring eyes of the waiters, he took her in his arms. Both of them were trembling.

144

"Oh, Christ, Laura, why now? Why not before—why not when I needed you . . ."

His expression changed: very gently, he took her face in his hands and kissed her.

"Don't you understand, Laura? We're all damaged—in some essential way. All of us. Luther Martin is dying of cancer and he won't quit. He hides his pain in the flag and goes on plotting and planning and killing. Cy Harper loves power and believes in his superiority so much that he confuses himself with God. He's got nothing but contempt for everybody. Emily was mad as a hatter, so she's exactly where she belongs. That one loved to kill—I'll bet it gave her orgasms. Lundquist was a zombie, a man without feelings, a sleepwalker. Wyeth couldn't decide if he was a man or a woman, he had so many lovers of both sexes, I don't know how he kept track of them. Fonesca—watch out for that one, Laura—he's the kinkiest of them all. Just ask his old football coach, who's rotting away in a VA hospital. West? Somebody burned his personal God and he'll never get revenge enough. Worst thing of all, he blames himself for letting the Preacher get killed. And Jonas, he's a computer— and his wires are all fucked up. All we've got, Laura, is our anger, so don't try to make any sense out of it. Everybody dies."

Suddenly he kissed her again. Laura reached up, putting her arms around him and touching the back of his neck with her hands. They explored each other, their mouths and tongues searching desperately for affection, if not for love. Then, like two survivors of a wreck, they leaned against each other at the rail. They were beginning again.

On the way back to the Mandarin, Laura lay against Gault, who held her gently to cushion the shocks the battered old cab took from the equally ancient road. They moved like sleep-walkers through the lobby, then took the elevator to the seventeenth floor and entered Gault's room.

The moon was shining through the gauze curtains; for a moment, they stood facing each other in the faint light. Then he drew her toward him and they kissed—gently at first, until the violence of their need engulfed and drowned them both.

Hours later, they lay in each other's arms, still safe and within the protective embrace of that emotion neither of them had felt for so long. Finally, Laura fell asleep.

It was as deep, as peaceful a sleep as she had ever known. Gault lay awake, his eyes staring into the blackness of the room, and he cried—silently, profoundly, bitterly.

7 SINGER

The most difficult part of making a positional queen sacrifice lies in foretelling how much activity the opponent's queen will develop.

Normally, rook, bishop and pawn will balance a queen, if there are no widely scattered pawns for her to attack. However, a queen loose on an open board may easily overcome a formal deficit in material.

The most favorable situation for sacrificing a queen arises when the board is crowded with pieces whose control of many squares makes it hard for the opponent to use his queen effectively.

—ROBERT BYRNE, "Chess"
The New York Times, December 11, 1977

THE CITY OF NEW YORK was suffering from the same presummer heat wave that had engulfed Washington a few days earlier. Singer sat in his study, clothed only in his underwear, still perspiring heavily. He was uncomfortable, overweight, and depressed, wondering what had ever possessed him to engage in this madness. He felt surrounded by death—Wyeth, Lundquist, probably Rhinehauer. In the sweltering humidity of this May afternoon, he found himself thinking of Grace.

He missed his wife terribly and often wondered why it was

so difficult to recall her clothes, her voice, even her face. It disturbed him—especially since his sense of loss, rather than diminishing, had increased over the five years since her death. What he could remember—with damnable clarity—was the progress of her disease, from the time when Grace just complained of headaches, infrequently in the beginning and then with greater regularity. This in itself was unusual, for both of them had been too happily occupied with their lives and with each other to indulge in the minor aches and pains that are for so many people the voices of a more general dissatisfaction.

As the headaches increased in frequency and severity, Morton urged his wife to consult their family physician and good friend, Morris Schulman. Singer could still remember Schulman's exact words. "Nothing to worry about, Grace. Tension. And after all, we're none of us getting any younger. You should get out more. Maybe you need a change of scene. Mort works too hard anyway. I'll give you something for those migraines, and why don't you come again in about two or three weeks? Anyway, Lily's expecting you for supper on the seventeenth, isn't she?"

She was indeed. So it began. A celebrative lunch at the Plaza, followed by two years during which the headaches grew worse. Grace would lie in bed, a cold rag steeped in vinegar on her forehead. Singer could smell it still. She was losing weight, along with her beauty and her independence. Periods of time when the pain disappeared did not succeed in quieting Singer's fear. And so, once these periods grew more infrequent—and as he seemed unable to communicate his anxiety to Dr. Schulman —Singer pressed Grace to see another doctor.

Together they went to a younger doctor, one whose office was as cold as the man himself. Singer recalled how angry he was that a nurse had conducted most of the examination. And there were, of course, the machines—probing, and, in the end, discovering.

A week later, in the afternoon of a fall day, Singer, surrounded by diplomas attesting to the professional excellence of this young man, listened to his wife's death sentence. He heard words, phrases that told him nothing and everything: inoperable, metastasis, mass, very advanced, the right hemisphere. Singer sat remembering, in this day's heat, remembering until the anger that had filled him then returned. Along with the frustration which accompanied this computerized practitioner's refusal to either inform Singer how long the malignancy had been growing or to so much as suggest any fault on the part of his colleague, the good Dr. Morris Schulman.

The days that followed had returned, at night, for five years. We'll give her something to help the pain, but in a very short time it stopped helping. She lost weight until it seemed there was nothing left to lose; her memory failed, to be replaced by hallucinations and fantasies. She became incontinent, soiling her bed clothes and herself constantly. He cleaned her himself lovingly and patiently. He sat by her bed and she never knew he was there.

When he finally left the hospital for the last time, he was long past tears—long past everything but hate and anger.

The doorbell rang; it was the courier he had requested from Washington. He sent two messages. To Martin:

Coles and Gault have joined forces. Fonesca and West are close to something. Jonas expects to have conclusive information soon. I think we are making some progress.

And to Harper:

Queen and Knight operating in tandem. All squares and lines are covered. Will castle as soon as possible. Suggest closed communications from now on.

He sat in front of his television set until 1:00 A.M., oblivious to the efforts of Johnny Carson. He could not rid himself of the feeling that his opponent was pressing an advantage.

Nor could he escape the consequences of the events he had set in motion.

File 816-77-9211 (U-41)

NAME:	Daniel Walter Fonesca
DATE OF BIRTH:	April 8, 1948
PLACE OF BIRTH:	Missoula, Montana
PARENTS:	Lawrence William Fonesca Jessica Amy Fonesca (Hearne)
SIBLINGS:	Florence Jane Fonesca (35) Bruce Marvin Fonesca (32)
MARITAL STATUS:	Married. Louise Nancy (Minella) (see attached Biog. File 67-YRT)
EDUCATION:	Ida M. Lamson Elementary School (1954–1962) Missoula High School (1962–1966) University of Colorado at Boulder (1966–1970) (Level: 86 average)
EMPLOYMENT:	Warren Dude Ranch, Jackson Hole, Wyoming (1969–1970)
COMPANY:	1970
U:	1974

PHYSICAL DATA:

Height:	6′ 4″
Weight:	190 lbs.
Complexion:	Fair
Hair:	Blond
IDENTIFYING MARKS:	Missing index finger, left hand—service connected, 1972 Small horizontal scar over left eye 4″ scar just below right shoulder
LANGUAGES:	Japanese, Korean, Thai, Russian
RATING:	178-4

Summary and Review (MLS)
Project: UNICORN

I think it is important to just call attention to a central contradiction. Fonesca seems on the surface to be almost a stereotype of a Robert Redford ideal: handsome, rugged, and extremely popular with just about everyone. But as you will note, alongside this profile there seems a pattern of random violence —unprovoked, unmotivated, and totally inappropriate to the situation. All the following details should be regarded in light of this dichotomy. In short, the figures don't add up.

Fonesca's father, Lawrence William, has lived all of his life in and around Missoula. He grew up on a small horse ranch and, upon graduating from high school, married a neighbor's daughter, Jessica Amy Hearne. He worked with his father, running the ranch; in 1930 his father died and he became its sole owner. An interview with Sanford Merle—an employee of the Fonesca ranch, now over seventy but still alert and active—describes the Fonesca home life during Danny's youth as "difficult." When pressed for details, the old man recounts a litany of physical abuse coupled with silence and isolation between husband and wife. It seems the elder Fonesca used his hands quite freely on his wife and children and then retreated into long periods of absence or silence. It is altogether possible that Lawrence Fonesca was responsible for crippling Jessica, who was hospitalized in 1958 with a ruptured spleen and a broken hip. The story told by Daniel's father centered about a fall from a horse, but it was a well-known fact (odd enough to be the subject of a barroom discussion) that Mrs. Fonesca did not ride at all. Sanford Merle hinted that Lawrence Fonesca was the "horse." (See Interview 57VR.)

Scholastically Danny was always near the center, but his career in school sports borders on the legendary. He batted and pitched the Missoula Blue Jays to three consecutive state Little League championships and one trip to the national finals in Pennsylvania. In this climactic series (Danny was eleven at the time) he pitched two no-hit, no-run games and hit six home runs (despite these heroics, his team lost). In high school Daniel captained all three varsity teams (football, basketball, baseball), a feat unequaled before or since. In his four years at Missoula High, he led his teams to three consecutive state championships in football alone.

Although he seems to have been much in demand by colleges all over the country, he chose to continue his spectacular exploits at the State University at Boulder, Colorado. His academic record there is undistinguished except for a decided penchant for Oriental languages—unusual for a student majoring in education and anticipating, I would guess, a career as a coach. The only other item worth noting during his college years is the extent of his sexual activity. If I am to give credence to the attached interviews (File 43-671), our agent made good use of his athletic fame—one wonders how he found time or energy to attend classes and engage in sports. There is convincing evidence that Fonesca fathered at least three children during his four years at Boulder (File 43-675).

Let me now extract what I consider the single most interesting item in the Fonesca file covering this period. In his junior year, during summer football practice, Fonesca developed an antipathy for an assistant coach, Harvey Krim. Krim was an ex-pro football star standing 6' 6" and weighing over 250 lbs. Fonesca's dislike seems to have been rooted in the style of sarcasm Krim employed to motivate his athletes to greater efforts. During a scrimmage, Krim joined the line opposite Fonesca to make an instructional point. In the ensuing action Fonesca "accidentally" broke Krim's back, necessitating an emergency operation that unfortunately was bungled, leaving Krim paralyzed for life. The following are excerpts from a Company-conducted dialogue with Krim at the VA hospital in Denver and with Norris Raim, Fonesca's roommate, who was playing on the line at the time of the incident.

Krim—February 4, 1971 (interview conducted by Laughton, 143-67-4948): "The son of a bitch knew exactly what he was doing. Christ, I was in great shape and pros don't have that kind of accident. He went straight for me and put his knee down on my back *after* the play was dead—and he knew just how to do it. And I'll tell you something else, when he visited me in the hospital after the goddamned operation he stuck his mouth in my ear and said, 'Remember me, fat man, next time you see a pretty girl. You're dead below the belt.' And then he starts his act, apologizing and crying. Shit, nobody believed me—my wife took off and I've been in this dung heap ever since . . ." (At this point our interviewer reports Krim broke down completely and the meeting was terminated.)

Raim—February 10, 1971 (interview conducted by 767-92-1530): "I lived with Danny for two years and we got along great but—I never told this to anybody, I always thought he had something loose somewhere. He talked to himself—you know, very low level—and he never got over anybody who did anything to him he didn't like. There was this girl he knocked up. She said she'd blow the whistle on him and the next day she shows up with a broken arm. And that Krim number, Jesus, that scared me because I was next to him at right tackle just before, and I swear he said, 'Krim's dead.' Then 'hup' and Krim is—well, practically. I moved out at the end of the term and Danny never talked to me again . . ."

I assume that this testimony and its implications were not looked upon unfavorably by your Company. I find it a bit frightening. In any case, it seems that your recruiting program had eyes everywhere—two weeks before graduation and before he was to begin work as a coach and gym teacher at Missoula High, Danny Fonesca was visited by one of your sales representatives, Robert Milnes (562-99-0134). The following is an excerpt from his report:

"At first he thought we had a case of mistaken identity—then it took me a week to get him interested. Then I told him of the national need, of how close to the edge our country was. I scared the shit out of him when I told him how we were going down the tube all over the world because we didn't have enough people who cared. I asked him who he thought scratched Kennedy and Wallace and I even suggested the 'not by accident' bit as per inflation and crime and a general collapse of our national life. He got this look in his eyes, and I knew we had him . . ."

Fonesca took a two-week solo trip down the white waters of the Salmon River in Idaho and suddenly shows up at your offices in Washington ready to go to work. Note the attached

153

training records: not only does he perform incredibly well in karate, judo, pistol range, etc., but in six months he's mastered Japanese. Now to his record with the Company.

Contrary to what might have been expected, Fonesca demonstrated almost from the beginning a first-rate head to go with his awesome physical skills. His earliest opportunity to display his talents occurs during the Pakistan-India conflagration in December of 1971. Fonesca was in the area as a nonmanagerial associate for Gorton (392-44-6613), scratched by the Chinese as soon as hostilities began. Fonesca seized the initiative and, despite his youth and inexperience, impressed the agency by assuming a unilateral decision-making role consistent with what he understood to be Company policy. Once it was evident that our "ally" Agha Mohammad Yahya Khan had no constituency and could not possibly win, Fonesca diverted a massive supply of U.S. equipment to the late-lamented Sheik Mujibur Rahman and personally arranged the surrender of Pakistan by forcing General Niazi to surrender his 70,000 men to the Indian commander, Lt. General Jagjit Singh Aurora. He then eliminated Yahya Khan's two top advisers and arranged for the U.S. to support Ali Bhutto in his grab for power. In all, an impressive week's work for an agent only six months with the Company.

As you can see, from this point on, he becomes our top man in Asia and in March of 1974 is rewarded with membership in Unicorn. His credits include elimination of Rahman (Bangladesh) and control of subsequent coups; insulation of our friend Admiral Sa-Ngad in Thailand and subsequent destruction of our enemy General Prasert Thamuasiri; and, of course, his brilliant handling of the kidnapping of the leader of the Korean opposition party in Tokyo, eliminating a major foe of our ally General Chung Hee Park. He also contributed most effectively to the assassination of Park's wife, who was in the employ of the General's enemies (see attached file labeled Korea—Park: Kim, Chung-Sun, Top Secret).

I might also call your attention to the fact that just before being "elevated" to Unicorn, Fonesca met and married Nancy Minella. (Photograph and biography attached, File X7-495.) As you can see, she is rather plain, but on the record is a very intelligent young lady. She is a graduate of Georgetown University and was working as a copywriter for Raiken, Smith, Inc., a good, small D.C. advertising agency. Fonesca met her in a Georgetown singles bar called Chumley's and courted her with exceptional persuasiveness. They were married in a civil ceremony five months after the first meeting. She keeps his house in Tokyo.

A careful reading of our electronic surveillance leads me to the inescapable conclusion that the gentle Mrs. Fonesca knows her husband works for the Company but believes him to hold a nonactive administrative post. (This is, of course, consistent with policy as regards married agents.) (Directive 4973651-XUSST-1, Addenda 99.)

I have spent long hours exploring Fonesca's intake interviews and psychiatric sessions but have failed to extract anything of real interest. He seems motivated by a genuine, almost embarrassing patriotism and sees himself as a soldier in the front lines defending an embattled country. His bizarre penchant for violence seems in recent years to be quiescent other than what would normally (can I use this word in this context?) be expected in his line of work. All in all, he is a very effective agent (see the details of the organization he works with in Tokyo—"Yamaguchi-Gumi").

Conclusions (MLS):

A strange young man. Frankly, he disturbs me because he is so filled with contradictions. I have no idea what makes him go. I guess I'm saying I wouldn't want him as a friend or an enemy. (Shades of Harvey Krim.)

8 FONESCA

The most difficult type of position to play is that in which both sides simultaneously attack on opposite wings. Many of the top players prefer to avoid this situation, believing that the outcome is unfathomable and akin to gambling, but there are others who wouldn't want it any other way.

What is especially tricky is the shifting back and forth from attack to defense, giving the game an irregular pace and requiring close calculation of complex tactics. One can never be sure that the opponent will not suddenly drop his attack and go over to a winning, all-out defense.

—ROBERT BYRNE, "Chess"
The New York Times, March 16, 1971

ALTHOUGH DANIEL FONESCA HAD, from the time he became the youngest agent ever to join Unicorn, operated successfully through a carefully constructed personal network within the Yamaguchi-Gumi, Japan's largest crime syndicate, he had never attempted to make direct personal contact with Harushige Ikeda, Tokyo's "Mayor of the Night."

Working out of a well-established base in downtown Tokyo, Fonesca had served the Yamaguchi-Gumi over the past four years on a strictly *quid pro quo* basis; in return for two highly proficient bodyguards and a constant flow of information, Fonesca had arranged every year for the deposit of one million laundered dollars in Ikeda's Swiss account. The Company considered this leverage in the Far Eastern arena a bargain at any price. There were as well the free-lance dealings. For delivering to Fonesca the guard around the late, unlamented, and anti-American Sheik Mujibur Rahman, Ikeda and his organization received a random sampling of prestigious Uzi automatic rifles and hand grenades. And in gratitude for the kidnapping of a dissident Korean politician in Tokyo and the assassination in Seoul of Chung Hee Park's lovely but scheming wife, an American wholesaler provided the Yamaguchi-Gumi with fifteen million dollars' worth of high-grade heroin for distribution throughout Japan and Korea. Daniel Fonesca, in his four years as a Unicorn, had not only meticulously orchestrated this collaboration but also used this organization as the base for his own impressive success in the Far East.

Fonesca had left Singer's meeting in Washington with a strong conviction that the clue to the Unicorn deaths could be found in charting the events of the past decade and comparing them with the activities of all the agents, dead and alive. The key was a brilliant Japanese Kendo expert who, in addition to his skill with swords, had achieved something of a reputation as a mathematical genius. The old man was consultant to Japan's special intelligence branch; his analyses and suggested conclusions were consistently and remarkably accurate.

Within a week, the ancient swordsman—unable, because of poor health, to receive Daniel personally—dictated a letter:

There is but one significant element in the history of your current problems. It is somewhat obscure, but is more readily grasped if viewed in an historical context. The Unicorn deaths increased twofold beginning in 1969, a year in which three new agents were welcomed to your group. Two of the three had suffered great sorrows, and both seem to have directed their anger at those they held responsible for their loss. You have assumed the objects of their fury to be your mutual enemies on the other side, but it does not do to assume. Perhaps this matter of assassination appears complex because the Unicorns profess as a group to share objectives. One best approaches the difficult enigma by asking the unexpected, and by eliminating as a base of reasoning truths which are merely accepted. Your claim that there is no visible motive is one which I prefer to challenge; I suggest that you examine the interstices in your *individual* views of the enemy. In your calling, a different perspective is quite often a dangerous one. You might begin with the gentleman whose teacher died so badly. Then you can examine the black man. It also might be wise to inspect once more the manipulative roles played by Mr. Harper and Mr. Martin.

Unfortunately, the energies expended by Fonesca's friends in enlisting the cooperation of the proud old Kendo master proved excessive. He died at the age of seventy-five in a Tokyo hospital before Fonesca could arrange a personal interview; as a result, elements of the note remained unclarified.

The young agent, newly established in a home converted by the Gumi into a virtual fortress, plotted an immediate course of action. For the considerable rental on these secure accommodations, he paid in his own currency—information concerning the transfer of funds from the President of the Sony Corporation to Takio Yoshida, the new leader of the opposition party and an ascending political star. Having fulfilled his obligations, Fonesca decided to pursue dates rather than people, believing that careful research would uncover facts that would more clearly identify the person and the motive.

He included in his research a trip back to Washington. At first he came up empty. The motives of the remaining agents seemed clear, and the dates and the times of their operations revealed little, if anything, that was suspicious or false. Morgan West had, somehow, consistently operated so individually and talked to so few people that there was no record of his attitudes or opinions concerning the death of the man he had been hired to protect. Jonas, Gault, and Coles had all operated with great success within the prescribed Unicorn procedures; no inconsistencies were indicated by the analysis of their assignments as compared with the dates and locations of the Unicorn deaths.

Cyrus Harper functioned, not surprisingly, behind a curtain of secrecy that totally concealed his opinions and actions during the nine critical years of Unicorn's decimation. Martin's record seemed without blemish or suspicion; it was, however, difficult to fix his location at critical times.

Fonesca's most interesting piece of information came from a young woman whom he had, years earlier, placed high in the TS files. Acting on Fonesca's request, she searched all the relevant files and compared them against Singer's dossiers. They all checked out. She then went through the "dead" file on her own initiative and unearthed a fact that had obviously been consigned to oblivion in the graveyard of useless information that occupies six square blocks four stories underground in Virginia. The note, dated 10/12/68, was eloquent: "Removed mass quarter-inch in diameter from prostate gland. Biopsy positive. Metastasis negative. Prognosis good." The location of the surgical procedure was given as the Maurice Hachmann Private Pavilion, of Rockville General Hospital in Maryland. The surgeon of record was Royce Berthold.

It was clear to Fonesca that the attending physician, a Dr. Hans Frueling, had attached this to the medical report to protect his own future with the Company; should the prognosis prove mistakenly optimistic, it could not be said that he handed Luther Martin over to cancer. Most likely, Martin himself had discovered and removed the addendum. The employee in charge of the Company's records also protected himself by burying one copy in the obsolete files instead of destroying them all.

Fonesca considered it fascinating, if inconclusive, that Martin had begun to die at the same time as the Unicorns. The young agent returned to Japan, where he felt reasonably safe, and followed the advice of the dead swordsman by scrutinizing all available information on the subject of Michael Trevor Gault.

Before knowing of his Unicorn status, Fonesca had identified Gault as the agency "eye" and had never felt comfortable with him; he had found him, on their two or three collaborations, to be both hostile and patronizing. Fonesca's examination focused on the events and people involved in Gault's origins with the Company. Central to the story of the Craigies were the mysterious Chinese agents supposedly responsible for their deaths as well as that of Singleton, the double agent. What Fonesca required was a source of accurate information concerning Chinese action in Washington during 1969. He was not unaware that the leader of the Gumi had direct access to such knowledge.

At the dead end of his resources, Fonesca elected to gamble. Fully believing that his life was at risk, Fonesca regarded his demand for a face-to-face meeting with Ikeda less a gamble than a necessity. Yet he knew that if the "Mayor" felt compromised because of the meeting, he would never leave the room alive.

Fonesca had already decided to force the conference on Ikeda by blackmail. No one, as far as he knew, had ever attempted to coerce Ikeda; such a threat was a calculated risk that could terminate his promising career as U-41 with great ease. His request was carefully worded and the confrontation was mutually advantageous, as crucial to Ikeda as it was to himself.

After a week of silence, the arrangements were made. A time, three days later, and a place, Ikeda's home, were set. Fonesca, aware that his plan was now irreversible, informed Singer that he was awaiting substantive information and approaching resolution. This was consistent with his method of operation, which centered about giving bits and pieces of information to his superiors and never quite revealing the whole truth about his motives and actions. In all things Fonesca was a loner. Certainly he was not overjoyed that Singer had sent Gault to Tokyo. He wanted no interference. Stalling, he left a message for Gault at the New Otani, telling him to wait there until contacted. Fonesca felt both confident of and resigned to the entire operation; he came alive when in command and now had only to wait for his meeting with Harushige Ikeda.

The brilliant morning light of Hong Kong flooded Room 7117 of the Mandarin Hotel. As Laura awakened, she felt the returning flood of feelings from the previous night; Gault kissed her, then pulled away from her embrace. He seemed suddenly withdrawn, as if embarrassed by his words and actions on the boat. Laura was also disturbed by the vague awareness that she had forgotten a detail of Michael's story, a fragment lodged in her subconscious mind that now had fallen loose just beneath the surface. As she tried to recall the exact words, they slipped into the recess of memory and were lost.

They showered separately and silently dressed. Laura could not understand the distance that had surfaced between them overnight—it was as though he had removed himself to another place.

"What's next, Mike?"

"I'm supposed to go to Tokyo today. Fonesca's got something hot that he can't handle alone. He called and asked me to back him up."

"When did you know this?"

"Yesterday. I just didn't want to talk death and danger last night at dinner. I figured I could tell you today and then we both could go over."

"There's something else, Mike. I picked up a first-rate Chinese line yesterday, a top grade-A Chinese double. He swears I'll have answers to all our questions today or tomorrow."

He smiled. "So we both keep our little secrets. Just what questions do you want answered?"

"Mike, I didn't know until last night how far I could trust you, if at all. Now I just want to stay here forever and forget the whole stupid business. I've fallen for you, Mike, heavy as hell, and you know it."

For a moment he just stared at her, without expression. It was as if he had not heard what she had said. Then he moved away toward the window. He turned and spoke quietly. "Yes, I do know and it scares the living shit out of me, Laura. I feel the same way and it makes us very vulnerable. There's no place for it in our business and now it's too late. There's no going back. But I'll tell you this, my darling, if we don't settle this

161

business quickly, we won't live to enjoy what we've got."

The words were what she had longed to hear but somehow there was something missing. He returned her to the job at hand.

"What's your Chinese connection looking for?"

"The same thing Lundquist found, something that happened in D.C. in 1969 involving Chinese agents. One of ours was named Singleton, who's dead. More than a few things don't add up, so my man's going to open up the Peking records."

He thought for a moment. "We'll separate and take our chances. I'll go see what the Jock's got. I just wish I liked him better—I think he's the craziest of us all. You can stay here until you get what you need and then follow me to Tokyo. Do you have any local protection?"

"Singer gave me a drop at the hotel, but by the time I got there it was blown. I've been promised a new one today."

"OK, when you get it, ask for a total protect. If they won't or can't do it, get Singer on the horn. And, Laura, don't wander around until your Chinese mailgram arrives. I'll be at the New Otani under the name of Trevor. The assistant manager, Hiroshi Mori, is mine and guaranteed safe. There'll be a room waiting in your name. If I'm not in leave a message that I can understand and please, Laura, don't get careless." He kissed her on the forehead.

Without lingering, Laura returned to the Peninsula to await contact from both her new control and Mr. Loo. Michael Gault took the two o'clock Cathay Pacific flight to Tokyo.

Harushige Ikeda was a burly, powerfully built man starting to turn soft. What had once been a strong, if squat, frame was now hung with fat. Wearing a satin smoking jacket and holding a long ivory cigarette filter, he turned his magenta-tinted glasses on Fonesca. His study, which few Westerners had ever seen, was crowded with stuffed animals, predominantly birds, though most obvious was the large black bear, standing upright as if poised for attack.

Fonesca—who had been kept waiting over two and a half

hours, a deliberate and unusual insult in Japan—now sat quietly, waiting for Ikeda to speak.

He was finally addressed in a hoarse, sibilant whisper that made no attempt to conceal the anger behind it. "I hope for your sake, Mr. Fonesca, that I have misinterpreted your message."

Ikeda's security guards, who had carefully searched Fonesca, stood silently in the far corner of the large room.

"You did not misunderstand me, Ikeda-San. I am sure you have read my message correctly."

The American's use of the familiar form of address was rude in the extreme.

"Unless you can explain every bit of this," said Ikeda, "you are in worse danger than you know."

He motioned for the two bodyguards to leave the room so that Fonesca could explain in privacy.

The agent's nerves held, and he proceeded without hesitation. "My organization is threatened with total extinction. I need help of a kind only you can give. The risk is great, and I knew of no reward that would be worthy of your assistance. I must therefore resort to the only gift I have to offer—the gift of silence."

"What is it you *think* you know, Mr. Fonesca?" he whispered.

For the first time, Fonesca noticed that both joints were missing from one of Ikeda's little fingers. In the tradition of the Gumi, mistakes are atoned for by removing a finger at the first knuckle, the second offense being paid for with the second section of the same finger.

Fonesca tried to engage the cold eyes behind the tinted lenses. "You personally arranged the entire Lockheed affair through your Kuromaku. You did this outside your own Gumi, so that you could destroy the Prime Minister and his government. A personal vendetta is a direct violation of the most sacred law in your organization. The Prime Minister was so foolish as to insult your sister by refusing to marry her. That was twenty-five years ago. You helped him to power in order

163

to destroy him. What would the Yakuza do if they were to learn of this?"

Ikeda showed no emotion. "You have, of course, incontrovertible proof of what you are saying?"

Fonesca continued as though without interruption. "Misuro Taoka, the son of your old friend, has in his possession all of the papers, including the recorded and sworn testimony of Kodama. I know precisely how it was done, and I have known for two years. I kept silent, for I knew that some day I might have to use this sword. I am sorry, Ikeda-San, but my present need takes priority over our association."

Ikeda's expression did not change. He drew deeply on his long cigarette. Although he gave no noticeable sign, his two bodyguards moved silently into the room; they had stripped to the waist, revealing the intricate tatoos that covered their backs and chests.

"What is it you wish to know?" said Ikeda.

"Washington, D.C., 1969. We are told that two Chinese agents kidnapped, tortured, and killed a man named Phillip Craigie."

Fonesca paused, as he opened his briefcase.

"All the relevant information is in this envelope. There is neither a trace of the Chinese nor any real reason for their interest in Dr. Craigie. The reason given in the case history is nonsense; the entire story strikes me as Company invention. What I ask is that you and your organization find the Chinese connection, if there is one—tell me what really happened. I know you own Wang Lin-Fu and am aware that he was, in 1969, the Peking control in Washington. Call in your debts now and you have my silence forever."

Ikeda stared at Fonesca for a moment. "I would not wish to be the company that insures your life, Mr. Fonesca. You are such a young man, and a very foolish one to risk so much. I will, of course, do as you ask. I will also repay you—if it takes one hundred years. My debts burden me until discharged. You are, my friend, dead. The price of what you have purchased from me is something you cannot afford." His eyes narrowed. "Yet as long as your knowledge remains compelling, I cannot act. But do not think that you will be safe forever. Things change, and what is scandalous today becomes honorable tomorrow."

He rose, walked to an ornate but delicate table, and wrote an address on a small pad.

"Tomorrow morning at seven o'clock you will be in Kyoto, at the temple called Sanjusangendo. You will be joined by a close friend and associate of mine—Shigeko Ikari, a very old man who served this nation very well in 1930 as we attempted to annex China. He is now chief priest of the temple and enjoys a life far more serene than you or I am ever likely to know. He will have the information you seek. This meeting is the end of your association with the Yamaguchi-Gumi. I wish you a long life, Mr. Fonesca. At least until we meet again, which, my friend, we most certainly will."

Fonesca left the room immediately, easily discarded his young Japanese tail, and disappeared among the crowds flowing into the Tokyo subway system in the late afternoon.

Following Gault's departure for Tokyo, Laura Coles was approached just as she emerged from the Peninsula's dining room. The man, who wore a three-piece dark navy suit, had a full head of white hair and spoke with a slight German accent.

"Miss Coles?"

Laura nodded.

"I am Heinz Darmstadt with the Chase Manhattan Bank of Hong Kong. I understand that you wish to arrange for the transfer of a considerable amount of U.S. currency for the purchase of a work of art. I have been asked by our branch in Washington to assist you in every way possible."

"Chase"—the code word for her new drop, if used in an unexpected way.

"Very good, Mr. Darmstadt. I've been waiting to hear from you."

They walked to a deserted corner of the large lobby and sat down. The German ordered coffee.

"What specifically can we offer, Miss Coles?"

"I will require a letter of credit for $500,000, and I may need to draw on this amount on very short notice. I suspect the gallery prefers a cash transaction, so I'll demand continuous and careful, but subtle, supervision."

"Certainly, Miss Coles. I'm sure this can be arranged. Your superior at the museum—a Mr. Singer, I believe—has authorized us to do whatever is necessary to insure the success of this venture."

Darmstadt finished his coffee as they concluded the details of Laura's protection. Eight of the Company's best local agents, working in two-man teams, would have Laura in sight at all times. In addition, a second set of agents would check her trail for anyone who appeared too interested in the activities of an American art dealer. Following agency jargon, the extent of Laura's protection was indicated by a sum of money, $500,000 being the "maximum protect" that would envelop her for the remainder of her stay in Hong Kong. Singer had delivered, despite the strain on the local resources evidenced by Loo.

She spent the next hour enjoying her cover. She purchased a dramatic black and gold cheung-sam that clung to her body and offered an intriguing glimpse of her long legs, and an extraordinarily beautiful amethyst ring.

As she approached the Peninsula shortly after four, Laura was accosted in the circular driveway by an elderly woman; an American wearing a garish flowered print dress and a wide-brimmed yellow hat that covered a berrypatch of dyed curls. Her voice was a disagreeable mixture of bourbon and magnolia. "Honey, can you help me out?"

Before Laura could disengage herself, the woman had unfurled a huge street map of Hong Kong, efficiently blocking an escape.

"Ah'm tryin' to find the cutest little place where me and Gladys had supper last night. We had somethin' they call Beggah's Chicken. Ah think the restaurant's called Tien Heung Lau, or something like that." The name came out sounding like Ten Hung Low. "It's out off that big street with the Jewish name—Nathan Road. Ah've got the address right here."

She now began to empty her huge yellow purse onto the hood of a parked car.

"Here it is—138 Woo Sung Road. The trouble is, Ah just cain't read maps when Ah don't have my readin' glasses. Could you just find it for me on the map and mark it like a nice little girl?"

She thrust the map into Laura's hands and planted her bulk between the hotel entrance and Laura, leaving her no option but to look for the address among the maze of streets and names.

The woman kept up a steady stream of chatter. "Know how they make that funny old dish? They actually put it in a dirty clay pot that you and I wouldn't touch at home and they cook it over a fire and then they bury it in the ground until that ole clay pot is black as a niggah baby's bottom. You know why it's called Beggah's Chicken?" She answered her without waiting for Laura's reply. "Well, the beggahs used to steal a chicken, cook it up real quick in a cheap clay pot, and bury it to hide it from their friends and then come back and eat it. Ah tell you, honey, it is *de*-licious."

Just as Laura had located and marked the address on the large map that was now spread out over the hood of the parked car, she understood and began to laugh. Dear God, it was Loo's courier.

"O.K., I get the message. You can stop playing Amanda Wingfield. Now what have you got for me?"

The woman, not appreciating Laura's reaction, refused to modify her charade. She looked at the spot marked on the map.

"Well, I do thank you, honey. I've got to go now and pick up Gladys. Could Ah repay your kindness and invite you to come with us to Ten Hung Low tonight, around seven? I promise you'll enjoy it. By the way, mah name is Hortense Folger."

Laura sighed, resigned to the game.

"Anything you say, Hortense. But I don't think I can take any more jasmine and juleps."

The broad smile on the woman's round, wrinkled face

stayed in place. "Fuck off, you little cunt. When I'm risking my life to give *you* a message, you just do as you're told."

Flouncing her pleated skirt and rattling the crown of pink daisies that ringed her yellow bonnet, Hortense Folger turned and entered the hotel, leaving Laura holding the map with the place of their meeting clearly circled.

The young man who had been following Fonesca for four weeks smiled to himself as he watched the tall, blond agent disappear into the stairwell leading to the main subway station of the Marunouchi line. Gault's instructions had brought about the desired results.

Sukisaburo Kishi was arguably the best shadow in the world. Although only thirty-one, he had been developing his unusual talent since he was fifteen. He had begun his career by working for an elite Japanese private detective service as an office boy. The firm had specialized in providing angry wives with sufficient information concerning their executive husbands' sexual proclivities so as to encourage a greater appreciation of family life. Pressed into service by the sudden illness of one of the firm's best operatives, Kishi demonstrated a natural ability for surveillance. Before he was twenty-five, he had become so proficient that he found he could command a salary higher than most of the firm's older detectives. Acting on this discovery, he began following his calling on a free-lance basis, limiting his work to surveillance only. Known in the world of corporate and international espionage as the "invisible man," Kishi was much in demand; his income in the previous year had reached an unprecedented peak of $150,000.00.

Kishi was a born voyeur. He loved the work, taking secret delight in his ability to attach himself to someone so completely that he became an alter ego. Even when following Japan's top security agents and police officials, he had passed unnoticed. Those employed in related fields, however, were keenly aware of his talents.

He had occasionally handled special assignments for Gault

over the past four years. For this, perhaps his most important assignment, Gault's plan was simple, dictated largely by the actions of others. Once the attractive young file clerk at Langley had told Gault what Fonesca had been doing in the Company basement, he had anticipated every move the agent made. Again using the clerk, Gault had made certain that Luther Martin's physical problem was brought to Fonesca's attention. When Fonesca gave up his search in Washington and boarded the flight to Tokyo, Gault had contacted Kishi and requested his specialty—complete surveillance. The strategy was designed to take full advantage of what was both Fonesca's major strength and his greatest weakness: his arrogant confidence.

Kishi was to follow Fonesca, remaining invisible only until the agent's plan of operation became clear. This occurred the moment Fonesca began meeting with Ikeda's representatives; Gault was certain that Fonesca was seeking help from the Gumi on the highest possible level and assumed, since he was aware of Ikeda's access to Wang Lin-Fu, that Fonesca was following Lundquist's trail. The dying words of the old swordsman having been passed along to Gault, it was obvious that Fonesca was moving toward the truth.

Since Gault lacked the means with which to persuade Ikeda to hand Fonesca a rather confusing fairy tale, he instructed Kishi to let himself be spotted; he was gambling on his hunch that Fonesca's ego would interpret the detection of this shadow as evidence of his own consummate skills and would further assume, thanks to the timing, that the trailer was one of Ikeda's men.

Kishi was told to let Fonesca believe he had been discarded following the meeting with Ikeda; the Japanese actually kept Fonesca under close observation until he boarded the train at the Shinjuki station. The enterprising young shadow then established himself at a sushi bar across the street from the Gumi headquarters, where he passed the time enjoying a small sampling of the bar's sashimi.

Nearly an hour had passed when he was joined by one of

the huge bodyguards present at the end of the meeting between Ikeda and Fonesca. The man had agreed to compromise himself in return for Kishi's promise that his four-year-old son who had disappeared the day before would be returned unharmed. His information was brief and to the point:

"Kyoto, Sanjusangendo, seven o'clock tomorrow morning, the old priest—Ikari."

The bodyguard had some sushi and beer and returned to his post without further discussion. Kishi continued eating for another fifteen minutes.

Kishi knew that the man would, tonight or tomorrow, kill himself in atonement for his unforgivable sin. He put the bodyguard safely out of his mind, paid his bill, and walked the crowded Ginza to the post-office branch next to the Isetan department store. He called the New Otani and asked for Mr. Michaels, the name Gault used for his friends and employees. Trevor was reserved for his enemies.

"Michaels."

"Kishi, *gokigen ikaga desuka.*"

"Yes, Suki, what do you have?"

"What you want, Michael. Exactly what you want."

In perfect English Kishi reported the details of Fonesca's scheduled meeting in Kyoto. Gault, in turn, arranged for Kishi's final payment and removed him from further involvement.

"One more thing, Suki. I would, if I were you, take a long vacation in some remote place. Kagoshima? Perhaps. I would, in any case, disappear for a few months. Wakarimasu?"

"*Hai.* I will do as you suggest, Michael."

His business completed, Kishi left the post office and returned to his modest home. There he made arrangements to collect his money and leave Japan—not for the few months that Gault had suggested, but forever. He was, above all, a realist. The moment he had discovered that his work for Gault would place him in an adversary relationship with Ikeda and the Gumi, he knew he could never again prosper, or survive, in Japan. Within thirty-six hours, he was established in a new home, with an entirely new identity, in Honolulu. Sukisaburo Kishi intended to live to a venerable age.

Laura sat in angry silence in the simple interior of the tiny restaurant on Woo Sung Road. She watched Hortense Folger and Gladys Maltz devour two chickens, slivers of a bamboo vegetable, and huge quantities of other unidentifiable Chinese edibles. The old bitch refused to discuss business until she finished her meal. Throughout dinner, in fact, the woman insisted on her cover, telling slightly off-color jokes with the embarrassed charm of an Atlanta debutante at her own cotillion. Finally, without in any way compromising her portrait of the prebellum South, she gave Laura what she had come for.

"The fat man says hello, honey, and he hopes he never sees you again."

Laura stared coldly at the woman. "What else does he say, Hortense?"

"In good time, Laura sweet, in good time."

Gladys, a blousy, bosomy old harridan with a foul complexion and white, lifeless hair, continued to eat during the conversation.

Laura put her hand on Hortense Folger's. "*Now*, Hortense, or I get up and go."

"Don't get your pretty little bottom in a sling, Laura honey. Here it is, short and sweet, direct from Peking—the big wok. Your Swedish friend was pickin' at the death of somebody named Craigie. Your company gives out like it was a Chink action, but it wasn't. There was no Chinese involvement." With the last sentence, Laura noticed, her accent disappeared.

"Singleton was the agent of your company who in the fairy tale was supposed to have sold Craigie to the Chinese, but like the kid said to shoeless Joe Jackson, say it ain't so. Well, it isn't. Singleton had something to do with research in a very hush project. He turned up dead about two weeks after Craigie and his wife. They found him in a basement in D.C. with his balls smashed and plenty of other damage. Loo says he can guarantee there was no Chinese in it at all—and that, Laura baby, is that."

The woman placed one of her chopsticks on Laura's hand and dug into the flesh until Laura released her. Laura sat dazed, trying to make some sense out of what she had been told. She had no reason to think that Loo was lying, which meant that Gault had been badly deceived by the Company. But why? There was something here that just didn't make sense. Wheels within wheels. Laura needed time to try and put it all together; without a word to the two women, she left the restaurant and returned to her hotel. Once there, she made a reservation on the morning flight to Tokyo.

Immediately following his meeting with Ikeda, Fonesca returned to his operating base, packed a small overnight case, and sent a note to his home telling his wife that he would be out of the city for a few days. He armed himself with a snubnosed .38 caliber Smith and Wesson, and a tiny two-shot Derringer strapped to his calf. He also carried a set of heavy-duty steel knuckles which were, given his considerable strength, as lethal as the guns.

With only ten minutes to spare, he caught the eight o'clock Bullet train scheduled to arrive at Kyoto's central station at ten-thirty. On the train, he studied the ground plan of the Sanjusangendo Hall and memorized each exit and entrance.

With the punctuality characteristic of Japanese mass transportation, the train pulled into Kyoto's central station precisely on time. In the hazy, misty night, Fonesca walked the few blocks to the Tawaraya Inn, a six-hundred-year-old Ryokan where he was well known and protected. Once safely in his apartment, he checked the rooms for taps and placed a call to the New Otani to inquire whether Mr. Trevor was still a guest. There was a short delay while the hotel switchboard located Mr. Trevor's room; finally Fonesca got a ring.

"Trevor."

"Welcome to our neck of the woods, Mike."

"Thanks. What's the program?"

172

"Just stay put until I call. Tomorrow, maybe around noon."
Gault said, "Where are you?"

"That's not important now. I'll give you everything later."

"Singer said you wanted a backup. I'm not much help stuck in a hotel room waiting for the phone to ring."

"Play it my way for a little while. You'll hear from me soon."

He hung up before Gault could argue, left a call for 5:00 A.M., undressed, and went immediately to bed. One of Danny Fonesca's great attributes was his total command over his body; he could move from wakefulness to profound sleep in a matter of minutes, and was never conscious of having dreamed.

He would not have slept so deeply and securely had he known that Michael Gault had followed him from Tokyo, had arranged the transfer of all incoming calls to his Tokyo hotel room on to his new quarters in Kyoto. Two of Gault's personal employees were, in fact, posted at both entrances to the Inn awaiting any motion on the part of U-41. At 4:00 A.M., Gault relieved his agents and waited himself for Fonesca in the dampness of that early morning.

Fonesca rose at five, awakened by the gentle presence of the young Japanese woman who was in charge of his room. He bathed in a deep, vertical cedar tub filled with very hot water, and ate a breakfast of dried fish, cold bamboo shoots, and raw egg yolk. He did fifteen minutes of intensive exercise, as he had done every day of his life since he was twelve.

Fonesca, who felt very close to the answer to the Unicorn deaths, thought briefly of calling Singer to share with him his plans for the next few hours. He decided against it; he had never placed much trust in Jews, and he harbored a basic distaste for men like Morton Singer with their soft, overweight bodies and patronizing, intellectual attitudes. Maybe, Fonesca thought, I'm just pissed that somebody like that was put in charge in the first place.

At six-thirty, Fonesca left the Tawaraya for his appointment at the Great Hall of Sanjusangendo. He arrived at the main entrance to the temple a few minutes before seven, discarded his shoes, and approached an aged caretaker who was preparing to relight the candles and the incense that were supposed to burn eternally. In fluent Japanese, he informed the old man that he had an appointment with the chief priest and would wait in the long, narrow hall that housed a thousand and one smiling Buddhas.

In the soft light of early morning and the uncertain candlelight, the effect of this seemingly endless row of statues was both threatening and ominous. The structure itself had been built in the thirteenth century to house the statue of the thousand-handed Goddess and had seen no alteration for six hundred years. The footfall on the old wooden floors announced all arrivals and departures. Fonesca waited. In the shadows, the Buddhist priests hovered like wraiths, pausing to pray and then fading into the darkness.

After a half hour had passed, a shrouded figure approached him, the face totally hidden under the hood.

"You wish to see me?"

"*Hai*, I am sent by a friend."

"I know, Mr. Fonesca. We can speak your language if it will be easier for you. Our meeting will not be long. I am, as you may know, no longer involved in worldly matters, but I owe my old friend this last gift."

"What can you tell me?"

"I myself can tell you nothing. My words are simply those of another speaking through me."

They were whispering, as if under accusation by those statues that stood side by side in a single row, their golden veneer reflecting the myriad candles.

"I am assured that there was no Chinese action connected with the death of the professor and his wife. When the Chinese in Washington learned, from their plant inside your Company, that they were blamed in the official history of those deaths, they were most upset and feared retaliation for something they had not done. As you know, Chinese policy at that time was to nourish the new relationship with your President, and all foreign units were clearly instructed to act in accordance with the new spirit embraced by Mr. Chou and his cabal. Because of this, the Chinese cell in Washington conducted their own examination into the deaths of Dr. Craigie and, subsequently, his wife. They found a very closed box: your Company had erased the matter beyond retrieval. My principal offers speculation based on his not inconsiderable experience and agility of mind; so I suggest you listen with an open ear. He thinks that your own agency was somehow responsible for those deaths and that they sought afterward, for some unknown reason, to provide a fiction that would withstand the most astute of probes. My speaker suggests that perhaps some terrible error was made and that someone or some group was searching in the ashes.

"There are further items, both of more than passing interest. First, someone else arrived on the scene, shortly after the Craigies had perished, and was taking a very close look at the entire affair. This person was then outside the Company. Second, Singleton was a top-echelon executive handling a special research project dealing with what you euphemistically call mind-control. This agent disappeared one morning from his office, was taken under duress to the Negro quarter of the city, severely misused, and then killed. There is, however, no official record of his death."

"Who the hell was Craigie?"

"Exactly what he appeared to be. An inoffensive, if slightly naïve pacifist with a gift for codes. My informants found no evidence whatsoever that he was anything else."

"It still doesn't make much sense," said Fonesca, "except that Gault's been chasing the wrong enemy. He joined us for the wrong reason. Well, O.K., please thank the Mayor for me and tell him his secret is safe. Absolutely safe, forever—the price is paid."

The old priest smiled without warmth or humor.

"He knows that, Mr. Fonesca, he knows that. He also knows . . ."

175

The smile froze. The old man fell like a marionette whose strings have suddenly been released. A pool of fresh blood appeared in the center of his back. There had been no sound of a shot. Before he could react, Fonesca felt a searing pain across his cheek and the warmth of blood sliding down his mouth, chin, and neck. The second bullet had grazed his face—it felt as if he had been slashed by a shard of glass. He had drawn his gun within a second after the priest had fallen and thrown himself onto the floor behind one of the giant statues. Pressed against the pedestal, he waited for the sound that would locate his assailant. So muffled was the shot that the black-robed priests at the far end of the room continued their early morning devotions without alarm. The crumpled body of Shigeko Ikari, the spy who had sought peace in the Eightfold Path and the Four Noble Truths, lay in the shadows like a discarded pile of rags.

Ten minutes passed. Fonesca knew that the killer would make no further attempt on his life, but would simply wait for him in front of the only exit to the long rectangular hall. He also knew he could not stay where he was. Very carefully, a single step at a time, avoiding any pressure that would announce his movement on the warped wooden floor, he moved from statue to statue until he reached the middle of the room where a young priest was lighting incense.

With a single blow, he reached out, broke the man's neck, and drew the body back into the shadows. In a matter of seconds, Fonesca had stripped the dead man of his robe and transformed himself into a stooped holy man. He completed the task of lighting the joss sticks and lit a dozen more candles as he kept the entire room under observation. He reasoned that his attacker, not being certain if he were one of the priests or not, would scarcely risk firing again. The entire side of his face felt numb. The blood continued to flow from the wound, but he used the cowl of the robe to hide both his face and the blood.

Just as he neared the entrance to the hall, the doorway filled with what seemed like an invading army. An early morning tour group of large, noisy Swedes poured through the entrance, led by a uniformed Japanese woman carrying a flag identifying herself and her group. They blocked Fonesca's exit and stood, a hundred strong, listening to the tour guide's exposition of how a thousand and one statues came to inhabit the hall.

Fonesca began to thread his way through the group, his head bowed reverently, his pistol ready for instant use. He never felt the Kendo naifu, the short dueling knife that entered his back and his heart, twisted to insure maximum damage. As Danny Fonesca slipped to the floor in the few seconds of life that remained to him, he turned, caught a glimpse of the hooded face of his attacker—and understood everything.

9 GAULT & SINGER

The player who falls behind early in a match is well advised to throw everything into making up the lost ground as soon as possible.

—ROBERT BYRNE, "Chess"
The New York Times

IN THE HYSTERIA that scattered the Swedish tourists and their Japanese leader, Michael Trevor Gault left the great hall of Sanjusangendo and boarded a trolley for the station, where he bought a ticket for the Bullet train to Tokyo. He paused at the phone center and placed a long-distance call to Hong Kong. A Chinese voice answered.

"Central 4."

"This is Michaels. Where is she?"

"The lady took the Thai Flight 466 to Tokyo. It arrives at 1:30 your time."

"Fine. Tell Fung I'm very pleased."

He moved swiftly from the station and hailed a cab. It was now a little after nine. With any luck he'd be at the airport in Osaka by 10:30 and catch the 11:00 A.M. JAL flight. Gault would arrive at the New Otani just ahead of Laura, who faced customs and a taxi ride through heavy Tokyo traffic.

During the ride out of Kyoto on the modern highway to Osaka, Gault evaluated the situation. For the moment, Operation Unicorn was safe.

He had inflicted a major loss on the enemy and could report to Singer that their plan was proceeding on schedule. Everything depended on the old man's living up to his reputation. Gault was now free to initiate the second phase of the operation. The only danger was that there was so little time left.

Singer's appointment with the President had been confirmed for nine o'clock in the morning. It was a little after ten-thirty when the President's secretary apologetically invited him into the Oval Office. The President was on the phone, concluding what had obviously been a lengthy conversation. He motioned for Singer to sit opposite him, and for another twenty minutes Singer waited, trying uncomfortably to find a place to fix his attention so he would seem not to be listening to what was said.

He wondered why men in high places were invariably unable to keep to the schedule that they themselves controlled. Finally, the President concluded his business, swiveled his chair in the direction of his visitor, and fixed his intense blue eyes on the accountant.

"I'm very sorry, Mr. Singer. I just can't seem to stay on schedule. When I was chasing after this job I thought all that was needed to run this country was a little intelligence and discipline. Now I know better. Anyway, what can I do for you?"

Suddenly, Singer wasn't at all sure that this meeting was such a good idea. "I appreciate your fitting me into your schedule, Mr. President, but I think what we need to discuss is of the utmost urgency."

God, he thought, I must sound like a pompous ass.

Before he could go on, the President interrupted him. "I'm sure it is, Mr. Singer, but wouldn't it have been better to have discussed it first with Cy Harper or Colonel Martin? I generally don't like going out of channels unless there's a damn good reason."

Singer absorbed this mild reproof without comment. He had been prepared for it.

The President continued. "When you called my secretary,

Mr. Singer, you indicated that this matter wouldn't wait, and I believe you said you wanted to meet without informing either Cy or Luther. I've respected that request. Now you've got to make sure I won't be sorry that I've violated my own chain of command."

Singer responded with confidence. "I appreciate that, sir. But when I'm finished, I'm sure you will agree that I had no other choice."

"O.K., Mr. Singer. Or can I call you Morton?"

Surprised by this gesture, Singer fumbled among the papers he held on his lap. His mother, Regina, had always measured success by who addressed you by your first name. He found himself remembering one of her last remarks: "The Mayor, Mortie, the Mayor put his hand on your blessed father's shoulder and called him Isaac."

"Please, Mr. President. I'd be honored."

"Fine. Now let's just hear what it is that's got you upset, Morton." The President took off his jacket, placed it over a nearby chair, and returned to his seat.

Singer opened the folder he had been holding and, without looking at the President, began the explanation that he had so nervously rehearsed. "Mr. President, I'm in a very complicated and difficult situation. As you know, I was requested by an old and good friend, Cy Harper, to look into what appeared to be a profound threat to the security of this nation. Through Harper I was introduced to Colonel Martin, whom I've come to respect enormously. The three of us—three old men, if you will—have been working very closely together. I thought at first that it would be simple. I devised and implemented a plan of attack based on my analysis of the facts as I knew them. It was, frankly, an unmitigated disaster which revealed the size of my conceit and which suggested that I was out of my league. Two agents, three actually, were eliminated almost before I got started—two killed and one disappeared."

"There is still no trace of Miss Rhinehauer?" asked the President.

So he does keep his hand in, thought Singer.

"Absolutely none. In any case, as we regrouped I began to take a more careful look around. Frankly, sir, I disliked and was frightened by what I saw. I've got no taste for violence, Mr. President, and I felt threatened. I still do. Anyway, I restudied the whole thing, and this time I put everybody under scrutiny—anyone who was involved with Unicorn as far back as its inception in 1949."

"Including Cy and Luther?" asked the President.

"Including Cy and Luther," said Singer. "But wherever I looked, I didn't like what I found. You see, what I had fogotten in my patriotic pride at having been asked to help was that the people who were being tracked down and killed weren't nice people, by any civilized standards. They and others like them have, for almost thirty years, done all the dirty work that we now say we're ashamed of. The Unicorns are in fact responsible for a staggering list of crimes against humanity in the name of democracy. Which finally led me to the right question: what was to prevent one of them, or a group of them, from turning inward like a snake eating its own tail?"

"But why, Morton?"

"Mr. President, if we knew why, we'd know who. The point is that I decided to isolate myself because there was no one whom I could really trust. I set in motion a decoy action; I told a lot of people a lot of different things. I persuaded Cy and Luther to join me in choosing one of our Unicorns to serve as a Judas goat—*after* the chosen agent and I had agreed upon the move as a feint. I was concerned at the enthusiasm with which these two men accepted this, essentially a sacrifice of one of our absolute best.

"I then entered into two-way partnerships with the other remaining Unicorns—Fonesca, West, Coles, and Jonas. I told each of them that I suspected one of the others and invited their help in exposing the suspect. This was designed to convince the actual enemy that I was a doddering old fool sniffing up the wrong tree. I then arranged for the agent I had chosen as my real ally and offered as the supposed sacrifice to use his not inconsiderable personal net to keep a close watch on each of the others.

"Every one of our agents now had a tail, which meant I was in a position to compare all the reports and see who was lying. If one of the agents was the killer, he or she would have to leave the surveillance and travel, to kill the agent I had named as the suspect. My own surrogate, the bait, had the resources to cover them all, including Cy and Luther, who have been under my total surveillance for the past months. As a result of certain information he has passed on to me, I now have an unpleasant feeling that our difficulties may emanate from the very top—Luther or Cy, or both of them."

Singer paused, but the President offered no visible reaction. Singer drew a breath and went on.

"The Unicorn deaths began some time in 1969. Whoever is responsible had to know the identity and whereabouts of all agents at all times. Martin and Harper were incomprehensibly slow in coming to a conclusion that any junior computer analyst would have spotted as a direct attack on the agency. It was obvious to me, an inexperienced outsider, the first time through. Why not them? What took so long? Only one agent, my surrogate Michael Gault, raised any outcry, and it was his pressure that helped force my two colleagues into action. Finally, a counterattack is mounted, at Gault's insistence, and an aging CPA arrives on the scene. Query: why me? And this is not false modesty, Mr. President, not by any means. I'm very good at what I do, but what I do is quite different from what Unicorn does. I began to suspect very early on that I was being set up. It's like a crooked bank hiring an honest, independent auditor they don't think much of—they believe they can fool him.

"Consider this. No sooner do I get started than my every move is anticipated. Wyeth is killed within two days of receiving my dossiers. I suspect he saw something in them I missed. Lundquist suggested that we meet privately after the general Unicorn conference—he was on the trail of something interesting, and twelve hours later he's dead. Who else did this singularly closed-mouthed man talk to? Rhinehauer takes off immediately after the meeting; so far as I know, no one knew of her plans besides me. She disappears inside of a week. She could conceivably be using the Agatha Christie ploy from *Ten Little Indians,* but I think not—too many dead bodies among her old friends in Paris. My instinct says she's out of it permanently. So, Mr. President, as distasteful as it may be, I'm taking a very hard look at Cy and Luther."

"And just what do you want of me, Morton?"

He seemed profoundly depressed—and angry. Singer thought for a moment that were this soft-spoken Georgia farmer a Greek king, he, Singer, might share the fate of too many unmourned bearers of ill tidings. He sighed, then said what it was he had come to say.

"I feel at last that I have a sense of this game and that I can predict the pattern of play. As to the outcome, let's say it is still in doubt. I am not yet sure enough of all the hidden factors, and, as I said, the role and motives of my two colleagues are still obscure. If I'm wrong this time, I'll be responsible for additional deaths. And as I get closer to checkmate, the possibility that my opponent may choose to erase me is very real. I felt you should know what is happening just in case I do not survive my own success."

The President smiled gently. "Do you want a bodyguard, Morton?"

"Hardly, sir, though I appreciate the offer. Our faceless opponent has demonstrated an impressive ability to circumvent protective shields—we've got a lot of ungrateful dead to testify how useless a bodyguard would be. No, if I don't win the game soon, I probably won't outlive it. And in that case, I would, if I were you, look very carefully at my two venerable associates." He paused for a moment and then added, "I'm sorry to have had to add to your burdens."

The President raised his hand, deprecating Singer's concern. "It comes with the job, Morton. I sometimes wish . . ."

He stopped as though not quite prepared to indulge his

strictly personal thoughts. "Are you sorry you got into this, Morton?"

Singer thought before he answered. "Yes, in a way, Mr. President. Like everyone else, I had a vague notion of the power game we've been playing since the end of World War II, but now I know the details. I've used my access to read documents that are hidden away in the cellar at Langley—a rather complete history of thirty years of deceit and murder. Lumumba, Hammarskjöld, Mboya, Allende, Trujillo, King, and a hundred other less important figures. Ridiculous attempts on Castro's life that probably got our own President killed. The alliances with bad leaders and worse governments. The spying, the torture, the killing. I ask myself why I should risk anything to preserve the corps of killers behind this."

He paused, drained by his outburst, and then added a question of his own.

"Let me ask you something, Mr. President. You campaigned for this office on a moral and ethical platform. You kept saying that we were a 'good' people. Do you still believe it?"

The Southerner accepted the challenge.

"Yes, I do, Morton. If I didn't, I think I'd voluntarily follow the course my predecessor was forced to take; I'd quit. I agree that what we've done in the name of national security has hurt us badly, but I still do believe that there is a bedrock of decency in this country, and I'm just trying to cut away the dirt around it. It *is* there, Morton."

The President seemed to have had a rebirth of energy; his eyes were bright with conviction, and Singer was mesmerized.

"Morton, they stopped me from appointing a bright, honest civilian to head up the agency, but this doesn't mean I must tolerate that agency. You get us healthy again and I'll make you a promise. I'll use all the power of this office to clear away the dirt, and you'll see that I'm not mistaken about that decency. You'll see it for yourself, Morton."

They talked a few minutes more, working out a method for Singer to have instant access to the President. Then the two men shook hands and the meeting was over. Singer left the White house feeling more confident than he had at any time since Emily Rhinehauer had disappeared.

File 942-37-6498

Morgan Lincoln West, Jr. (U-39)

DATE OF BIRTH:	December 5, 1925
PLACE OF BIRTH:	Atlanta, Georgia
PARENTS:	Morgan Lincoln West
	Clara Charlotte West (Stiles) (Deceased 1974)
SIBLINGS:	John Franklin West (49)
	Joseph Lee West (Deceased 1962)
	Barbara Ann West (45)
	Merry Alice West (Deceased 1942)
MARITAL STATUS:	Single
EDUCATION:	Central Elementary School (1931–1939)
	Booker T. Washington High School (1939–1943)
EMPLOYMENT:	Jordan's Grocery, Atlanta (1942)
	Blue Star Trucking, Atlanta (1949–1950)
	Pennsylvania Railroad (1950–1952)
	Southern Christian Leadership Conference (1952–1968)
U.S. ARMY:	1943–1948 (444th Truck Battalion)
	ETO (Bronze Star, 5 Battle Stars)
COMPANY:	1969
U:	1971

PHYSICAL DATA:
Height:	6′ 6″
Weight:	245 lbs.
Complexion:	Dark
Hair:	None

IDENTIFYING MARKS:	Appendicitis scar (1936) Scar tissue (burn) lower abdomen Bullet Wound (scars—6) (see pages 5–9, Addenda 67F, for details)
LANGUAGES:	Swahili
RATING:	201-9
NOTE:	See Addenda 4-4C134 (Jail sentences in Atlanta, Montgomery, Birmingham, Little Rock, and Jackson connected with SNCC activities.)

Summary and Review (MLS)
Project: UNICORN

This agent was born and spent most of his childhood and adolescence in the heart of Atlanta's black ghetto. His father was the son of a sharecropper living in Coombs, about thirty miles west of Columbus. Seeing nothing worthy of emulation in his own father's life, West Sr. married and promptly moved to Atlanta in search of improved prospects. These did not materialize; at the age of eighteen, West Sr. started work as a porter for the Southern Railway System, and his wife entered what was to become her life's work, domestic service. Between them, they produced a sufficient income to raise a family of seven in poverty.

In high school, West Jr.'s grades were average, he made friends easily, and because of his size was an excellent football player for a mediocre team. During his senior year, he worked after school at a grocery store as a stock boy, for which he received three dollars a week. In 1943, our Unicorn was drafted into the Army and took his basic training at Fort Benning, Georgia. He was then assigned to the Quartermaster Corps as a truck driver. He went overseas in late 1943, landed two days after D day with the Ninth "Q" Truck Battalion (later to be known as The Red-Ball Express), and spent the rest of the war moving men and equipment across Europe. All our records indicate that he was well-liked by his fellow soldiers and courageous under fire; his commanding officer (Dilworth, Watson, Col.) also testifies to his extreme willingness to assume and accomplish any task whatsoever (Interview GW-USA File 1414).

Following V-E day, West remained in Germany. As part of the army of occupation, he was stationed in a variety of supply depots; he managed in each place to establish himself quite comfortably in a civilian apartment with an attractive white mistress (Interviews 16F-H-I, File 19313-Y). These liaisons at first caused some friction with white troops, but West's size and strength effectively ended most discussion.

There is only one incident of particular interest during this period. In Berlin, West was entertaining his then current roommate at a Berlin nightclub frequented by white officers stationed in that city. A Major Walter Sinclair ordered West to leave so he could have the table. West complied without serious protest, though the incident was replete with racial epithets. (Sinclair was probably drunk.) Four weeks later, Major Sinclair disappeared from sight and was never located (official designation MIA—See MP File 13649132). I think we can assume that West is not a forgiving man.

West was honorably discharged in May of 1948, and his return home helped shape the rest of his life. We have here a chronicle common to many black soldiers in similar circumstances. I've listed just a few highlights to illustrate the point. There were more.

1. May–December 1948 Unemployed
2. January 1949 Driver's Helper. Blue Star Truckin (Atlanta) @ $39.50 per week
3. March 1950 Discharged for constant fighting with white fellow workers (Interview Craig Colton, V.P. Blue Star Trucking; now resident Golden Age Nursing Home, Atlanta).
4. April 1950 Arrested for attempting entrance to white restrooms at Greyhound Terminal, Atlanta.
5. Between this first arrest and May of 1952, West was arrested, charged, and jailed twenty-six times. Each incident involved a black-white confrontation. Finally, on May 30, 1952, West boarded a bus on Peachtree Street in Atlanta

and insisted on sitting in the white section. After considerable struggle, he was forcibly ejected by three policemen and the bus driver. West, convicted of disorderly conduct and resisting arrest, was sentenced to six months on the prison farm at Rockland, Georgia.

While at Rockland, he met and became friendly with Ezekiel Hunter, who was serving a ninety-day sentence for a similar offense. Hunter, an executive with the Southern Christian Leadership Conference, was able to convince West that his energies could be better expended in other directions. (Interview 304 attached.) A portion of Hunter's interview describes a meeting arranged by Hunter between Martin Luther King, Jr., and our agent.

Excerpt:
". . . King kept us waiting almost four hours, and Morgan was getting hostile and impatient. When he finally invited us into his motel room, I knew King was going to do his number on West. He talked to West for over an hour and when he was finished, I tell you that big Nigger's life was changed forever. I've never seen anyone so paralyzed by love. When King said good-bye and put his arms around that huge man and kissed him, yeah kissed him, I thought Morg was gonna bust out and cry, or at least fall down and kiss King's feet. When we left the room, West turned to me and said, 'Zeke, help me to work for him. I want to be with that man, to guard him. Please help me.' And then he did cry, and so did I."

The rest, as they say, is history and it's all in the attached material. From that meeting on November 3, 1952, to April 4, 1968, Morgan West never left Dr. King's side. He was his bodyguard, his confidant, and his friend. I suspect this was the happiest period in West's life. We know how it ended. I suggest you carefully examine the attached photograph—taken the moment King was shot on that balcony in Memphis. The others are all looking for the killer, but West is crouched over the fallen body.

His psychiatric intake interview shows nothing: we can only speculate about the agony of loss, the guilt, the sense of failure that must have engulfed West. We have a six-day gap, and then West comes to the Company with an offer to help find the killer. Examination of File XX 141934, Title: King-Ray, Top Secret, shows that West, working free-lance, led us to Ray; his additional findings (attached) incontrovertibly prove the "conspiracy" theory. No other reading of West's material is possible. He names those who hired and controlled Ray, and he produces convincing evidence as to method and motive. Two distinguished United States senators, still at their posts, are clearly implicated.

Since no follow-up action was taken by this or any other agency, we must assume that West was suffering a very intense level of anger and frustration when your recruiting executive (36-379-212-Krall) offered him a job. All I can say is the man must have been extremely persuasive. In any case, West joined the Company in July of 1969. His subsequent career is, in many ways, incredible. In 1969–1970, his first year, he unsettles an entire continent—I count two revolutions, two political assassinations, one kidnapping, and the suppression of one "unfavorable" coup d'état. He learned Swahili, created a highly efficient African network, and shows evidence of being one of the most destructive physical forces I've ever encountered.

There is considerable evidence that West arranged the death and imprisonment of over three hundred left-leaning Nigerian officials who were attempting to subvert Gowon. The following is a direct quote from a Company man who worked with him in Kenya, Ethiopia, and Nigeria (see attached, 45-6713-419-Cohen).

"He is a mean, angry, dangerous son-of-a-bitch, but he's also absolutely safe. In Lagos, we found the hostile on Mao's payroll who was trying to embarrass the government with that stupid cement fiasco. Our man isolated him near the docks, where he was paying off Gowon's number two man. West put a bailing hook in the double, packed him in a crate, and had him shipped to the Chinks: then he took the payee, stuffed a stick of dynamite in his mouth, told the poor bastard why he was doing it—and sat with him for six hours. The man went crazy before West finally blew him up. Frankly, he scares the shit out of me . . ."

I think this gives us the picture. I find the following items curious and interesting.

(a) He keeps no permanent residence.

(b) He works *all* the time.

(c) He is sexually very active, but never keeps one woman for long.

(d) His covers are extremely flexible:

Nigeria—dock worker

Benghazi—UPI stringer

Cairo—rock musician touring with a currently "hot" group called appropriately "The Sick"

(e) Finally, we have no record that he has ever discussed King, much less the assassination, with anyone.

He was made the thirty-ninth Unicorn in October 1971. His assets center on his tremendous aggression, a penchant for first-person violence, and his highly devious and complex mind. (I find his triple turns in Ethiopia and Somalia fascinating. First he finished the old Ethiopian emperor, then he makes it impossible for his successors to succeed. Much of the present chaos there can be credited to our Mr. West.)

Conclusions:

He is like a lethal weapon which is not at all discriminating. His fury is random. In some ways, I fear this man above all the others, because there seem to be no operative restraints. In addition, he's got a head to go with the body. Let's watch him carefully.

10 WEST

Beginners do not have a monopoly on blunders. The finest players in the world have been known to leave a Pawn or Queen en prise. They have even been known to overlook a mate on the move. As a rule, however, a good player's lapses take a more sophisticated form.

He is more likely to *miscalculate*. Thinking, as such players do, in terms of a sequence of moves, he occasionally overlooks something that is going to happen near the end of this sequence. Thus, an enterprising player will sometimes give up material, thinking it will bring him profit a number of moves later. There is a defense, however, that he has not anticipated. Because of this, the plot turns out to be unsound.

A. I. HOROWITZ, *Learn Chess Quickly*

AT FIRST, MORGAN WEST, JR., had little or no interest in the tedious chronicle forwarded to him in Nairobi by Morton Singer. He had even considered not attending the meeting in Washington, but his curiosity prevailed. He recalled his amusement when he finally saw his club members in the flesh. All white, and all trying to look serious and professional.

He carefully avoided conversation, pretending to be totally immersed in a rereading of Singer's dossiers. For West, the meeting was without interest. He knew he was safe in Africa. The impregnable yet mobile compound he had so carefully established could not possibly be penetrated. Four men and two

191

women, the elite of East Africa's intelligence systems, were responsible for his full-time protection; when he moved from place to place, their job was to form the bell jar within which West was free from worry. This team, equipped with an arsenal of electronic gear and lethal weapons, searched out the ground ahead, guarded his flanks, covered his trail. No enemy had ever disturbed in any way the calm and concentration of Morgan West, Jr., who was then quite free to concentrate on the task at hand. His many successes had resulted as much from the fact that he could not be hurt as from his legendary strength and uncanny ability to plan and execute difficult intelligence operations.

West intended to return immediately to his compound on the outskirts of Nairobi. In the planning stages of a complex operation designed to remove Ian Smith as an obstacle to the administration's nonviolent solution in Rhodesia, he deeply resented this utter waste of time. Once the meeting ended, he went to his local headquarters deep inside Washington's ghetto to pack and assemble his protective entourage. Only moments later, West was both shocked and impressed by a short but persuasive note, hand delivered to the location judged by his infallible shield to be totally secure.

> Those hunting Unicorn are identical to your own enemies. Five minutes with me will convince you. I am offering a partnership. If interested, meet me at 5:00 A.M. tomorrow at the Monument. If you are not alone, there will be no meeting.

The one rule Morgan West had considered absolute was never to go anywhere without his security force. This time, however, the bait was too tempting—West's only enemy was the individual or group responsible for the death of Martin Luther King, Jr. He had, of course, delivered James Earl Ray and identified the cabal of five old men—among them the two white-haired senators—which had insisted on and paid for the death. But West knew even then that these were not his ultimate enemies; there remained those who had carefully arranged the killing. Those with enough skill to find and hire Ray, providing him with money and passports to insure his escape, an escape thwarted only by the unforeseen persistence of a black bodyguard.

His enemies, though caught unawares, responded brilliantly. When Ray had threatened to break his silence his captors were suborned and his escape arranged. In the deep woods that surrounded the prison, Ray paid the price for annulling his bargain. He was subjected to extreme physical persuasion, returned to prison and allowed to act out his pointless charade before the congressional committee. He would never again threaten those who stood safely hidden in the shadows behind those whom West had discovered. Knowing of their existence, West—frustrated at being deprived of the one link to those he sought—was extreme.

Morgan West, feeling chilled in the damp morning, sat alone on a bench in front of the Washington Monument. He was soon joined in the predawn darkness; and the ensuing conversation was as brief as the note that had summoned him. West was the first to speak.

"You got all of five minutes, and not one second more. I'm very unpredictable without my security blanket."

"I only need two minutes. It goes like this. The same people who are killing the Unicorns wasted the Dreamer."

Only West, in his role as bodyguard and friend, had ever referred to King by that code name. When King used the name himself, West knew the line or room was clean of FBI scans. The code had never failed them. Now, years later, with these two words from a perfect stranger, the entire nightmare of Memphis returned. West, suddenly dizzy and nauseous, tried desperately to conceal the weakness that flooded over him. He was grateful for the early morning darkness. His response was almost inaudible.

"Who?"

"The Cardinal and the Soldier."

"You're crazy, man."

"Hardly. The President had his right hand get rid of your leader. Once the preacher moved from Civil Rights to Vietnam, he was dead. Johnson was so paranoid by then that he would have killed anybody who could lead public opinion against him. They gave the job to J. Edgar, who hated King anyway, but he blew it. Johnson knew two men who had never failed and who had the power."

West was near collapse. All he could do was mumble.

"Oh, my Christ—oh, God, Unicorn killed him."

"No, Morgan." The voice turned gentle and reassuring. "They didn't even trust Unicorn for that. They set it up outside."

A warm spring rain had started at first light. West paused to look at the features of his informer. "Can you prove it?"

"Soon. And once I have the proof, I get them and you get your peace. Go home, Mr. West. When I've got the information, we act, but on one condition."

"What?"

"You act only under my orders. And I want them alive. Agreed?"

"Agreed."

West left, walking across the park and along the opposite side of the Monument in the direction of the Potomac. The man on the bench watched the black man disappear, and he smiled. He knew that Morgan West would never abide by his agreement, that he would personally sentence and execute the two men he now believed to be responsible for the death of his lost saint. Cy Harper and Luther Martin would answer to him now. The man walked from the bench to a car waiting at the curb. He was booked on the midmorning flight to Paris—Emily Rhinehauer required careful supervision. West would wait for word in Africa.

One month later, the documents that chronicled the assassination arrived in Nairobi. Alone in one of the stucco and straw huts which fill the sprawling slum on the edge of that city, West read the story under a kerosene lamp. Hoover's warning to Johnson regarding King's anti-Vietnam crusade; the minutes of a meeting attended by Johnson, Hoover, Harper, and Martin; another meeting after the old FBI chief had bungled the job. It was all there: the direct line from Harper to Martin, then to Ray, and on to the senators.

Morgan West gathered his protection and flew to Washington immediately, putting into motion the plan which would, inside of a dozen hours, break the security seal on two of the most closely guarded men in the city. Luther Martin would die first.

By the day's end Luther Martin felt overwhelmed. His nightly chemotherapy and deep radiation treatments, if they accomplished little else, did enable him to sleep well enough to feel some energy and confidence in the mornings. But by noon, pain had eroded his fleeting vitality, and it was all he could do to refuse the medication. Realizing that the task before him was by no means over, Martin needed to conserve the potency of these drugs; he could, however, hold out only until midafternoon. And then, after only a few hours of relief, the pain and exhaustion again seemed total.

He never had feared death, and he could manage pain. His nightmare was instead the loss of his ability to function with dignity and intelligence. For this disgraceful illness he would implement a soldier's solution, but not until he finished one last job. Unicorn.

To an uninformed observer, Martin's schedule would appear to be that of a robustly healthy, if slightly obsessive, man. As always, his workday started at 6:00 A.M., seven days a week. Reading the new documents and rereading the old, Luther was not about to let this matter blemish his career; if he could not ignore the pain, he would endure it. In the afternoons, he mulled over all possible strategies with his aide and companion of twenty-five years, Major Allistair Marshall. The two men spent countless hours at the same table in this large office, checking for mistakes and oversights in the gradual destruction of Unicorn.

In addition to serving as Luther's assistant and secretary, "Ally" Marshall was also the architect of Martin's safety. He had designed and supervised a complex and failsafe guardianship involving both electronic and human surveillance, free from any possibility of failure. Wherever he was, at home or at Langley, coming or going, Luther Martin was surrounded by the best of care.

Major Marshall was gravely troubled by the accelerating, now obvious deterioration evident in his superior. But he gave no sign of his concern as he entered, looking precisely as he had throughout this twenty-five-year association. He was always clean shaven, his uniform immaculate, and his now gray hair undisturbed. He saluted, as usual, and waited for the colonel to offer him a chair.

"Sit down, Ally, and let's clean up the day's work," Luther said wearily.

"Thank you, sir. What do you want to cover first?"

"I suppose it had better be Ethiopia. It's so goddamned screwed up you can't tell a player without ten scorecards."

Marshall hesitated as he reached for the file, then was surprised to hear himself address Martin as he never had before.

"Sir, why don't we just knock off for the rest of the day— you really don't look well."

The words seemed to destroy Martin. He slumped back in his chair as if emptied of all resolve. "Christ, Ally, I must really look like a corpse. Is it that obvious?"

"It is, sir. Can we take you home?"

"Fonesca's dead, Ally, and I think Unicorn is too. Singer's whistling in the wind and our superstars can't protect themselves and I'm too old and sick to do anything about it."

Marshall looked up and took a sharp breath. "When did you get the word on Danny?"

"A couple of hours ago. Singer called. And it's worse than just Danny. We can't locate West at all; for all we know, he may be down too. Coles and Gault got in this morning, and we've got them safe in the Silver Springs fort. Jonas is mad as hell about the twenty-four-hour watch we've put on him, and Cy Harper's ready to turn the whole thing over to the Security Council. I'll tell you, Ally, I never felt so goddamn worthless."

The major asked for details; in reporting them, Martin seemed to gain some vitality.

"We don't know much. He was found in a Jap temple in Kyoto with six inches of steel inside him. He was dressed like a priest and wandering around with a bunch of Swedish tourists. Singer claims Fonesca was getting very close, but who the hell knows."

He paused, drew a breath.

"Let's go home, Ally. I'm bushed."

At that moment, a voice came through the small speaker on Luther's desk. "Telephone for Colonel Martin, Code double 5V."

"Tell them he's gone," barked Marshall.

"No, Ally, I'll take it . . . Yes?"

He listened without changing expression.

"Understood. We'll deal with it."

Martin sat for some ten minutes without saying a word to the major. The color returned to his cheeks, he straightened his shoulders, and stood up. "Ally, we've got work to do. We're receiving some important visitors very soon. Come on."

The two men left Luther's office and entered the green room, which contained all computer portals and communication outlets. Only a handful of executives had access. Within thirty minutes, Martin and Marshall had designed a welcome for their guests.

Morgan West's execution of Luther Martin would be a masterpiece of simplicity. Having been supplied by his partner with the relevant details of Major Marshall's security program, West saw immediately that there were only five minutes of vulnerability. As they left Langley, Luther and his three-man escort would emerge from the elevator in the basement garage and walk in the uneven fluorescent light toward the bulletproof car. Underground garages were supported by pillars. West knew that he and his six-man assault force could, once inside, envelop the four men and drive out with Martin as hostage. West applied himself to the problem of gaining access to the garage for four armed men and two attractive, but equally lethal, women. All conspicuously black. His main asset was the plastic identity card, which gave him total clearance for the Executive Offices, and his status as a Unicorn.

At 4:30 an exodus occurs as the Company bureaucrats, clerks, and technicians depart Langley en masse. They lock their safes, shred their documents, and remove themselves with great dispatch; their cubicles empty as if by magic, with an efficiency unmatched by anything accomplished during the day. In addition, the night staff—the coders and decoders, the duty officers, the listeners, and the out-of-favor executives—arrive for the second of three workshifts. For approximately eight minutes, the garage attendants are inundated as they inspect identifications in and out.

Precisely at 4:35, the peak of the entering and exiting traffic, the black agent arrived in a brightly painted Volkswagen minibus which displayed a mural of Jacqueline Bisset reclining naked across the length of both sides. The four rows of seats on the inside of the van were empty, the six black executioners occupying instead the specially designed crawl-space between the floorboards and the base of the seats. By removing the frames and upholstery, West had created sufficient room for his colleagues, one under each seat.

The sentry, having held the post for five years, recognized West, logged his entry, and looked quickly inside the van before waving him into the garage. West drove the van into its most distant corner and immediately loosened two of the fluorescent overhead lights. He then entered the building, went to the third-floor men's room and waited, allowing enough time for the change of shifts to complete itself; at 5:15 he returned to the van and emptied his cargo. After strategically deploying his assistants, West climbed back inside the van and crouched on the floor, watching the elevator entrance.

While Morgan West, Jr., waited in the gloom of the Langley

garage, comforted by the knowledge that by noon tomorrow Luther Martin and Cy Harper would both be dead, Morton Singer, Laura Coles, and Michael Gault enjoyed a pitcher of Sangria on the back lawn of a lovely old home in Silver Springs, Maryland.

This meeting had all the outward signs of a peaceful gathering of old friends, perhaps even family. The street was lined with large trees which had already blossomed in the early spring. Gault watched Laura play the part of suburban hostess to perfection. He now felt that he might have seriously underestimated this woman. She had neither arrived at the New Otani nor taken the Thai flight from Hong Kong. Somewhere between that city and Tokyo, Laura Coles had dropped completely out of sight. When Gault had called Singer, he disclaimed any knowledge of her whereabouts and asked Gault to find out what he could about Fonesca's murder. After a week of wasted activity, he received a communication from Singer.

Come home. Coles here and well. We are near the end.

Two hours later, Mike Gault was on his way to Washington. Laura met him at the airport, and he embraced her with a passion that she had not expected.

"For God's sake, Laura, where the hell have you been?"

"Just looking, Mike. My Chinese connection gave me something I didn't understand. I switched planes at the Hong Kong airport and tried to find something here in Washington. I waited to tell you, because it had to do with the Craigies. Anyway, I came up empty."

Laura repeated Loo's information, but was disappointed in Mike's reaction. He agreed it was possible that the agency was covering up, that the Chinese might not have been involved, but said that he failed to see how this could relate to the Unicorn deaths of the past eight years.

As she described her two-week search for the truth about the Craigie deaths, he could not shake the feeling that she was holding something back. They drove toward Silver Springs, Gault wondering what Laura Coles had really been doing since he last saw her. Now, although the scene on the lawn behind the house was pastoral, a storm was rising on the horizon and the conversation was anything but peaceful.

Singer was too angry to mask his feelings. "My god, Mike, our little partnership has turned into a fiasco. Where the hell were you when Danny was killed?"

"Right where he told me to be. In my hotel room in Tokyo. Don't blame me, Morton. All these goddamn Unicorns want to go it alone. He wouldn't even tell me where he was."

Laura tried to intervene. "I don't think anything is gained by fighting each other. Why don't we get Jonas in from the Coast and call in West to see what we can do together? If Mike's right and it's Harper and Martin, we'll need them."

Singer, squinting against the sunlight, looked at the woman. "Laura, my dear, Jonas won't talk to me, let alone leave his retreat. He claims he's the only one smart enough to take care of himself and says he's safe so long as he stays where he is. And I can't blame him. As for West, it seems as if we've misplaced him."

Gault sat up in his chair. "What the hell does that mean?"

"It means he disappeared from his compound in Kenya along with his six shadows and nobody's seen him for forty-eight hours. I can't rouse him on the Red Alert code, so either he's been had or he's pulled out. At the moment, the three of us and Simon *are* the whole of the invincible team. I have to admit it looks more and more like Cy and Luther."

Gault got up and stood behind Laura. "O.K., Singer. What's our next move?"

"You and Laura stay here where I know you're safe. I can't cover all my pieces at once. I need a day or two to pick up some information. If Luther's our man he must be pretty confident by now, and that's how mistakes get made. As soon as I'm ready, we'll set up Luther; and if Cy's in it we'll get him too. The important thing is that I don't want to worry about the two of you for the next twenty-four hours."

Laura touched Mike's hand lightly. "But isn't this one of Luther's houses, Morton?"

"No, this one's mine. Neither Cy nor Luther has ever heard of it."

"And the watchdogs?"

"Also mine. Our protection comes from the top, and none of them has ever worked for the Company."

"So we're in cold storage," said Gault.

"For a day or so, yes. I can't afford to lose you. Go with me on this and I think we'll see it finished by Sunday."

The two agents agreed, if reluctantly. Singer set up a new communications code and described his elaborate design on Martin. As they labored over the details of their new plan, the storm suddenly arrived, announced by a thunderclap and shards of lightning. Then came the deluge washing away the heat and humidity, drenching the three of them before they could escape inside the house.

While Laura and Mike were finding dry clothes, Singer made a single telephone call.

"I was right, Cy. I don't understand it completely, but I am sure. Luther should be watched very carefully. This thing should be over, one way or the other, in a day. The only thing I need is absolute proof. Right now Jonas is the key. And watch yourself as well."

The rest of the brief conversation was given over to amenities between old friends who no longer quite trusted each other. Once again, as he had so many times since the beginning, Singer felt isolated and quite alone. He looked out of the large bay window at the furious rain, pulled on an old raincoat, grabbed his black umbrella, and left the house.

A dark sedan waited at the curb. He slumped in the back seat, soaked after the short walk from the house, and wondered what Simon Jonas had to tell him about Mike Gault and Phillip Craigie.

In the garage under Company headquarters, Morgan West

and his army of six could not hear the summer storm that swept the city—closing the airports, flooding the streets, and paralyzing evening traffic.

At 8:24, the elevator door opened, and four figures emerged. With a patience born of confidence, West waited without breathing until they had reached the center of the now deserted garage. He depressed a button on the tiny electronic control board that linked him to his six soldiers; like marionettes controlled by a single string, they appeared on all sides, rising up behind cars and stepping out from behind pillars. Within seconds, West was out of the van, his revolver leveled at the central figure.

He heard the echoing report of the six automatic rifles that took out his bodyguard. West didn't understand until it was too late. The man he faced was not Luther Martin, nor were the other three Martin's familiar escort. His finger hesitated on the trigger for the moment it took him to recognize his failure, which was all the time the four men needed. One sent West's pistol clattering to the concrete with a blow that nearly broke the black man's wrist, two of the others drew silenced magnums and placed the long-tubed barrels directly in front of his eyes, and the fourth man, used as Martin's double on several occasions, delivered a powerful kick to the agent's groin. Everything occurred simultaneously; the situation was reversed in seconds. As West fell, his hands and feet were instantly cuffed. He lay helpless on the dirty garage floor until he was carried to Luther Martin's sanctuary on the top floor of the building. The other six bodies, mutilated beyond recognition by the soft-headed bullets, were placed in the Langley incinerators. At 8:39, the sentries were notified to reopen the garage.

Once inside Luther Martin's special office, West was thrown against the wall and propped up like a straw man. Martin entered, flanked by Major Marshall and his two guards.

"Why, Morgan?"

"You killed King, you bastard. You and Harper."

"Quite so, but on orders from the highest possible source. His civil rights crusade was tired, so he decided to jazz it up by bitching about Vietnam. We couldn't let one black man make policy for the country, now could we? The minute he got out of his league, he was dead ... And I'm sorry, Morgan. So are you."

"How the fuck did you know what was going on?"

"My secret, Morgan. Let's just say I got word after you were all inside. All we had to do was close the doors."

"You doing Unicorn, old man?" West asked him.

"Is that a serious question, Morgan? I was about to ask you the same thing. I guess I've got my answer, and you've got yours."

Without further comment, Martin and his entourage walked out of the room, leaving Morgan West to wait alone for the Company physician.

File 038-44-6139 (U-36)

NAME:	Simon (NMI) Jonas
DATE OF BIRTH:	May 22, 1940
PLACE OF BIRTH:	Winachee, Washington
PARENTS:	Aaron Ezra Jonas (Deceased) Charlotte Elizabeth Jonas (Birch)
SIBLINGS:	None
MARITAL STATUS:	Married (1965). Audrey Rebecca Jonas (Seiden)
EDUCATION:	Winachee Elementary School (1945–1953) Chelan District High School (1953–1957) University of California (1957–1961) (B.A.) Stanford University, Palo Alto (1961–1962) (M.A.) California Institute of Technology (1962–1965) (Ph.D.)
EMPLOYMENT:	Brookings Institution (1965–1966)
COMPANY:	1967

PHYSICAL DATA:
Height: 5′ 8″
Weight: 145 lbs.
Complexion: Pale
Hair: Brown (sparse)

IDENTIFYING
MARKS: None

LANGUAGES: Russian, Chinese, French, German, Italian, Arabic, Spanish

RATING: 210-7 a

Summary and Review (MLS)
Project: UNICORN

I must say that the history of Simon Jonas, U-36, came as a welcome relief. As is obvious from the attached material, Mr. Jonas is a man who agrees, quite literally, with the ancient philosopher who declared that "the power of the mind is absolute."

Jonas was born on May 22, 1940, in Washington state, in a lovely area around Lake Chelan. His father owned a small and mildly successful real-estate agency. This agent's home life seems to have been stable and largely without incident. What is remarkable, however, is Jonas's academic record, from his kindergarten class to his doctoral dissertation (California Institute of Technology, June, 1965—document attached, "The Black Hole: An Eternal Darkness").

Jonas, if not a genius, is too close to it for me to differentiate. Consider the following:

(a) An average of 98.7 throughout high school and the highest S.A.T. scores in the history of the state.

(b) A 4.00 grade point average at Berkeley. Summa cum laude, Phi Beta Kappa, with highest honors in physics, mathematics, *and* Russian.

(c) A perfect record (100) for M.A. and Ph.D. His dissertation was published in thirteen languages and won the Faure-Xavier Prize as the outstanding thesis by a doctoral candidate.

It is simple enough to understand these figures, but rather more difficult to understand the man. Extensive interviews with neighbors, friends, teachers (File 990 QD) produce very little beyond the common admiration for his mind. He seems to have been a quiet, isolated child—there is no evidence of a single close friendship. Teachers do not recall him as being an active participant in class, and he never participated in sports. His father, Aaron Ezra Jonas, was active in the community (Rotary, Elks, 4-H, etc.) and ran for the State Assembly in 1952, losing badly. A decent, loving parent, he was singularly uncomfortable with his only child. Emerging from our long interview with Simon's mother, Charlotte Elizabeth Jonas, is the picture of a strange child, living largely within his own mind and unusually close to his mother. ". . . Simon preferred to stay indoors, with me—watching me cook, bake, and clean. We talked—how we talked! He wanted to know about everything. I guess I spent more time with Simon than I did with his father . . ." (See full interview 59400-V-Jonas, C. E.). She is now sixty-seven and has, for the past five years, lived at the Chelan Residence, an attractive condominium for Senior Citizens; Jonas pays all the bills but does not visit.

At Berkeley Jonas discovered friendship and sex, but formed no relationships that could be termed close. In his senior year, his father became ill with terminal cancer and killed himself. Now comes our first red flag. From the time Jonas learned of his father's illness up to and including the funeral, Simon Jonas did not return home. His time at Stanford (M.A.) and Cal Tech (Ph.D.) seems a logical extension of his undergraduate days. A few select friends, some female relationships, a lot of study, and an impressive record of scholarship.

Since our interviews revealed so little of value, I read some of Jonas's writing. Here, for the first time, I caught a glimpse of the man. I have attached a dozen papers, two of which I found particularly interesting. One is a term paper for a seminar on the works of William Faulkner, entitled "The Myth That We Are Human." In it, Jonas propounds the theory that writers like Faulkner create entire fictional worlds in which people give evidence of their humanity because there is no such evidence in the real world.

The second is a political science paper entitled "A State of Siege." Although brilliantly written, Jonas's acceptance of war, genocide, etc. as man's normal behavior is hardly original. What I find interesting is the terms in which he couches his conclusion. He manages to destroy completely a major thesis of so profound a mind as Hannah Arendt. "Our natural state, then, is one of death and destruction. Accept it, indulge in it, and enjoy it. Therein lies truth."

In 1965, Jonas married Audrey Rebecca Seiden, with whom he has three young children—Kelly, Melissa, and Kim. His family knows only that he is a "consultant to several government agencies" and that his work necessitates numerous absences over extended periods of time. Audrey Jonas, according to attached report 54-732, is currently engaged in an extramarital affair with Armando Ruiz (Mexican Davis Cup Team 1963–65), the tennis professional at the Seaside Tennis Club in La Jolla. We have no way of knowing whether Jonas is informed; our investigator suspects that he knows and doesn't care.

Upon receiving his doctorate, Jonas must have set a record for job offers from the business community. He chose instead to go to Brookings and ponder the "Black Hole," which he claims worried him. The Company is attracted to Jonas at this point, and John Fallow (194-37-3922) recruits him for a few freelance jobs. As far as I can tell, he was used as a one-person think tank. The Company fed in a specific problem and Jonas computed a solution in his head. He was damned good at it.

This seems to me a classic case of the right man for the right job. I needn't remind you that it was Jonas, more than anyone else, who rid us of Nasser and got us Sadat. (See attached file, Operation 49000R-TS.) His manipulation of the Lebanon situation is the perfect example of this agent's power to control events, using only his mind. Without ever leaving California, the man brought Sarkis to power, got the Syrians into the act as peace makers, arranged the influx of Israeli arms to the Lebanese right just when it looked as if Chamoun and his Christian Falangists were out of the game. Finally, he arranged the end of Kamal Jamblatt, the last hope of the Moslem left.

Note one highly significant omission. In all the attached

material you will find not a single instance when Jonas is personally involved in violence. Fascinating, I think, given the destruction for which he has been responsible.

Finally, consider this extract from his intake interview July 19, 1968. (Intake interview—S. Jonas, by 492-35-7771.)

Q: . . . you understand the basic nature of Unicorn.

A: Why insist on treating me like an idiot?

Q: It is essential that you understand exactly what the job is.

A: OK, Feldman, how's this? You've got a group of killers, the very best—brains, brawn, and no conscience. They work only when it's for all the marbles, and they never say no to anything.

Q: Good enough. Can you do it?

A: (Laughter) I've got an IQ over 200, seven languages, a doctorate in physics, and above all I can see what's going to happen before anyone else. I don't give a damn how good your Unicorns are—I'm better.

Q: Why do you want it?

A: I'm bored. The jobs I did for you last year were more fun than I've ever had. It was like pulling strings on a puppet; everyone did exactly as I predicted. I love it.

Q: Can you kill a man yourself?

A: I'll never have to. There're always people like you for that. By the way, Feldman, did you ever read the dictionary definition of "Unicorn"? I memorized it. ". . . a mythical creature resembling a horse and having a single horn in the center of its forehead; often symbolic of chastity or purity; capable of being tamed by a virgin and usually successful in evading capture . . ." OK, Feldman, I'm your virgin bucking to be a Unicorn . . .

That, gentlemen, is Simon Jonas, in some ways the strangest of a very strange group.

11 SIMON JONAS

Who would settle for the gain of a pawn when he could blast through to checkmate? No one, of course, if the choice is put that way. But in the uncertainty of over-the-board play, one often finds a pawn in the hand preferred to a mate in the bush.

—ROBERT BYRNE, "Chess"
The New York Times, July 18, 1977

SIMON JONAS, unlike his fellow agents, had been impressed with the quality of Singer's analysis of Unicorn's decimation. Following the Washington meeting, he had approached the accountant and requested a private meeting. Singer suggested his apartment in New York. Jonas offered instead to provide a small, private office at the National Science Foundation, whose sterility he could guarantee.

The meeting took place the day after Lundquist's death, just a few hours before Singer would return to New York. In a windowless office, furnished with a metal desk and two exceedingly uncomfortable chairs, Morton Singer listened to this slightly built, homely, and myopic genius propose a plan of action ideally suited to his unique talents.

Throughout this brief but productive session, Jonas spoke to Singer as if he were teaching calculus to remedial third-grade students.

He began by patiently explaining that, when dealing with a covert enemy, motive was the key to identity; he went on to suggest that motive could almost always be discovered by a thoughtful and detailed analysis of the facts. The computer, he explained patiently, is the most effective analytical tool, not simply because of its ability to store and instantaneously retrieve vast amounts of information, but because the machine is totally free of emotional involvement. Thus, said Jonas, computer conclusions are usually reliable *if* the facts used to program the machine are accurate.

The purpose of this lecture was its conclusion: he wanted Singer to know that he, Jonas, had added an important humanizing value to the computers he used so brilliantly. He had learned to apply his own insights into the human condition to the sterile facts. Singer listened without interruption, fascinated by the man's brilliance—and by the utter lack of personality. Jonas, on his part, was comfortable with the way an accountant thinks and works and perhaps even felt some kinship with this particular CPA; in any case, he proposed a joint enterprise. He would, he told Singer, need every single piece of information concerning the death of Unicorn, including more specifics than were contained in Singer's dossiers. If Jonas were to succeed, he would also require free access to all Langley computers and to any files that might be helpful.

Singer reflected as he listened, considering the possibility that Jonas was himself behind the deaths and was now trying to seduce him with an offer of partnership. Certainly this potentially valuable ally was equipped to implement such a delicate yet intelligent attack, but Singer decided to rely on something rather more personal. He decided to trust his intuition. Which was why, on the evening before Singer's departure for Paris in pursuit of Emily Rhinehauer, the aging accountant and the youthful genius joined forces.

Proceeding methodically and with an unbelievable amount of patience, Jonas began to search through an almost impenetrable jungle of information and data. Every single known or suspected fact concerning Unicorn was called forth from the dusty archives of the past. The quick and the dead, all the agents past and present, all those who had hated and loved them, all their victims and allies, all their achievements and failures were reviewed, understood, and examined by the merciless mind of Simon Jonas. It was the unique nature of his mind that he could absorb, retain, and organize such a tremendous quantity of information.

In the center of that furnace, the most obscure and intimate details that comprised the lives of Harper, Martin, and the remaining agents were reviewed and refined, and then scrutinized and understood by this strange and introverted man. Then, finally, the tidal wave of facts, dates, and information was programmed into this human computer.

The minutiae stored in countless computers and files at Langley staggered even Jonas, who took three full months to ingest the information. Singer had been in constant touch, relaying without delay the continuing movement and ongoing deaths of the Unicorn agents, both before and after Jonas departed Langley for his fortress high on a cliff at Big Sur. There, as always, he worked in a large, bare study lined with cedar and insulated with granite floors and ceilings. A window on the ocean side constituted an entire wall. The only sound he heard was the endless crashing of the surf on the rocks below.

For his convenience as well as their safety, his wife and children were exiled to his mother-in-law in Hawaii. Simon knew his wife would miss her lover and regretted having to interrupt her activities. He did not regret the fact that he was able to work without distractions for twenty hours a day. He ate little and slept less, yet he felt exhilarated. It had been some time since he had encountered an opponent of such intellectual quality, and Jonas had no doubt as to the outcome.

After three months at Big Sur, he felt ready to begin the process of retrieval, sensing a camouflaged pattern of conflict and inconsistency. In a way, the task had been made easier by the continuing slaughter: dead, you're out. Lundquist and Fonesca were now clues, not suspects; so, Jonas assumed, was Rhinehauer. Singer was no factor. In a closed set, relationships seldom appear random and are never without purpose. And now, only a subset of Unicorn remained. Harper, Martin, West, Coles, and Gault.

Jonas, having traversed fact with logic, extended himself beyond reason, addressing the people; and he was well aware that he preferred to recreate these lives from integers rather than pursuing them as had Singer. Whereas the accountant tried to understand these perverse lives, Jonas knew. Psychology, motive, reaction—all put forth as if in a biography. Obvious as the killer had become, the analyst waited for the necessary and conclusive step of proof. He flew to Washington on the red-eye flight out of San Francisco.

He had discovered the Black Files, coded 0-access-001, quite by accident two years before. Only five men had the power to open those doors and only Martin from the Unicorn group; chancing upon these files, Jonas lacked at that time the means to get to them. On this occasion, however, he was given carte blanche by Singer. After three days over the most restricted terminal at Langley, Jonas found confirmation of what he already suspected. He was not, however, ready to rule out a partnership between agent and control. He hurriedly reviewed Martin and Harper and then made a call from a pay phone outside the Washington Hilton. Singer answered this, U-36's priority line, on the second ring.

"Yes, Simon."

"I've got it. And I need to see you right away. I'm not sure I didn't pick up a tail sometime today."

"Who, Simon?"

"Not on the phone. It's too complicated, and I'm not absolutely sure our man doesn't have helpers. How soon can we meet?"

"I need to see Mike and Laura in about an hour in Maryland—they have to stay out of it for a few days. I can see you right after that, perhaps nine."

"O.K. Nine o'clock in my safe house at the Foundation. There'll be no record with night security."

"I'll be there, Simon."

Jonas hung up and called the Foundation to arrange for late entry into the building for Singer and himself. He then went to his suite and took a cold shower, satisfied that he had done what no one else could.

At the house in Silver Springs, Laura Coles was drying her hair. Gault watched from the window as Singer's car disappeared into the night and rain. He turned and looked at Laura, wearing only bikini pants and a transparent bra. Her long hair, still damp, hung in a straight line down her back and shoulders. She looked vulnerable, and Gault gathered her gently in his arms.

"The old man thinks we're in trouble, Laura."

"Are we, Mike?"

"Yes." And then he paused. "I know who it is, but I don't know what the hell to do about it."

Laura raised her head to look at Gault; her eyes were strangely unfocused.

"It's Harper and Martin, isn't it?"

"Yes, Laura, and they've taken out West."

"When, for Christ sake?"

"A little while ago. We're next, and they know where we are."

"No one even knew where West was, so how?"

"I don't know. Singer told me just before he left. He wants me to cover his tracks; once he picks up Jonas, they'll lay out the case against the two old bastards to Admiral Turner and the President. I'm the security force, but Singer is scared they'll get him before he can close it out."

"And me?" Her voice was so soft he could hardly understand.

"Stay here, unless Cy and Luther win it all. And if they do, get out and go as far and as deep as you can. I'll come and get you if I'm still alive. The meeting is set up inside Langley, so it could be sticky."

"How long should I wait, Mike?"

He held her tightly, stroking her damp hair. "Give us tonight. If you haven't heard anything by morning, you'll know that we're out. What are you carrying?"

"The pistol, my two pens, and the nails. I'm an arsenal."

"Good. You'll need all of it if I lose. Don't go out and don't, under any circumstances, let anybody in. If any of those jokers downstairs comes through your door, kill him. I don't know whose payroll they're on, Martin's or Singer's. If I call you, I'll use the name you got in high school."

"You know everything, don't you? You bastard," she laughed.

"That I do, darling." He kissed her for the first time since Hong Kong, then left the room without a word.

Laura watched from the window as he drove out of the driveway and into the furious rain.

Singer sat slumped in the rear of the army vehicle he had requisitioned, staring at the windshield wipers as they moved from side to side. The rain had not let up, and the windows were steamed on the inside. Fighting drowsiness, Singer again thought to locate all his pieces. To lose track of anyone now would be disastrous.

He had just spoken with Harper, who was with the President in the White House. Jonas was en route to their meeting at the Foundation. Laura and Mike were in seclusion at Silver Springs. That left only West and Martin outstanding.

Singer used the car's telephone to call his private message center: there was, as yet, still no trace of Morgan West. Singer then called Luther Martin.

An unfamiliar voice responded after several rings. "Extension 500 red."

"Who is this?" Singer demanded. The absolute rule was that only one party, the owner, could answer the red phone.

"You first, friend," the voice answered.

"This is Morton Singer, goddammit, and I want Colonel Martin. Now."

"This is Major Marshall, Mr. Singer." The voice, courteous

in the extreme, ignored Singer's outburst. "It's impossible to reach the Colonel just now. He's in an emergency meeting."

Singer spoke slowly and evenly. "Major Marshall, evidently I have not made myself clear. It is crucial that I speak with Luther immediately. I have the authority. You have no business on this phone. Unless Luther's dead, put him on."

There was a long pause. Marshall finally said, "Please hold for a moment, Mr. Singer. I'll see what I can do."

The phone clicked and Singer was left to listen to the faint beep of a call on hold. "You damn well better do something," he whispered.

"Sir?" the driver asked.

"Nothing." Just an old fool talking to himself.

Singer waited for five minutes as the car struggled through the rain-slowed traffic.

Finally, another click. "Luther here, Morton. What the hell's got your ass on fire?"

"Damn it, Luther, we're going into the last turn and I want to know where the hell everybody is. And it just might interest you to know that I still can't find our black ace in the hole."

"It might interest *you* to know that I was in the process of scratching the man you're looking for. He tried to take me out of the game."

"What the hell are you talking about?"

"Our man in Nairobi launched a major offensive on my home grounds an hour ago. He outmaneuvered our gate security with six assassins, each carrying enough fire power to conquer Zaire. They were waiting for me in the garage, but I got the drop on them and kicked their black asses to hell and back. Somehow West found out about Unicorn and King, so he was out of his mind."

"What about Unicorn and King?"

"Oh, shit, Morton. Don't you start. It's a long story, and I'm tired. You know where I am, so what else do you need?"

"Stay there until I call, probably within the hour. I may need you fast. Jonas says he's got it wrapped up."

"O.K., my friend. Good luck."

Singer replaced the receiver and tried to make sense out of what he'd just heard. A setup, he decided. Somebody had used West and then sold him out.

The rain let up to a drizzle as the car stopped in front of the National Science Foundation. Singer told the driver to wait across the street. Unapproached by the security guards, he went upstairs to Jonas's office. Sitting in the same metal chair that he had used at their first meeting, he waited under the fluorescent lights that gave his round face an unhealthy green cast. The room was stuffy, and he nodded off after five minutes.

He awakened with a start, disoriented at first, but vaguely aware of the sirens on the street. He looked at his watch and cursed the forty minutes he had lost. Already 9:45 and no Jonas. Singer's stomach was queasy and his neck sore. He dialed Martin.

"Yes."

"He's not here, Luther."

"Jonas is never late. Get out, Morton."

"I'm on my way. Stay there."

He hung up abruptly, put on his old raincoat, and scuttled down the seven flights of stairs. The halls and empty offices were silent and dark. He walked quickly out the front door, but his car and driver were gone. Half a block down the street was a group of silhouetted figures. An ambulance had backed onto the sidewalk and two police cars had blocked off traffic. Singer walked slowly toward the street lights, knowing what awaited him.

Simon Jonas lay on the pavement, staring up at the night sky. A fine copper wire was embedded deeply in his flesh around his neck. His hands clutched vainly at his throat. The street smelled strongly of feces and urine.

A young policeman approached Singer.

"You O.K., mister?"

"Yes," he muttered. "Thanks anyway, officer. What happened?"

"We don't really know. A cabbie stopped to let out a fare and saw him. It's a mess. We're waiting for homicide. You don't know him, do you?"

"No, I was just leaving my office."

Singer stepped away quickly and entered a phone booth a block away. Again, the clicks of the relay system.

"Jonas down. In front of the National Science Building. The police are here already."

"I'll clean it up. Do we move now, for God's sake?"

"Absolutely. I'll be with Luther within two hours."

"Cy coming?"

"Yes, we go for mate. There's no more time."

"That's what I've been saying all along."

Singer hung up and dialed Martin. "Jonas is out. Before I saw him."

"Shit."

"I'm on my way over. This is our last chance, Luther."

"I'll be waiting. How about Cy?"

"Call him and get him over there right away."

"Christ, Morton."

Singer hung up and looked out of the booth at the mist and made a final call to the Silver Springs house.

"Yes."

"This is Singer. Is Coles there?"

"Yes, sir. Should I put her on?"

"No. Keep her there and don't let her out of your sight. And *nobody* is to see or talk with her. Clear?"

"Yes, sir."

Singer hailed a cab and instructed the driver to cruise the area, assuming that his car and driver would be nearby but out of the line of possible police inquiry.

Laura lay on her bed for hours, watching the rain. Downstairs she heard a baseball game on the television, and the banter of her guard. She drifted into light sleep, waking periodically, dreaming in fragments—elliptical images of overwhelming sadness. Somewhere, far away, she was conscious of a ringing telephone and whispered conversation.

It was now close to ten o'clock. Someone turned off the television set, and she heard only the comforting sound of rain. Now and then a car went by, the arc of its headlights sweeping the room.

Suddenly there came the sound, muffled but unmistakable: the pops of a silenced pistol. Laura jumped from the bed, her gun already in hand, cautiously opened the door and walked to the edge of the stairs.

The four guards in the living room below her were sprawled at different angles on the floor and sofa. None of them was moving. Michael Gault stood in the middle of the room with a .45 Colt in his hand. He looked up at Laura and held a finger to his lips; they waited and watched, scarcely breathing, for what seemed like a long time. Then Gault walked softly up the stairs.

"Let's go, darling. We're blown. Martin got Jonas and Singer is under arrest at Langley. They'll be looking for us now. The jokers downstairs were Martin's, waiting for word to do us. Put yourself together and let's go."

Laura ran to him, crying. "I'm so scared, Mike. I don't want to die. Hold me . . ."

He picked her up as if she were a child, carried her down the hallway, and laid her gently on the bed. He rocked her in his arms and she thought again of their time together in Aberdeen. Then, in the flood of memory, she heard his exact words once more and she knew. She understood, at last, what had troubled her that night just before she drifted away into sleep. Gault was watching her face.

"We've got to go now, Laura. They'll be here very soon."

She did not move. He turned on the light by the bed and saw that she knew.

"When, Laura?"

"Just now, Mike. I just remembered."

"Remembered what, darling?"

She shivered again. "In Aberdeen, on the boat, you knew

what had happened to Rhinehauer. You said she was crazy—that she was where she belonged. What did you do to her, Mike?"

"I had her put away, Laura, in the madhouse. She was like the rest of you, a crazy killer. I had no choice but to commit her. Anyway, she's dead now—starved herself to death. They tried to feed her with tubes but they couldn't keep her alive. No one ever did it before in that place. It started a riot."

Laura stared in horror. He smiled, his eyes bright with excitement.

"Why?" she whispered.

"Let's say I'm making the world safe for democracy. Let's say I'm filled with fear and loathing. That I'm tired of the slaughterhouses, especially the goddamn agency. I'll keep at it until all the good ones are dead, the clerks will take it over, and then the agency itself is dead."

"And me?"

"Dead, Laura, like the others. As long as one of you is alive, I can't breathe."

"Mike, we could disappear, they'd never find us. You don't have to—"

"No sale, lollipop. Isn't that what they called you in high school, darling?"

Gault smiled, looking as if he expected an answer. She tried to blink away the tears, then covered her face with her hands. More than the fear and the loss, she felt hopeless in the face of Gault's sickness, hopeless in her feelings for him.

"But I loved you—and you loved me, I know you did. Doesn't that count for something? I was trying to help the week I disappeared, trying to find out what happened to your teacher. I loved you so much, Mike . . ."

"And I hated you for it, for making me feel like that. You smell like something dead—it was like fucking a corpse."

Laura jumped from the bed and threw her arms around Gault before he could move; she slashed at him, raking her nails on the flesh on his back and neck. She stopped crying, wanting to watch him die. He looked at her with surprise, but showed no pain. The smile on his face grew into a full, deep laugh. He finally stopped himself to speak.

"Oh, Laura, Laura. I had those nails of yours replaced that first night in Hong Kong, when you were safe asleep. Oh, yes, I was afraid of those nails, Laura. But, seriously now, I can't stay all night, as much as I'd like to. They're waiting for me up at the big house—and Luther's got a big surprise coming. And I've got the agency. I'm afraid I must go." He reached into the pocket of his jacket. "Good night, Laura."

The wires were in his hands.

PART III

END GAME

There is a fairly widely held notion among grandmasters that conservative play is the best policy when confronting an unknown opponent.

To take chances may be to play into the opponent's strength, whereas sticking to solid positional maneuvering is more likely to put him beyond his depth. Besides, if this doesn't succeed, there is always the end game, a realm where otherwise talented players often find themselves at sea.

—ROBERT BYRNE, "Chess"
The New York Times, July 17, 1977

12 SINGER & GAULT

It is all well and good to simplify when you are ahead
in material, but what if you are behind? The answer
follows logically: if you are unfortunate enough to be
behind in material, avoid exchanges and seek to com-
plicate the game. Try to secure compensation for your
loss by working up some sort of attack, always making
life as difficult as possible for your opponent. Maybe
he will make a mistake, or maybe you will discover
that you have really made a brilliant sacrifice, and had
adequate compensation for your material all the time!

A. I. HOROWITZ, *Learn Chess Quickly*

SINGER FOUND HIS CAR parked in an alley adjacent to the back
of the National Science Building. He got rid of the cab and
nodded to his driver.

"Did you see what happened, Lieutenant?"

"Not a thing, sir. I was watching the doorway like you told
me to, until I saw the police flashers in the rearview mirror. I
figured I'd better move and hope you'd find me instead of having
to answer a lot of questions."

"Good thinking, Lieutenant."

He sat back in his seat and closed his eyes for a moment.

"Where to, Mr. Singer?"

"This address first."

He handed the driver a slip of paper. "It's in Alexandria,
about three blocks from the highway. I'll be there just a few

minutes, then we've got to get back to the White House. I'll need ten or fifteen there. And I've got to be at the main office before midnight. Can we manage it?"

"Yes, sir, if you're not too long at each place."

He spent even less time in Alexandria than he anticipated, five or six minutes at the most.

As the driver propelled Singer's car back over the 14th Street Bridge, around the Monument, and toward the White House, Singer plotted the next thirty minutes; time enough, he hoped, to conclude the crucial part of his entire plan. The rain had stopped, and there was a refreshing coolness in the air. Singer cracked a window and felt immeasurably better. He had, without recognizing it, come to enjoy the challenge of the play. Now, for the first time, he saw the entire board. It was always easier to discern motive and purpose when only a few pieces remained. This was, after all, the beauty of the end game, and Singer had always been superb at it.

As the car passed through the White House gates, Singer wondered if this would be his last visit. He was escorted immediately to the small study on the ground floor by two secret servicemen. The door closed behind him. There were to be neither observers nor transcripts of this meeting. For some fifteen minutes, Morton Singer spoke quietly but forcefully to the President, the Vice-President, and the Chief Justice. When the meeting was over, he left as quickly as he had come, having achieved full agreement on the ultimate move. He reentered his waiting car and ordered his driver to take him to Langley.

He sat silently in the back of the car, reviewing his strategy. As they crossed the 14th Street Bridge into Virginia, Singer realized that he was being followed. A black Cadillac limousine was attempting to pass the smaller army vehicle. Without waiting for confirmation, he leaned forward.

"Lieutenant, we've got trouble. Take the left to the airport—*now!*"

Just at the fork that either bears right to Langley or loops left toward the airport, the lieutenant saw the large black car that was nearly alongside. He jammed his accelerator to the floor and turned sharply into the left fork; the smaller car slipped ahead of the Cadillac and straddled the center of the two-lane road, blocking any attempts at passing. This superbly executed improvisation, coming as it did on a blind turn, also sent the army car through the wooden barrier surrounding a road construction site.

Before Singer's driver could respond, the right front wheel was imbedded in a drainage trench, and the front axle of the car had been sheared in half. Realizing their situation, Singer hurled himself out of the car and flattened himself to the ground. The lieutenant remained slumped over the wheel, dazed when his head had hit the windshield as the car slammed through the barrier. The limousine sped past in the left lane, and the fragment grenade thrown through the passenger window of the army car shredded the inside of the vehicle.

Wedged between the car and the concrete wall, Singer saw the Cadillac disappear in the direction of the airport. The lieutenant was dead; the only undamaged piece of the car's interior was the telephone. Singer was just completing his call as six police cars left their posts at National Airport in response to the explosion. Once there, they found a dead young soldier, a demolished staff car, and one shaken but angry survivor.

An hour earlier in his small office in the White House, Cyrus Harper listened with considerable distaste to Luther Martin's opinions as to the violent death of Simon Jonas, and Morgan West's assault on his colleague and friend. Following this lengthy telephone conversation, he decided he approved fully in the disposition of the black Unicorn.

He completed several items passed along to him by the President, whom he continued to view as a neophyte, and then inquired if he might have a few minutes of the Chief Executive's time before the workday was officially over.

The response upset him. He was told that the President was in a closed meeting and afterward would go directly to bed. Was it something that could wait until morning? Since the matter was less than urgent, and because Harper did not want to risk foreclosure by a secretary, he told her that he'd see the President at their regular breakfast meeting. He locked his desk, placed a file folder in the safe, turned off the porcelain lamp he had brought down from his New York estate, and left his office for Singer's command performance at Company headquarters.

"What a damned mess," growled Harper, as Eric Seeman, his chauffeur of thirty years, turned the Daimler out of the White House gates and toward the city.

Seeman could sense without fail those rare occasions when a response was expected. This was not one of them.

It was so damned untidy, reflected Harper. The dead mounting, control passing to an old accountant, and on top of everything else spook meetings at midnight. When he had recommended Singer to the President, it was largely a diversion. While he enjoyed their mail-order chess matches and had been privately impressed by the accountant's handling of cases malfeasance and corruption in government, Harper could not seriously believe that old Morton would make any real headway in the Unicorn business.

He had sensed, however, that the new President was growing impatient; new faces and new appointments were, at least for this one, considered accomplishments. To Harper's mind, the hallmark of a pigmy: style over substance.

Unicorn was, in any case, finished. No way to replace all twenty-five top agents at once. He had no option but to talk the President into giving Luther and himself the task of reorganizing the whole agency. And Gault could front the operation; Harper had always sensed the right instincts in the man.

If Singer actually did have an answer, of course, he'd have to go—his knowledge made public could ruin everything. Harper had known that from the beginning. Poor Morton, no way he could walk away from this. Goddamned Congress, they're beginning to take themselves seriously. He jotted down a note on the small pad he always carried. He wrote with a delicate gold pen given to him by his father: Get Russ and Barry to paralyze the committee. He turned to watch the passing headlights that reflected on the beaded windows of the Daimler.

"Eric," he said abruptly. "Would you arrange a meeting of the 'six' at breakfast tomorrow? We're going to begin all over again."

"Yes, sir, and may I say it's time."

In the darkness of the car, the old man smiled.

And then, in silence, they drove to Langley.

A few minutes before midnight, Luther Martin sat alone in his large office, wondering how he would last through the night. Surrounded by the relics of a life spent in battle, he wondered where all the days had gone. The pain now was almost unbearable. The medication was close to useless. This was the third and, by far, the most severe attack since that awful discovery almost eight years ago. Each time he thought he had licked it, only to have it return, more insistent and more crippling than before.

He had asked Ally to pull the whole summary file on Unicorn. It lay on the table, its many blue tabs marking the dead. Luther Martin could not believe Unicorn had failed. The best unit he had ever commanded: responsive, capable, and totally without conscience. He had learned, as an intelligence officer on Patton's staff, that the only way to survive was to maintain the offensive—"attack, goddammit, always attack—cut their balls off before they get a chance to do it to you." For Luther Martin, Unicorn had been the intelligence version of Patton's battlefield philosophy.

The vigor he had regained while dealing with West was now only a dull ache. Martin stared at the blue tags which were the index of the Unicorn chronicle, the pain of this failure as sharp and bitter as the pain from the cancer. He remembered when Harper had first approached him with this Unicorn idea.

"Major Martin, could you come by the White House and take tea, or whatever your preference, with me? There's something I would like to share with you."

It had been not an invitation but a command, though issued by a civilized and urbane man. They sat in the same small office Harper still occupied almost three decades later.

". . . a group of men and women, Major, with you running them. Allen says you're very, very good. Think of the possibilities: no supervision, unlimited resources, absolutely no congressional interference. As far as everyone is concerned, Unicorn will not exist. Just you, me, and the President—and I'll handle that son of a bitch."

Here, finally, was someone who would and could do something, someone who saw things as he did. He recalled the long sessions as each agent was chosen and, over the years, the care and dedication with which replacements were made . . .

He did not look forward to this evening's session. Like all soldiers, he welcomed beginnings and hated endings.

He looked at the large antique clock on the wall that had been a gift from General MacArthur. It was time. He took two more pills, picked up his files, and went downstairs to the conference room to preside over the interment of Unicorn.

Gault drove into the Langley garage and took the private elevator directly to the conference room. The first arrival, he sat down at the head of the long oak table. It was Gault's show and he didn't want any one of them to lose sight of this fact.

He leaned back in the large leather conference chair and closed his eyes. He felt close to fulfillment and yet was aware that the next phase of his plan would be at least as difficult as the one he would complete this evening. But he had come a long way since that night so many days and years ago in that dirty cellar with Singleton.

He had been so patient, so willing to accept the occasional failure without panic or despair. Singer had been an unexpected asset and likable enough, but after tonight Gault would work alone. The closer he came to success, the greater the danger. No help. Actually, this was as he wished it, the way it had been from the beginning and, he supposed, the way it was meant to be.

The door to the conference room opened suddenly. Luther Martin came in first, followed by Cy Harper. They greeted Gault with unusual warmth.

"Good to see you, Mike," said Martin, as he gripped Gault's shoulders and sat down beside him.

Harper took the chair at the far end of the long table. A pitcher of ice water had been placed at each end, yellow pads and pencils in front of the twenty chairs. The three men seemed adrift in a sea of leather and oak.

"Did you get the word on Jonas?" asked Martin.

"No, Luther. What happened?"

"Somebody tied a copper scarf around his neck in front of the National Science Building. About five hours ago. He was on his way to Singer."

There was no response. It was almost as if Jonas's murder had just now occurred, in this room.

Harper broke the quiet with his soft, cultured voice. It carried with it a trace of irritation. "Singer's late. How much time do we want to give him?"

Martin picked up a phone at his end of the table. "Ally. Is Singer in the building yet?"

Before he had time to receive an answer, Singer entered the room, took off his coat, draped it over an empty chair, and sat down at the middle of the table. Without a word of greeting, he asked that all doors be locked and sealed. Gault was staring at him.

"And no tapes," he said. "No record in any form. Agreed?"

They had never, any of them, seen Morton Singer like this. The diffidence and the clumsiness were gone, and with them the humanity and the warmth. He repeated his question without raising his voice.

The others responded with wordless gestures of assent and waited.

Martin picked up the phone. "All systems shut down, Ally. Yes, *now*. And lock us up tight." He replaced the receiver and looked directly at Singer.

Singer began without preliminaries. Everyone here was, in effect, both a principal and a survivor. He spoke without looking at them, focusing instead on the papers before him.

"Thirty minutes ago, someone tried to prevent me from keeping this appointment. A very decent young man is now dead. He will be, I promise you, the final casualty in this outrageous business."

Martin looked up as if to speak, but Singer cut him off by simply raising his hand an inch off the table.

"Let me lay it out for you. After that first general meeting, I knew that there was no way to deal with this mess alone. I was an outsider investigating a closed club. From the beginning, I was also intrigued by the thought that Michael Gault was the only one to cry wolf—and, as well, had been trying to clean house for the past several years.

"I planned to approach him. Before I got the chance, he came to me with a proposition. An audacious plan, to which I agreed.

"Since that moment, he has been my surrogate in the field. We tried to keep track of all the agents, assuming the enemy would show himself sooner or later. Unfortunately, our antagonist used the peculiar virtues of Unicorn agents to circumvent our neat little plan. Mike trailed Emily Rhinehauer to Paris, but we lost her when she relied on private and criminal contacts. At this point, Mike suggested that I recommend him as a sacrifice to see if either of you two—" he looked toward Cy and Luther "—would protest the possible risk. On the contrary, you grabbed at the idea—not so much a word of caution from the two men who are, finally, responsible for these agents. O.K., that's how it was. Now, I'd like Mike to take over."

The phone rang and Martin grabbed the receiver. "Dammit, Ally, I thought I just told you . . . What? O.K., but no more for anyone."

"For you, Morton. It came in on the black line."

Singer reached for the phone. "What is it?" He listened and, without a word in reply, hung up. "Go ahead, Mike. There'll be no further interruptions."

Gault stared out at the three men. "It was so goddamn simple—once I knew where to look. For almost nine years, we'd been dying. No apparent reason. So the question always was who hated enough to waste us all. I looked around me at Singer's campfire, and it just didn't add up. Then I looked at two old men with a lot of power and connections, one watching that power slip slowly away, the other watching his life run out."

He paused, looking first at Harper, then at Luther.

"Two bitter old men, *sic transit gloria*. And I said to myself, these two are the only ones who always knew exactly who *and* where each Unicorn was. I told Singer what I thought, offering to use the people I'd gathered together over nine years. The idea was to watch the last Unicorns to see if any of them were working privately, moonlighting for Cy, or Luther, or both of them. In the meantime I put a total watch on both of you on this end.

"Somehow, I was always just a little late. By the time I caught up with Emily in Paris, she had joined the French Mafia. Christ, Bisquet must have had a hundred people trailing and leading her. And we had an old frog detective put on her to boot. She disappears anyway. Mysteriously.

"I figured Laura was next on the hit parade because she had something solid, and so I tied on to her. When Fonesca started to make his move, I arranged for Singer to cover Laura and tried to keep Fonesca in sight. But Fonesca wanted to run alone, so he tricked me. He kept me waiting in a Tokyo hotel while he was in Kyoto getting himself killed. By this time, Morton and I were pretty sure. Except for which one of you it was.

"It had to be—you two pulled all the strings. You signed Morton up because you thought he was a dummy and because you knew the President would go for him—the thing sounded like one of those tricky appointments of his that no one expects, that goes against the cliché.

"So we only had to figure out which one, or both, and why.

For that we turned to the resident computer, and he comes up with the answers. Morton tells you both that old Jonas has come through, without saying where the meeting was. But once again, we're not good enough. One of you planted that driver on Morton; this kid came direct from army intelligence, so Singer thinks he's safe. As soon as the kid sees where the meeting is going down, he calls somebody and Jonas is dead. So, again the last question—who and why?"

Now he stopped and permitted the quiet to close in on both Harper and Martin. Neither of them moved. Mike drew a short breath and continued his attack. His voice lowered, he looked directly at Martin.

"Luther, my good friend and sponsor, honest and beloved protector of the republic. You . . ."

He almost spit these last words. Martin seemed paralyzed.

"You. I left Silver Springs this evening to cover Mort. He told me to stay put, but I had a hunch. I was parked in front of the building and took a look at Jonas right after Mort. The necklace was yours, Luther, the one you taught me to use, and I'm the only one who would recognize it. I guess there just wasn't time to get someone else to do it—right, Luther? God, sick as you are, you still had the balls to do it yourself.

"As soon as I saw that necklace, I went over to your shop and waited until you came out. That big black car is hard to miss—the one you use for special occasions, like meetings in the park with old friends. And I watched you take out the only one who could finger you, Luther, the one who tipped you off, Mort's driver. I was too far back to help, but I saw Morton get out O.K. . . . But not bad, Luther. For a dying man, not bad at all."

Martin's voice was hoarse, and he was breathing rapidly. "And my motive, Mike. What in hell was my motive?"

"The oldest one in the world, Luther. You're scared of the final bill. Danny Fonesca fell over the fact that you started to die a long time ago—1969, to be exact. You wanted to even up accounts. Hell, Luther, you might have started Unicorn, but in the end you couldn't live with it. So when the doctors gave you the word, you tried to make it right by killing them all. Like a father raising a killer child and then taking the law into his own hands. Destroy Unicorn and maybe, just maybe, you could at least die with clean hands."

Martin turned and grabbed Gault's shoulder. "Bullshit, Mike, and you know it." His lips were almost colorless, and he was trembling.

Gault shook Luther's hand loose. "Should I read it, Luther?"

Martin sagged when he saw what Mike had taken from the files. "Where in the holy name of God did you get that, you bastard?"

Gault allowed himself a faint smile. "You taught me everything I know, Luther. How about it? Do I read it, or do you tell us why?"

Luther seemed to have suffered a stroke. He stared unseeing at the piece of paper in Gault's hand.

The room was breaking under the silence. Gault shrugged and spoke. "O.K. This is a letter from Luther to Father Donald Xavier Gervase, a Jesuit priest, now almost ninety years old, but surviving the rigors of age and illness at the Loyola Seminary a few miles outside of Assisi. Father Gervase baptized Luther, gave him his first Communion, and until his retreat to the seminary was and always had been Luther's family priest. This letter—" Gault again held it in front of Martin, who had not moved "—was written in 1968, just two months after Dr. Freuling confirmed his diagnosis and notified Luther. I'll just read one section of this letter."

It is not that I am afraid of death, or even of pain. I am, you see, afraid to face my God. Everything I have done was for what I believe to be a just and good cause, but I see how the killing has become my way of life. I'm not ready, Father, to go to God with all that blood on my hands. Comfort me, Father, I need your wisdom.

Gault put the letter down and addressed Harper as if Singer did not exist. "You see, Cy, Luther is too good a Catholic to live or die with what he believed to be a mortal sin. He couldn't stop what we were doing, so he continued to run us and kill us at the same time. You might say he ran us to death. He's crazy, anyone would be after nine years of chemotherapy, cobalt radiation, surgery—and hiding it all from you and Marshall. He wanted just enough time to finish the job. Only the pain-killers are left, but they're no good and there's no more time."

All that could be heard was the clock set into the wall behind Harper.

Martin looked first at Singer, then at his old companion of so many battles. "Cy, for the love of God, you can't believe this. Sure, I've had second thoughts—haven't you? But I could never kill my own men." He turned to Singer. "Morton, do you believe any of this crap?"

Gault spoke before either Harper or Singer could respond. The next few minutes were critical.

"It's all here, Luther. Day by day, I've tracked you. I've watched you with each death. And when Singer started, you began to move too fast. Your gut wouldn't give you much more time, and you were much easier to trace. You were in Paris the week before Wyeth was killed, and the stunt man Roux had worked as your contractor three times before. You had Company people in Bisquet's organization for five years, so it was easy to set Emily up. God knows what you did to her.

"Fonesca reported to you directly, and I've got copies of all his messages. You knew exactly who he was meeting and where. Did you tell him to nail me down in Tokyo?"

He threw a sheaf of coded communications in front of Martin, who just stared at Gault.

"The Chilean net owes you everything for the Allende operation, so I suspect they kept you up to date on Laura. When you couldn't buy Steiner, you scratched him. By the way, old man, I recognized the slant that tried to keep Laura away from Hong Kong. He was one of ours—or should I say yours?"

Gault stood up and walked behind Martin's chair.

"What else, Luther? Lundquist? You couldn't get anybody that close to him, but you're still good enough to have done that alone. You're the only man alive he'd turn his back on. That left just Laura and me, Luther, and I figured we didn't have much chance with four of your boys taking care of us. I know you thought they were yours, Morton, but don't bet on it. I say they're his."

Gault sat down facing Martin and Singer again took control of the meeting. It was close to one o'clock.

"Persuasive, Mike, very persuasive. Cy, I'm sorry we were so slow, but that's it. I'm sold, and I think you will be too when you go over the material Mike's put together."

Without warning, Martin jumped to his feet and moved to the door with surprising swiftness. "Not me, you bastards, you don't set me up."

As he reached for the knob, Harper touched a button beneath the tabletop. The door was thrown open, and Major Marshall, flanked by four uniformed soldiers, blocked Luther's path.

"Ally," he shouted. "For God's sake, help me—I'm being set up!"

Saliva appeared at the corners of his mouth. As if by some final effort of will, Luther hurled himself directly at the soldiers. They held him, pinning his flailing arms. He collapsed like a rag doll and began to whimper like a child. "I didn't. Christ, I didn't. I couldn't, Cy, you know that. Allie, don't do this to me . . ."

Harper finally spoke. "Get him out of here. What the devil are you standing there for—the man's a traitor. Get him out of here!"

The soldiers carried the old man from the room.

"What do we do with him, Cy?" asked Singer.

"Let me worry about that, Mort. You've done your job. He hasn't much time in any case. Walter Reed, maybe. He's mad, of course."

Gault's face hadn't changed expression once during Luther's

agony. Harper walked over and sat down next to him. "Mike, I know how difficult this was for you, but it had to be done. We all loved and respected the man that was Luther Martin, but I think that man's been dead for a long time. He was a casualty of the war." He touched Gault gently on the hand. "But, damn it, Mike, that war is still going on. You and I can give some purpose to Luther's tragedy. We can remake the whole agency and run it the way it needs to be run. I'm not a young man, Mike, and I would feel infinitely more secure if I knew that you would head up a new Unicorn and, since I still have some influence with the President, perhaps a new agency."

Gault looked directly at the emaciated old man, felt the full force of his passion and commitment. Singer watched from the far end of the table. Gault nodded. "Of course, Cy. I'd be honored."

Harper's dry, weathered face broke into a smile.

Gault got up, shook Harper's hand, gathered his files, and left. He walked down the long, gray corridor to the office that had, for nearly thirty years, been the exclusive province of Luther Martin. He sat down at Martin's desk and pressed the key on his intercom. Marshall entered, almost before Gault had returned the key to the off position, and stood at attention.

"Relax, Major," said Gault. "I'm not a soldier."

"Thank you, sir."

"Thank you for the letter, Major. That did it."

"I had no choice. I've always put my country first. Always . . ."

Gault smiled. "That's why I trust you, Major. O.K., we'll be working very closely together from here on in. I'll want you to help me in much the same way you helped Luther for so many years."

"I'll try, sir." Marshall looked pleased.

"Two things before you close up tonight."

"Sir?"

"First, I want a twenty-four-hour watch on Harper. He's a dangerous man and I'm afraid we're going to have to scratch him. We'll need the name and availability of our top contractor. It won't be easy to hit Harper; he spends so much time at the White House. Also, of course, it will be purely accidental."

"And?" said Marshall.

"I also want the old Jew covered, but no negative action. Let me have a daily log on who he sees, what he does, where he goes . . . everything. If he does what he ought to do and gets out now, he'll live to a ripe old age. If he starts acting like he enjoys this work, he goes too."

Marshall nodded and turned to leave.

"One last thing, Major. I'll be in very early tomorrow. First thing, call the President. I want an appointment as soon as possible. No notification to the Admiral, he's a front and will be treated as such. Understood?"

"Fully, sir."

"And, Ally . . ."

"Sir?"

"Please, the name is Mike. Thanks again."

Marshall smiled and left the room.

Gault leaned back in the chair, closed his eyes, and whispered aloud. "We're on our way, Phil. We're on our goddamn way."

He sat for an hour, exhausted. It was close to three before he turned out the lights and went home.

13 SINGER

There is no surer incentive to action in chess than the
sight of the enemy King out in the center of the board,
far from the protection of his own men. When the King
is checkmated, the game is over, and so no cost can be
too high to prevent him from crawling back under
cover.

A. I. Horowitz, *Learn Chess Quickly*

Singer stood at his window enjoying the signs of the approaching summer. The smog hung over the buildings and streets, the
moist June air an open invitation to shirt sleeves, T-shirts,
and shorts. New York slowed perceptibly in the face of the on-
coming heat that would, in another month, send people out of
the city like lemmings in their lust for the sea.

Singer turned away from the window and returned to his
desk. He reread the six-page report that had been delivered to
him that morning by courier from Washington. It was what he
had been waiting for: seventy-two names and addresses; in effect,
the postscript of the Unicorn affair. He had made one short telephone call to Washington and now would only wait. The appointment had been confirmed for eight o'clock, leaving Singer
nearly an hour. He had little appetite for what he would do in the
next few hours, but there was no alternative. Once more he reviewed the single file that lay open on his desk.

At precisely eight o'clock, the chimes played out their name-
less melody that had always delighted Grace.

Singer rose slowly from his desk, went to the door, and greeted his guest. "Come in, Mike." He stepped aside to let Gault pass into the living room. The two men stood awkwardly in the center of the large room. "Sit down, sit down. We'll be here for a while."

Gault moved instead toward the windows and then turned to Singer. "What in the hell is this, Morton?"

"What do you mean, Mike?"

"Come on, Morton. You know goddamn well what I'm talking about. I get your message that if I'm not in New York tonight, the truth about Phil Craigie goes to the President. I don't have the vaguest idea what you're talking about."

"But you're here."

"We're friends, Morton. If you wanted to see me, all you had to do was ask. My office knows you've got an open line to me any time, any place. Christ, we saved the whole damn thing—in my book that counts for something. So why all the nonsense?"

"Sit down and we'll talk."

The two men sat facing each other, Singer in the deep leather chair that was his favorite and Gault in a straight-back frame chair that was as uncomfortable as it looked. Gault waited for Singer's explanation.

. . . they had come to Phil in late October, when the leaves fell quickly, red and gold across the campus. There were two of them: a slight, soft-spoken young man with a humility that Phillip Craigie found especially appealing, and a quiet, attractive black woman.

They found the Professor walking home at the end of a long day, and introduced themselves without seeming presumptuous. Carl Whitefield and Elizabeth Adam. They walked with Craigie to his home, where they sat by a low fire until afternoon had turned into twilight and then into evening. Maureen had served cheese and wine while they listened carefully to their guests' proposal.

At first, the Professor was surprised, even angry that they would come to him. They must surely have known of his feelings about Vietnam and war in general, of his opposition to this government and, in particular, this President. And his feelings about the work done by their employers had been publicly expressed, time and time again. Why, then, were these pleasant young people wasting their time?

Yet the visitors spoke reasonably and patiently to Phillip and Maureen. They not only understood, they, in fact, agreed with many of his views. But there were other factors; these two Company representatives were disarmingly candid about the open Chinese wire which could yield a life-saving stream of information. But, alas, it was in code—a code so devious and complex that neither their resident specialists nor the computers could break it.

And so it had been proposed that a brain trust similar to Los Alamos be formed, not of nuclear scientists but of cryptologists, six or seven of the best in the nation. All would come to Washington for a few months and brainstorm this Chinese conundrum. Craigie loved the intricacies of letter and number and, even as an amateur, came recommended.

Would he come? Their request was not that he alter or compromise his ideals but simply that he help his country in a time of need. Here was, put simply, a chance to save American lives in Southeast Asia. After they left, the Craigies sat for hours in front of the dying fire and shared the pain of the conflict the evening's visit had brought them. In the end, they decided to go to Washington—the Professor did not, on balance, see how he could in good conscience refuse.

Whitefield and Adam were pleased with their success and, as requested, leased a modest house in Chevy Chase for the Craigies, who would pay their own way and arrive in a week. Months later, Carl Whitefield was killed by a hit-and-run driver and Elizabeth Adam died from an overdose of sleeping pills.

A week after their decision, Phillip and Maureen took up residence near the nation's capital. He was given a small cubicle at Langley in which to work. And he was cautioned against revealing the nature of this work; since it was only for a few months, he saw no reason to inform anyone, not even the soldier whom he had come to regard as a son. Craigie knew he would be back in Maine before the letter ever reached Vietnam.

240

"It's finished, Mike."

"Mort, what *are* you talking about?"

"The game we've been playing."

"If you don't get to the point, I'm going home. I've got too much work to waste time listening to riddles."

"I knew it was you, Mike, as soon as I got word that Fonesca had been killed. Up to then, you'd done a brilliant job of pointing me in the wrong direction. Your logic on Luther and Cy was just the kind of reasoning you knew I'd respond to. After you finished with me, it was the only motive that made any sense.

"You also had insurance. You knew my employers would never let me see the files on the real story of the Craigies. The agency was so anxious to bury the truth that it did your work for you. And even if I had been lucky or smart enough to find out, there was no chance I would realize that you knew from the beginning.

"I was doing your job for you as well. You fed me the bait, and I made the case against Luther."

Singer rose from the leather chair and walked slowly toward the window. It was beginning to get dark, and a few lights pierced the haze of the summer evening.

. . . *on a cold winter morning, Kenneth Singleton laid his complaints before Cyrus Harper and Luther Martin. He spoke of the frustrations over the long years spent trying to learn how lysergic acid could best be put to use in the national interest. After his wearying recitation, Martin and Harper appreciated this frustration—but what might he require? Surely the dispossessed person generally used by the Company could be appropriated for scientific purposes. No, Singleton impressed upon them the fact that a complex drug deserved a worthy subject. He wanted a sampling of the white, educated class. And the selection process was not as difficult as one might think; there were, at Langley, numerous free-lance civilians, generally the best in their field, who came and went with great frequency. No one would notice them; nor could they be linked with the Company—after all, they were not steady employees and their work was highly classified. Their physical presence at Langley made the task of administering the drug and observing its effects simple indeed.*

To Martin and Harper there seemed no risk to this solution, and the subjects were civilians. Singleton's request was readily approved, and shortly thereafter a group of people from various projects became, unawares, a part of an interesting and novel experiment.

"I think you've gone crazy, Mort."

Singer ignored the interruption and showed Gault his back as he looked out over the city. He continued without turning around. "If there hadn't been such time pressure, Mike, I really believe you would have made it. I suppose you were afraid Luther would die before you could set him up. And it's so difficult to accuse a recently enshrined hero. All of your hard work would have been wasted."

Gault had not stirred from the small, uncomfortable chair. His eyes were almost continually closed. "How did you figure it out?"

"Your trouble, Mike, is that you treat everybody with contempt. I'll tell you how I figured it out, and I want you to hear all of it. I'm not a very smart spy, but I'm no idiot either. You should have assumed, given the loss of Wyeth, Lundquist, and Emily, that I would take a long look at how and why Fonesca died. And the key to that was who he was meeting and what he was trying to find out. The rankest amateur would do a complete search of all his messages in and out. Didn't it occur to you that there were no communiqués from Danny to either Luther or Cy? We were covering those two anyway.

"A simple backtrack picked up Ikeda and your Japanese shadow. Kishi didn't compromise you, but it didn't take a quantum leap to reconstruct Fonesca's moves. From the time Danny got his instructions from Ikeda late in the afternoon of May seventh to the time he was killed early the next morning, there was absolutely no word from him. No way Luther, or anybody else this side of the Pacific, could have found out where he was going in time to act on it.

"Show me one lie in a ledger and I question every other figure. You told me Danny was had by Luther's people, but it felt wrong. The message check confirmed it. My immediate reaction was an accountant's; I went back over everything. I talked to Laura without indicating what I was after. I found out you had approached her, not vice versa as you maintained. You told her I sent you to back up Danny, not that he had asked for you. Tangled webs to unravel. I just checked everything, from the very beginning, and suddenly it was all there.

"Yes, Luther was in Paris the week before Wyeth was killed —you sent for him. But you were there when the accident happened. And while Roux did Company work ten years ago, he did five jobs for you personally in the last three years, and you weren't even operating in Europe. I found from the lady with the baby carriage that you were sleeping with Wyeth the morning he died. God, Mike, isn't there anything you'd stop at?"

Gault smiled, remembering how David had kissed him good-bye.

"No, Morton, there isn't."

Craigie could neither describe nor explain what was attacking his concentration. There was, first, a simple lethargy and then a few brief but alarming dreams. Then sleeplessness and anxiety, waves of unreasonable and sudden panic. He grew thin, his handsome, rough face became less definite. His gentle spirit broke in moments of unreasoned anger—he actually struck her, splitting her lip and drawing blood. And the dreams appeared, more often and increasingly bizarre. His work on the code was forgotten as he spent his days staring into space. He followed the channels of his mind, haunted by ghosts, wraiths, childhood furies.

Ironically, for help he turned to his employers; the Company psychiatrist went through the motions but refused to divulge the existence, much less the purpose, of the experiment. In the end, Craigie grew silent and despondent, ignoring her most loving supplications. Alarmed beyond reason, she called the Company, spoke to a concerned and compassionate superior. Yes, they had noticed the change; and yes, they all were worried about it; yes, of course he would do what he could. What he could do was

"Lundquist, your great, good friend. Yes, Luther could have gotten that close to him. But couldn't you believe that even an asshole like Mort Singer would check on Luther's whereabouts that evening after the meeting?"

Singer paused, wanting Gault to answer or at least show some reaction.

"You got a bad break on that one. Luther was taking his regular cobalt treatment in Rockville. You didn't know he was dying under the name of L. Milton. His stand-in went home from Langley that night, and you thought to set him up for the Lundquist killing because your observer reported him at home alone. A convenient chapter for your fiction. And if not Luther, who, who else *could* get the big Swede to turn his back? That's easy, Mike—his closest friend. You see, it's all in knowing what questions to ask. What did he want, Mike? And why did you kill him so soon?"

Gault sighed. "He asked me if I knew the real story on the Craigies. He'd stumbled over it and wanted me to clear myself. I had no choice. But I loved him, Mort, more than anyone." Gault's face was flushed and he perspired profusely in the evening swelter of the apartment.

Singer continued without pause. "And I remembered who recommended du Plessis when Emily asked me for a 'safe' inside man, and who had access to Bisquet's club. You, Mike, not Luther. You were the Company internal man; these were all your people. It took me a lot of fancy digging in a very short period of time to find that out.

"By the way, du Plessis shot himself this morning and Gangelle's in custody. Too late for Emily, but at least the good doctor won't bury anybody else. Were you aware that all his patients were donated by people who wanted them put away? Not people needing therapy, just inconveniences."

Gault spoke as if to himself. "Gangelle was my creation. I set him up and kept him safely in business. Just part of the network I worked on for nine years. Nine years without really needing him. I let him moonlight so he'd be there when I did need him."

. . . early one evening, he silently left Chevy Chase and drove to New York. Followed closely by Singleton's assistants, he checked into the St. Moritz, insisting on a room overlooking Central Park. He was given a suite on the twenty-sixth floor. In an infrequent moment of lucidity, he saw that he had lost his mind. Suspecting a tumor or a rare brain disease, he felt unwilling and unable to burden her with this horror.

The two guardians concerned entered the suite just as the Professor completed a final message to his wife. Frightened by the sudden appearance of strangers Craigie hurled himself outward, shattering glass and, seconds later, dying twenty-six floors below.

Singleton's colleagues, deeply disturbed, called home for instructions. Within the hour, Craigie was entered in the Company archives as "unstable, manic depressive, suicide." Project Lotus was abandoned. Cy Harper was preoccupied with indoctrinating a new President. Luther Martin noted on Singleton's memo that "this kite should have no tails—set up a slant cover that will survive a long, hard look."

"Is that it, Morton?"

Gault suddenly stood up and began to pace the room. Singer moved to his desk and sat down. He selected one file and turned the pages.

"Just about, Mike. The Chinese who was inside Laura's car at the JFK Center belonged to you and was relatively easy to identify. Once I knew where to look, that is. And I assume you removed Steiner."

Gault laughed at length, for the first time. "He loved her. I tried to buy him, but he really loved her. Which made it easy —he never figured I'd kill him. We had this witty little chat in Laura's garage right before she went to meet you; when he said no for the fifth time, I put the wires around his neck. I thought Laura would keep out of Hong Kong if I put him in the trunk. But the joke is that she didn't love him." Gault laughed again, but Singer could sense the fury that was rising in him. "If you knew after Fonesca, Mort, why the hell didn't you move then?"

"It was still possible that Cy and Luther, either one or both, were running you. I made the stupid assumption you could be watched and had four good men on the job. Jonus was my last ace. He was certain to come up with the answers I needed. But I didn't know you'd planted the driver on me—Christ, I really liked that boy—so I was sure you'd stay with Laura since you couldn't know where and when I was meeting Simon."

"My mistake. The young lieutenant called you from the car, didn't he? That's why he wasn't in front when I came out. He was covering your rear."

"Right again, Mort. He was selling nickel and dime intelligence to the Russians, which I happened to find out while I was chasing Helms. Nothing important, really, but enough to have him by the balls. I tapped in on your request for a clean bodyguard and a friend at army intelligence put him on the job. Easy when you know how."

Gault stopped pacing and stood in front of the empty fireplace under Grace's portrait.

Singer sighed. "One question, Mike. Why Laura? I'm just romantic enough to have believed you couldn't hurt her. Foolish enough, I guess."

"That was the call you got while we were trussing up Luther?"

"Yes, and I had a hard time not showing it. How the hell did you get by my men?"

"No sweat, Singer, none at all. Your guards thought I was gone for the night, so they were all sitting around the TV set when I walked in. Only one of them even got his gun out."

"And Laura?"

"For Christ's sake, old man, grow up. I made a very small slip in Hong Kong, and she remembered it because she was in love. Otherwise, she could've lived, I suppose. Anyway, it doesn't really matter. Take away the pretty face and body and the dreams, and she was like all the others. Nobody'll miss her."

". . . you set up West."

"Beautifully."

"And me, Mike. The hit and run on the way to Langley. Why? You couldn't have been afraid of me."

"Well, now, you were beginning to worry me, old man. I didn't much like all the private meetings and telephone calls. Too much going on I didn't know about. I thought that maybe I'd underrated you, and it would be safer if you were gone. It was an ad lib and besides, the driver had to go anyway. It seemed like a good idea at the time."

Singer smiled. "Surprised when I walked in?"

"You bet. You're pretty tricky, Morton. For a fat ass. Was that whole scene with Luther for my benefit?"

"Entirely. We had to let you run until we had the names of everyone you owned." Singer showed Gault the papers that had arrived that morning from Washington. "Who's who, Mike. Names *and* addresses. We also know that you had a contract on Cy and that I was next."

"Marshall? That boot-licker would waste his mother for a star."

"You can't really believe he'd turn on Luther. Martin's his whole life; he *is* Marshall's mother. Ally was our ace in the hole."

Gault went to the windows, turned his back on Singer, and stared out at the night.

. . . they informed her with consummate tact. Three of them, specialists in the graveyard detail. They talked of heroism, of service to the nation, they told her there would be funds available. They asked what else they could do. She stared at them without response. They left. For a few hours she evoked the magic of memory, recalling their love and their life together. No children now to comfort her because they had wanted all their time to themselves, jealous of every moment spent apart.

She reread the last message—fragments of a Thomas poem they both loved. The denial of the finality of death. In these minutes, she considered the future and rejected it.

"Tell me about it, Mike."

"I really don't care to," said Gault. "You must know what they meant to me. He and Maureen were my parents, and this fucking Company just threw them away."

"And so you decided that all these deaths were a fitting memorial to those two lives?"

Gault's eyes filled, his face twisted in sorrow and pain. "You don't understand, goddammit. If the Chinese had done it, there would have at least been a fucking reason. But this was sheer waste. Well, I'm going to waste this agency. And when I'm done, there'll be an end to this dying. It will be quiet."

His body shook, and Singer watched him cry.

. . . he left Maine for Washington and demanded a reason. He said a man like Phil Craigie doesn't take his own life, and he threatened to go public unless they told him about it.

He believed their fairy tale and he said nothing, because he would himself hunt down the Chinese. Without pause, he would enact justice. He bought those who were available and threatened those who were not. Some he killed. With a unique skill and a special brilliance born in Southeast Asia, he looked deeply and long into the darkness. He patiently endured a hundred disappointments and false leads. In the end he found nothing.

No Chinese, no kidnapping, no murder, no evidence that Phil had cracked the Peking code. And it was at this dead end that he discovered truth. He reached Singleton and one afternoon they talked. In this agent's words of sympathy, admiration, and concern, Gault heard the resonance of deceit. A phrase, an incomplete thought—at the end of that first meeting, he knew that Singleton's life was over.

He waited, that same evening, near the stop sign that halted the traffic leaving Langley. When the right car paused at the sign, he simply stepped inside, pointed a .45mm Colt at the man's groin, and urged him to proceed to a cellar on the outskirts of the city.

The two men talked again in that dank basement. But this time Kenneth Singleton was far more candid, if somewhat less urbane. When it was all over, Gault knew why and how the Craigies had died—and what he must do to survive. In the fourteen hours it took Singleton to die, the Unicorn deaths were born.

Gault knelt before Singer like a child, the tears still streaming down his face. "Mort, help me do it. We'll bring it off, you and I. We're a great team. We'll do it all alone . . ."

Singer moved away from the kneeling man. "Mike, you're so obsessed that you can't see what you've done with Craigie's life, his dream. You're a pacifist turned killer. I'm sorry for you, Mike, genuinely sorry for what these bastards did to your friends and to you. It was unforgivable and it has to stop, but not your way."

Gault stopped crying and got up. "You lousy Jew. You're like all the rest. Do you really think you can stop me? You're a dead man—now."

His fury exploded in the room. The wires flashed in his hands, as though materialized by a magician.

Singer did not move. "Not this time, Mike."

They rushed out of the bedroom and study. They took away his wires and pinned his arms behind him, but not before he had snapped the throat of one man and ruptured the spleen of another. They held Michael Gault until his screams had stopped, then took him from the room.

Harper stepped into the living room and sat down next to Singer on the couch.

"Are you all right, Morton?"

"Physically undamaged, Cy, but I'm afraid that young man is going to haunt my nights for a long time." He shook his head as if to dispel the memory of what had happened. "How's Luther?" he asked.

"As well as we might expect. His performance took a lot out of him. He's at Reed and is, I'm told, reasonably comfortable."

"How long?"

"A month or two, at best."

For the next few minutes, the two old men sat facing each other. Then Singer got up and put on a few lights.

Harper glanced at him. "So that's it, Morton."

"Not quite, Cy."

"Oh? And what, exactly, does that mean?"

"It means, quite simply, that I'm not satisfied to let you wash your hands in Mike Gault's agony."

"Either I'm a bit more dense than I'm prepared to admit, Mort, or that isn't very simple. What's the bottom line?"

"That you get out of government, Cy. Retire with all due honor. Stay out. It's time, you know."

"You're not serious, Morton." Harper was on his feet.

Singer ignored him. "The agency will be reshaped by new men with a different set of values. Patriotic, yes, but with a sense of perspective. I'm no child—we're going to gather the information we need, but we won't shape events to suit our needs. The killing and dirty tricks are done. No more Unicorns, ever. The mythical beast is extinct. You know, Cy, the beauty of chess is that no one has ever been hurt playing it."

Harper smiled. "You've very naïve, my friend, even if you are old. I've no intention of stepping down. We wouldn't last ten years with your attitude. But this is all academic. You can't win, Morton."

"I can try, Cy. Just before our last meeting at Langley, I made two visits. I stopped in Alexandria to talk with a senator who is both honest and highly intelligent. His reputation for integrity is beyond question. He was a presidential possibility, but no longer holds that ambition. Actually, I just stopped to drop off the total record of this agency over the past thirty years, as well as all the Unicorn files."

Harper turned ashen. "In the name of God, why did you do that?"

"A life insurance policy, Cy. My second visit was to the White House. I told the President and two others, the top three, my terms for not making these facts public. All the facts of how for at least three decades this agency has manipulated men and governments and murdered in the name of peace. And it took less than ten minutes to get written agreement on your retirement and a new approach to intelligence. And in a few months there'll be a new head for the agency—someone whose strength and integrity are rooted in a morality we've come to think is obsolete. It's over, Cy—all over."

Harper towered over the seated accountant. "Pretty good for an amateur, Morton. But it will never happen. I'll never permit it."

Singer stood up and faced him. "It has happened, Cy. And you have nothing further to say about it."

Harper stared at Singer for a moment, then turned quickly and walked out without a word.

Singer sank into his deep leather chair.

When Mrs. Perlmutter arrived in the morning, she found Morton Singer sound asleep in his chair. He held in his right hand the chess piece he had removed from the board, the black bishop. Mrs. Perlmutter went quietly about her work, wondering why a man of Mr. Singer's age would keep such hours.

DATE DUE

FE 20 '81			
MR 6 '81			
MR 14 '84			
MR 14 '84			
OC 8 '85			